THE LONESOME CHISHOLM TRAIL

THE LONESOME CHISHOLM TRAIL

Johnny D. Boggs

First published in the US by Five Star

This hardback edition 2013
by AudioGO Ltd
by arrangement with
Golden West Literary Agency

ISBN 978 1 471 32117 7

British Library Cataloguing in Publication Data available.

Printed and bound in Great Britain by
MPG Books Group Limited

For Lisa

Chapter One

He was exactly what I envisioned as a Texas cowboy, a tall, handsome man with straight white teeth and a Stetson Boss of the Plains as black as a crow's wing. With his shining blue eyes, high black boots, and crimson bib-front shirt, he looked as if he had stepped off the cover of a Beadle's half-dime novel. Of course, he carried a sidearm, a new model Colt revolver, fast becoming the choice of weapon for plainsmen everywhere.

And it was pointed right at me.

"Now, Ty," he said, maintaining his smile and friendly voice while leveling that long-barreled .45-caliber cannon. "Just ease that money belt off and put it on your saddle."

I had dismounted to nature's call for the first time since we had left San Antonio. When I came out of the bushes, I was dumbfounded to find my new friend pointing his Colt at me. Now the shock was wearing off, and I realized the man who called himself Rip Ford had intended to waylay me all this time. With a dry throat and sick stomach, I loosened the belt that held the only money to my name—not that it was much.

After placing the belt on the saddle, I stepped back from the spare horse he had loaned me. He shifted the gun to his left hand, then deftly picked up the reins to the roan I had been riding. He smiled again and, with his gun barrel, motioned toward the canteen on the roan's saddle horn. I took the canteen and waited.

"I don't want you to think badly of me, Ty," he said, "and I ain't one to leave a greenhorn without any water. Better take that blanket, too. It's apt to get a mite chilly tonight." I unlashed the heavy wool blanket strapped behind the saddle's cantle and threw it over my shoulder.

"I just need a stake, Ty. Now you just wait here by the road and someone's bound to come along by morn and take you back to San Antone or down the road. You can tell all your friends that you was robbed by the great Rip Ford." He laughed at that, holstered his gun, and kicked his horse into a trot, pulling the roan behind him.

"You'd leave a body in the middle of nowhere without a horse!" I cried, finally finding my voice.

"Hell, Tyrell," he called back. "It's my horse."

When he had disappeared down the road, I sat down and studied my options, none of which I liked. It would be dark soon, and the thoughts of Indians, wild animals, and snakes didn't make me comfortable. Here I was, a sixteen-year-old orphan, penniless and alone, with only a blanket, half a canteen of water, and the clothes I wore—and most of those were stolen. I thought about walking back to San Antonio but dismissed the idea, realizing I could easily get lost at one of the many crossroads we had traveled. Rip Ford—and I was starting to doubt that was his real name—was right. My best bet was to wait, so I settled down for a cold night, alone in South Texas, suddenly wishing I had never left Florence, South Carolina.

The shock of being robbed soon wore off, gradually replaced by anger, then of foolishness for being suckered like that. I had let a stranger charm me, befriend me, rob me, and leave me stranded. I should have never stepped inside that saloon.

* * * * *

It was the music that had drawn me there—a rich baritone voice and soft guitar strumming that carried above the sounds of glasses clinking and laughter inside the building and traffic in the streets. I was on the wrong side of San Antonio, and I knew it, but I was looking for my uncle, or directions to his ranch, and had been unable to find anyone who knew him in the city proper. Now I was in the rowdy part of town—what the locals called Hell's Half Acre—and, remembering his letters to my mother, I knew this was his element.

Stepping into The Clipper, I smiled. The place was full of cowboys, women in frilly dresses, and an assortment of rawhide-looking men. This was the West I had imagined. To my right, sitting on a stool and leaning against the far wall, was the source of the music. He was a dark-haired young man in a yellow shirt and blue pants, smiling as he sang to a small gathering of cowboys and dance-hall girls, the latter hanging onto his every word.

I spent my years pushin' cattle
Down that lonesome Chisholm Trail.
Herdin' all those doggies
Through wind and rain and hail.
The only thing I ever owned
Was a horse and a gun.
Keep on drivin' 'em
Until the day is done.

I leaned against the bar and listened to him sing. His voice and boyish good looks were those of an actor, but his boots were worn and brown, and the spurs hooked on the stool gave him away as a cowboy. Why he was singing in a saloon in the red-light district, I had no idea.

"What'll it be, sport?" a booming voice sounded behind me.

Turning, I saw a burly bartender with mutton-chop whiskers and a scarred forehead. "Whisky," I said dryly, caught up in the moment. He nodded, uncorked a bottle, and filled a shot glass of some reddish-looking liquid, then waited.

I pulled up my shirt and found my money belt, withdrew a Yankee greenback, and handed it to him. When he gave me my change, I quickly put it back in the belt and reached for the shot glass. Quick death is better than slow death, I thought, and gulped the whisky. It burned its way down and exploded in my stomach. I leaned against the bar and coughed.

Whisky wasn't new to me; I had stolen sips from my father's private stock, and stills were common around Florence. But this wasn't what I would call whisky.

The man to my left laughed and summed up my thoughts perfectly: "That rotgut goes down about as smooth as coal oil."

Through watery eyes, I saw him. He had blond hair, a neatly trimmed mustache, blue eyes that reminded me of my mother's, and a smile that immediately put you at ease. After he tipped back his black Stetson, he held out his right hand. "Rip Ford," he said.

"Tyrell Breen, but most folks just call me Ty." We shook hands, and he ordered two more shots, tossing the bartender some silver. I sipped my drink this time while he downed his in a flash.

"Where you from, Ty?" he asked. "If you don't mind tellin'."

I told him I was from South Carolina. I told him a lot more, the whisky loosening my tongue quickly on an empty stomach. I was looking for my uncle's ranch, his name was Clifford Rynders, the ranch was somewhere south of San Antonio, which I knew from the letters he used to write my mother. Uncle Cliff had no idea I was coming, and no one I had met in town had ever heard of him, let alone knew where he lived.

"Damned if the citizens of San Antone ain't about the dumbest hogs on this earth," he said. "Hell, Ty, I know Boss Rynders, been up the trail to Kansas with him, and seen the elephant with him more times than I can count."

"Seen the elephant" was foreign to me, but I recognized the nickname "Boss" and most of Uncle Cliff's letters had been about the trail to Kansas, so I figured Rip Ford wasn't lying. A weight was lifted from my shoulders, and I blurted: "Could you take me to him?"

He laughed and slapped my back, then ordered two more whiskies even though my glass was almost full. "Be right proud to, Ty. You aim to try cowboyin'?"

"I had hoped to," I said honestly. "I've never done it before, but I can ride a horse."

His voice cackled, and I felt like the sixteen-year-old fool that I was. It wasn't actually a lie; I had ridden horses before, and, when Mama would read from Uncle Cliff's letters, I had envisioned myself riding side by side with her brother on the Texas plains. I had bought and read Beadle's novels, substituting Clifford Darius Rynders for Kit Carson, Wild Bill, and the other heroes in print.

"Ridin' a cow pony is part of it," he said, "but first we got to get you outfitted proper."

Suddenly I was aware of my own clothing, and, standing next to this tall Texan in his fancy-stitched boots, I realized my wardrobe had "Easterner" stamped all over it: a pair of worn brogans and a dusty linen coat. The gray slouch hat I wore, while no Boss of the Plains, would pass, I figured, as would my cotton shirt and jeans.

But when I said as much, Rip frowned suddenly and pointed at my Levi's. "Boy," he said in all seriousness, "a Texas cowboy wouldn't be caught dead in a pair of jeans. Them's sodbuster's pants."

We finished our drinks—he drank my third shot—and stumbled out of The Clipper, leaving the girls and singing cowboy behind, and headed back to the respectable side of town. I was lightheaded from the whisky, practically giddy as we stumbled into the store with huge block letters that could be seen clear across town:

JAS. A. ADAMS & CO. DRY GOODS
Christian Businessman
Clothing, Boots, Shoes & Hats

A girl, maybe my age, approached us, and my newfound friend swept his hat off his head and placed it on a pile of silk and cotton scarves. "Might I help you?" she asked.

"I certainly hope so, lovely lady," Rip said, "for this is the fourth, no fifth, establishment we've been to today and so far have been met by nothing except contempt and rudeness. San Antonio, I'm afraid, is leaving a rotten taste in my mouth."

I was flabbergasted by Rip's boldness, too drunk and stunned to believe the whopper he was telling. But the wide-eyed young girl believed his every word. The only rotten taste in my mouth was from the rotgut served at The Clipper.

"Ma'am," Rip said, "this poor boy I found crying his eyes out after Comanches killed his ma and pa and burned his house. The only thing he has left to his name are the clothes on his back, and I've been searching this whole town over looking for donations, just a pair of boots, some pants, and stuff.

"No one, not a soul, has even lifted a finger to help him, and his parents one of the pillars of South Texas. The Corbetts. I'm sure you've heard of them."

She nodded, although I would bet the Corbetts were about as well known as Tyrell Breen, and glanced at me, and maybe my bloodshot eyes convinced her that I had been crying over my departed mother and father. Or perhaps the thought of dead parents hit me hard, because, even though Rip Ford couldn't have known, it was true.

"That's just terrible," she said. "You poor boy." But she was staring at Rip again, eyes sparkling, cooing like a schoolgirl. Rip was a handsome man, I'd give her that, and he definitely was a charmer.

"Perhaps, dear young lady, you could somehow donate some worn boots, just some pants, maybe a clean shirt he can wear to his parents' funeral. Anything will help, ma'am, and it'll leave a much better feeling of San Antonio for us."

"Well," she said, "you really should talk to my father about this, and he's gone home to eat but should. . . ."

Rip sighed in mock exasperation, and I knew he had her.

Fifteen minutes later, I walked out in a pair of black boots and drill pants, the seat and inside thighs reinforced with canvas for riding, and carried an extra shirt and long johns underneath my arm. I kept my hat and coat, and left behind my brogans and Levi's.

Rip donned his Stetson and smiled. "Bless you, young lady," he said. "Now we'll remember San Antonio more fondly. The Culbertsons would have been honored."

"Culbertsons?" she said. "I thought it was Corbetts."

I froze in my tracks, but Rip didn't miss a beat. "The Culbertsons are his only kin, up in Waco. Good Christian folks and wonderful people, but they couldn't even light a candle compared to you."

With that we were gone, off to the livery with my purloined goods. I suddenly felt guilty. My dad had been a businessman much like the young girl's father, and this had been my first real taste of robbery, not counting Dad's whisky stock, of course.

"Relax, Ty," Rip said. "Never spend your own money when you can get it for free. That goes for clothes, horses, whisky, even women."

I stepped back and smoothed my shirt. "What do you think?" I asked.

"Put a pair of leggin's on you and some spurs, and you'll be the terror of the Chisholm Trail," he said.

"Yeah," I said, and noticed his bandanna, a piece of beautiful blue silk that complemented his eyes.

"Only wish I had a scarf," I said, suddenly greedy.

Rip's eyes brightened, and he carefully took off his Stetson, reached into the crown, and withdrew a red cotton square. "For you, pard," he said, and handed it to me.

"Rip!" I yelled. "You stole this. I mean, you just charmed that lady out of these duds, but this . . ."—I pointed at the bandanna—"this is just outright thievery."

"Yeah," he said. "Pretty damned smooth, too."

And slowly I found myself taking the bandanna and tying it across my neck, adjusting it so the knot fell on my left shoulder, in the same fashion as Rip.

"Now," he said, "let's go find your uncle."

Chapter Two

I jumped, awakened by some strange noise, and fumbled in the darkness while trying to remember where I was. Somewhere an owl hooted and I settled back down, trying to remember my dream. I had been back in South Carolina, sitting by the fireplace as Mama read one of Uncle Cliff's letters. She adored him, but my father never put much stock in my mother's only brother, partly because they had never met.

Clifford Rynders left home in upstate South Carolina when he was about my age, hunting in Tennessee, farming in Georgia, and freighting in Charleston before finally drifting southwest, where he joined the First Mississippi Regiment and went off to fight in Mexico. After the war, he wrote that he was going to see "what the hubbub is about in Texas before coming home." He never returned to South Carolina.

His letters weren't often, always written in someone else's hand "because my writing isn't fit to read," and were usually vivid and full of adventure. He chopped cotton a while, and by and by discovered the cattle business, driving herds to California in the 1850s, to Louisiana during the late war.

But after the war, when I was old enough really to understand, the cattle industry exploded in Texas. He wrote of driving longhorns from South Texas to mythical places such as Sedalia, Baxter Springs, and Abilene, of Indians and stampedes and skies blacked out by locusts. He told of the ranch he had started south of San Antonio, said I should come out and join him, that life was wonderful in Texas.

The letters stopped in 1872, shortly before my mother died in childbirth. The baby died, too, and we buried Martha Elizabeth Rynders Breen and Daniel Clifford Breen in the family plot.

My father was someone I always thought of as a survivor. He had served in the Hampton Legion during the war, was wounded twice by Yankees, at Bull Run and Chickamauga, and somehow managed to restart his business after the surrender and profit despite the carpetbagger rule in the South. But the autumn after Mama's death, the powerful Jay Cooke and Company failed and sent the entire country into a terrible financial panic. The money stopped, my father's business was ruined, and before Christmas he was dead.

I thought of Rip Ford now, and of my money belt. The currency and silver inside were all I had to my name, but I was thinking of something else in that piece of leather. It was a letter from James Donald Breen, the last one he wrote:

Dear Tyrell:

A few hundred dollars and a Navy Colt are not all that I expected to leave my only son, but times are hard and one's dreams don't always come true.

You are 16 years old, a man now, and if I have one wish for you it is to look to the future better than your father did. Nothing lasts forever.

Remember that and always plan ahead.

I wouldn't suggest staying in South Carolina, Ty, for I see nothing to hold you here. Many of our friends left for Texas after the Lost Cause and now I

wish we had joined your Uncle Clifford. Look him up if you would and give him your mother's love. Maybe there's a good life to be found out West.

Tyrell, I cannot ask you to forgive me for this, but maybe someday you will understand. I was never good at failure and painfully regret that I am failing you now.

I won't ask you to shun John Barleycorn or Demimondes or even cards. Be your own man, son, and be a better one than me.

I love you dearly.

Your loving father,
James

He had carried that Navy Colt .36 revolver throughout the war and often bragged that it never failed him.

A neighbor found him in his office at his desk, the letter in an envelope in his coat pocket. The first percussion cap had misfired, but the second shot worked perfectly, and a small lead ball entered my father's brain and killed him instantly.

Tears streamed down my face as I lay shivering underneath the wool blanket. The past few months were still fuzzy in my mind. I had tried to settle all of my family's affairs before leaving Florence by train, carrying only a few clothes, my father's Confederate campaign hat, and a money belt containing a few hundred dollars. I had sold the Colt revolver, though. The gun my father had committed suicide with was nothing I wanted to keep.

By rail I traveled to Columbia. From there, it was a mix of trains, wagons, boats, coaches, and my own feet—what I came to call the "ankle express"—as I moved through Atlanta, Nashville, Memphis, Little Rock, Jefferson, Dallas, Waco, Austin, and finally San Antonio. And now I was alone and lost.

And so a day that saw me excited and happy for the first time in years ended with me crying myself to sleep.

I woke at dawn and studied the countryside of brush and hard rock for movement. Nothing. Hunger chewed at my stomach, and I suddenly worried that no one might travel down the road for days. I tried to remember the towns nearby, ones that Rip Ford had mentioned after we left San Antonio. Floresville, he had said. Goliad. Ulvade. I had no idea which direction they were, or even how far, but I was certain of San Antonio's location now that it was daylight. Of course, I'd have to guess at the crossroads when I came to them, but anything beat waiting.

So I picked up the canteen and blanket and started walking north along the road. Less than an hour later, I stopped to rest my already blistered feet. Cowboy boots, I learned, were not meant for walking.

After a long gulp from the canteen, I sighed. Last night I thought I was going to freeze to death, and now it was mid-morning and I was baking. And this, I had to tell myself, was early March. Now I remembered a line from one of Uncle Cliff's letters: "There are four seasons out here: deadly heat, deadly cold, deadly wind, and deadly rain."

Birds chirped and insects hummed, and I listened for a minute, enjoying the peace. Suddenly, I heard something different. I concentrated, trying to identify the new sound. Finally, I shot up and screamed: "Someone's singing!"

The voice was coming from the north. I stumbled that way, at last saw him in the distance, and began waving frantically and yelling. He was just a spot at first, but slowly came into focus. A bay horse, a hat the color of wet adobe, and a bright yellow shirt. The voice became clearer, and I recognized it and the song:

I spent long days in the saddle
Thinkin' of grabbing some land,
Maybe buyin' some stock,
And havin' my own brand.
But it's a dream I know
That will never come true.
Dust I'll be eatin'
Until I'm ninety-two.

He saw me, and the singing stopped as he kicked his horse into a gallop and rode toward me, reining to a stop but not dismounting.

"Hey, pilgrim," he said, "you fall outta the sky or somethin'?"

I couldn't help but laugh at my good fortune. It was the singer from The Clipper, and his guitar was wrapped in canvas and strapped to his saddlebags. He swung a leg over the saddle horn as I told him my plight, from seeing him in The Clipper, to meeting up with Rip Ford, about my Uncle Cliff Rynders, and finally about being robbed. I did, however, leave out the detail of the chicanery at the Jas. A. Adams & Co. store.

The cowboy pushed back his hat and began rolling a smoke, then offered me the makings, which I politely declined. After a few drags, he finally spoke.

"Wish I could help you out about your robber, pilgrim, but I can't say I rightly remember you from The Clipper. I had my eye on this green-eyed . . . well. . . ." He took another puff and laughed. "Rip Ford, eh?"

"That's what he called himself."

"Well, he sure wasn't Rip Ford, but it's a right funny name to be usin' as a highwayman."

"Why?" I asked. "Who is Rip Ford?"

The cowboy flicked away his cigarette and frowned. "Boy, you really are a pilgrim. Rip Ford just happens to be about the by-God most famous Texas Ranger in the world. Only Texican I can think of that could carry his boots would be the late Sam Houston."

Sam Houston I had heard of, at least, so I didn't feel like a total fool. I realized I hadn't introduced myself, so I held out my hand and told him my name.

"Jesse Trace," he said, and gave my hand a couple of awkward pumps. "So you're kin to Boss Rynders?"

Now, I perked up. "Do you know him?"

Jesse Trace smiled, adjusted his position in the saddle, and kicked his left boot free from the stirrup, then held out his left hand. "Yessir," he said, "now hop aboard, young Tyrell. His place is just down the road apiece. We'll be there by late afternoon."

We rode on, me behind him, clutching his sides and careful not to bounce into his guitar too much. He kept calling me pilgrim, boy, and sonny, although he seemed to be only in his mid-twenties. He asked more about the bandit who called himself Rip Ford, and I described him as best I could, but Trace said he could not recollect seeing him.

"He had a roan horse and rode a big black one," I said, and I felt him jerk in what I first assumed was recognition. But he shook his head.

"Nope. Don't ring a bell."

He shifted the subject to Clifford Rynders, and I told him what I was doing, about the letters, the death of my parents—the details of which I omitted—and his big ranch, and my dreams of being a cowboy.

"He don't know you're comin'?" he asked.

"I wrote him," I said, "but I'm not sure he ever got the letter. Mail delivery in South Carolina isn't great these days."

"Ain't great in Texas, neither," he said. "Fact is you'd probably be better off at conversin' with smoke like them Injuns. 'Course, they don't really talk with that smoke like them jim-dandies write in those five-penny books." He thought about that for a moment, adding: "But there might be a song there."

"You write your own songs?" I asked, trying to file away the fact that smoke signals weren't anything like telegraphs.

"Yup," he said, "mostly when I'm ridin' along like this, or when I'm on a drive . . . providin' I ain't ridin' drag."

"Why not then?"

He laughed. "Ridin' drag you best keep your mouth shut, unless you like eatin' dust."

"Tell me about Uncle Cliff," I said.

"He's your uncle, sonny. You ought to know all there is."

"But I've never met him. He left South Carolina long before I was born."

Jesse Trace shook his head. "You left home, traveled a thousand miles maybe, to join up with an uncle you ain't never met and who probably don't know you're comin'. Sonny, you got grit. I'll say that about you."

I backtracked a bit. "He invited me out in one of his letters."

"Well, I'm sure Boss Rynders is at his place. He don't leave much these days unless. . . ." He was suddenly quiet.

"What?" I asked, thinking the worse. Something had happened, something that explained why he had quit writing, not that his letters had been like clockwork. But it had been almost two years. At least he wasn't dead, a thought that had never occurred to me before I left Florence.

"Tyrell," he said, "you'll find out everything shortly." A few minutes later, he laughed. "He was a man to ride the river with, though, sure enough. Man had sass and sand and tougher than an ornery old mossy horn. But get that herd in, in Abilene or wherever, and he'd help us turn the badger loose. We seen the elephant, sure enough."

"Seen the elephant?" I asked.

"Just an expression, pilgrim," he said. "Findin' adventure, sorta, seein' what the hell's over the next rise."

I nodded. "Must be a song there," I said.

Trace reined to a stop and thought, then kicked the bay into a walk. He hummed some bars, threw out some words, but after a few minutes gave up. "Good idea, sonny, but I just can't rope the words today."

After that we were silent for most of the day, talking occasionally to break up the monotony of the ride. Around noon, we dismounted and rested the bay while eating jerky and hard biscuits. It was the only food I had eaten in days, and, although not much, my stomach was grateful.

For the rest of the day, I worried about meeting Uncle Cliff. He had been a hero when I was a child, but most of what I knew about him was what I made up after Mama read his letters. I had pictured him as some feudal lord in a faraway place called Texas, looking over his demesne. But what if he had been crippled in an accident, or what if he simply had no use for a greenhorn kid from South Carolina, blood kin or not?

Jesse Trace had called it "grit" to come out like this. Suddenly, I thought of another word—stupid.

We turned off the main road a few hours later. After another hour, we heard dogs barking, then saw the shack. It was small and made of adobe, with a well, small corral, privy, and lean-to. Three horses stood in the corral, watching us approach, while two hounds ran into the middle of the yard and continued barking. They were gaunt animals, dirty and mean. Another glance at the corral told me the horses were in the same emaciated condition.

The bay horse we rode didn't seem to mind the dogs, and Jesse reined to a stop a few yards from the house. The dogs stopped barking and backed off from the horse, aware of its deadly hoofs, but continued to growl.

A haggard-looking man stumbled from the house, grabbing hold to a porch beam with one hand to keep from falling. In his right hand he held a pistol at his side.

"Who are you and what do you want?" he bellowed.

"Boy," Trace whispered. "Meet your Uncle Cliff."

Chapter Three

Clifford D. Rynders never had a daguerreotype made of him, so I could only imagine what he looked like, using the Beadle's covers as examples more than my mother's descriptions. I had pictured him as a tall, straight-shooting man with a brace of revolvers and a gallant white horse. The man standing in front of us, though, could barely mount a horse in his current condition. Uncle Cliff was nothing but a drunk.

He was tall, I guessed, but it was hard to tell with him slumping. His dark eyes were like my mother's, and I recognized the prominent Roman nose she had often described. But any similarities ended there. Beard stubble and dirt covered his face, and his hair, dark and streaked with silver, looked more like a bird's nest. He stood in his stocking feet, with a pair of tan canvas pants held up by one suspender strap; the other strap dangled next to his left leg. The shirt he wore was muslin, and I doubted if it had seen water since the last time it rained. He squinted and yelled again.

"It's me, Boss Rynders. Jesse Trace. I just come a-callin' and brung you your nephew, Tyrell Breen."

A smile slowly formed on Rynders's face, not from recognition of my name, but of Trace's. He carefully stepped off the porch, hooked the loose suspender over his shoulder, and finally shoved the revolver into his waistband after missing the first couple of tries.

"Jesse Trace," he said, walking toward us. He grabbed the bay's bridle and patted the horse's neck, and I caught the heavy scent of whisky and stale sweat. "Light down, old hand, and we'll sit a spell."

We dismounted and Uncle Cliff led the bay to the porch, then he stumbled onto an oak keg that served as a chair. "Jesse," he said, "be a good hand and bring out my bottle and some glasses. I'm just tuckered out."

"Sure, Boss Rynders," Trace said, and disappeared into the adobe shack, leaving me alone with my drunken uncle.

It didn't really matter, though, because he had yet to notice me.

Trace returned in a minute with three tin cups and a bottle containing only a few fingers of amber fluid. He handed the bottle to my uncle, then placed the cups on an empty crate marked **ARBUCKLE'S**.

Uncle Cliff let a few drops of whisky fall into one cup and handed it to Trace, polished off the remaining whisky in the bottle with one swig, and sighed heavily.

Trace looked at his cup and decided, I guess, that there wasn't enough whisky to make it worthwhile so he handed the cup to his drunken host, who must have figured that any whisky was enough whisky. He downed it quickly, then belched.

"What brings you out this way?" Uncle Cliff said.

"I brought you your nephew from South Carolina, Tyrell Breen." He motioned to me. This time, Uncle Cliff glanced my way and nodded, but his gaze quickly returned to Trace.

"Say, Jesse, old hand," he said, slurring his words. "You wouldn't happen to have some sippin' liquor or something in your war bag would you? I find myself suddenly dry."

Jesse shook his head. "Sorry, Boss Rynders, but I'm headin' down to join a herd for Mister Simpson, and you know how he feels about that scamper juice."

"Sure, sure," he said, patting Trace's knee. They were quiet for a few minutes, then Uncle Cliff asked: "Doug Simpson, you say?"

"Yessir."

"How many head?"

"Ain't rightly sure. He didn't make a drive last year, you remember?"

Uncle Cliff nodded. "Who's your trail boss?"

"Jonas Taylor. From what I hear, he's a fair man."

He nodded again, then smiled. "I reckon the Gen'ral will be leadin' you?"

Trace laughed and said: "If it's a Douglas Simpson herd, you can sure bet it'll be Gen'ral Houston. How many times y'all been up the trail together?"

Now Uncle Cliff laughed. "I ain't sure, but I recall last time in Abilene a preacher wanted to marry us."

At this, Jesse Trace hooted and slapped his knee, and, although I had no idea what they were talking about, I found myself laughing, too.

After a few moments of silence, Uncle Cliff asked again: "You sure you ain't got no bug juice, old hand? Hell, I'd even settle for some tequila."

Jesse Trace shook his head. "Afraid not, Boss. I just got some jerky and biscuits, and my guitar."

Uncle Cliff stood up, apparently satisfied that there was no whisky among us. "Well, old hand, stay off any widow-makers and give the Gen'ral my regards." He staggered into his shack. Minutes later we heard snoring.

Trace stood up and walked his horse to the well. He filled a bucket and let his bay drink, then made sure the horses in the corral had plenty of water and grain. Finally he reached into his saddlebags and tossed the two dogs some biscuits, which they greedily devoured.

After which, he spoke to me. "Well, boy, there you have it. He's been like this almost two years now. Workin' when he has to so he can buy rotgut, stealin' the bug juice, I reckon, when he can't." He shook his head in disgust. "I hear tell he helped some Mex farmer last summer. The Boss Rynders I knew wouldn't lift a finger to help a sodbuster. Hell, no cowman would."

"What happened to him?" I asked.

"Well, I don't know the long and short of it. They say he lost a herd to some thieves in Kansas. But you'll have to get that from him." He mounted his horse. "That is, if you aim to stay on?"

I sighed. "I have no place to go."

"Well, then take care of him, if he'll let you. He can be as cranky as some belly-cheatin' cook at times, but he knows cattle. If you aim to be a cowboy and can keep him off the scamper juice, he's the man to teach you." Trace reached into his saddlebags and handed me the last of his jerky and biscuits. "Better take these, Tyrell. I'll be eatin' high on the hog by tomorrow, and you ain't likely to get a square meal around here."

After taking the food, I looked around the spread and had to agree with Trace. "Yeah," I said, "I wonder what he has been eating."

"I don't know," Trace replied, "but there were three dogs the last time I was here." My jaw opened, and Trace smiled.

"Just joshin', boy," he said, and spurred his horse into a trot.

I ate a few biscuits and some jerky, then made the mistake

of looking at the two dogs, which had quickly taken a liking to me and were staring with pleading eyes. So I emptied the sack of food onto the dirt, and the dogs went to work on the last of the biscuits and dried meat.

As dusk approached, I wandered around the spread, keeping away from the main house lest Uncle Cliff awake and send a bullet my direction. It was a miserable place in the middle of nowhere in need of repairs that would take months to complete, but the well water was cool, and the sunset turned the sky orange and red and cast a warm glow on the ground.

But when the colors faded, darkness brought a chill, so I found my blanket and stretched out in the lean-to with the dogs, my newfound friends, nearby. I closed my eyes, trying to comprehend my run of bad luck, then felt something bite my leg. Then again. And again. I suddenly jumped up, startling the dogs, and brushed off fleas, walking around while I scratched at parasites, real and imagined.

Finally I sat down and leaned against the well and nodded off for a few minutes at a time, drifting into a deep sleep a few hours before dawn.

The sun was well up by the time Uncle Cliff stumbled from his shack, but I had been awake for hours, waiting for him. He made his way to the well, drew a bucket, and washed his face between hacking coughs and groans. I was off to the side, near the corral, and managed to summon enough courage to clear my throat. He glanced my way, squinted, and then said in a dry voice: "Who the hell are you?"

"I'm Tyrell Breen," I said, "your nephew from South Carolina." I waited, unsure if the name meant anything to him after all that John Barleycorn.

"Martha's boy?" he asked after a minute.

I sighed with relief. "Yes, sir."

"Where's your pa?"

Frowning, I replied: "Gone to Glory."

Uncle Cliff snorted and guffawed, and I was taken aback. "Gone to Hell, more than likely, that skinflint of a bastard."

My ears reddened with anger, and I wanted to storm away, but I knew I had nowhere to go, and hoped it was just the whisky, the hangover, and such talking. Uncle Cliff took a long drink of water, washed his face some more, then stared at me again for a while, I guess trying to determine if I were a hallucination induced from whisky like those elephants my half-dime novels said drunks saw.

"What in the hell are you doin' here?" he finally asked.

I swallowed, and told him of his invitation, of my letter informing him of my arrival, of my experiences in San Antonio with Rip Ford and along the trail with Jesse Trace.

After which, he shrugged and stumbled back into the house, where I heard him crash on his bed.

The rest of the morning I spent wondering what I would do. I walked around the spread and slowly discovered that, although in need of work, this ranch could be a good place. It had good water, some wood, and I even saw some quail and rabbits. But it definitely needed more than a drunk to run it.

By mid-afternoon I found myself sitting on my uncle's porch, scratching one of the dogs' ears. I heard noise from inside the shack, saw Uncle Cliff step out on the porch and glance my way. He stared at me again while he scratched his head.

"Tyrell?" he finally asked.

"Yes, sir."

He laughed, and his eyes seemed to smile. "Thought I was havin' a dream," he said as he shook his head. He held out his right hand, and I took it, smiling, and he stepped back and sized me up. "I heard about Martha. She was a fine woman. And you say your pa passed on?"

"Yes, sir," I said, "carpetbaggers, the Panic. It just did him in."

He nodded. "Where you bound?"

My hopes sank at the question. This was my destination, and, since I was out of money, it was my only place. I struggled to find the words, finally blurting: "I had hoped to stay here."

"Should had writ somethin' first, Ty, or at least let me know you was comin'. Then I could tell you not to leave Florence."

"I did write," I told him, "and you had invited me out in one of your letters years back, said you had started a big ranch and everything. Mama was real proud of you, even my father."

Uncle Cliff sat on a crate and shook his head. "Ain't much I can offer you, Ty. My cards are on the table, boy. Ain't got nothin' in the hole. But I ain't never been a man to turn someone away without some chow. Hope you like canned tomatoes and coffee."

I told him I could eat coffee beans whole, and he smiled as he stood and motioned me inside. He started a fire in the stove as I filled a blue enamel coffee pot with water from the well. Then he grabbed a can of Arbuckle's coffee and pulled out a handful of whole beans.

"Let me see your bandanna, Ty," he said, and I unloosened my scarf and handed it to him, figuring he would use it as a glove or oven mitt. But instead he wrapped the coffee beans in my stolen piece of cotton and shoved it in the pot, which he put on the stove.

"C'mon, boy," he said. "We'll do some chores while the coffee boils." Dumbfounded, I followed him outside.

Of course, *we* did not do some chores. *I* did all of the chores: chopping wood with a dull axe, feeding and watering the stock, cleaning up the shack a bit while Uncle Cliff sat and watched and talked. I didn't mind, though, for he had seemed to accept me now that he was sober and no longer hung over.

I was sweeping out the place when I noticed a familiar envelope, unopened, sitting behind an empty bottle of rye. It was the letter I had sent him before leaving Florence. I put the broom aside and picked it up, then shoved it at him, yelling: "This is my letter! The one I wrote you saying I was coming. You didn't even open it!"

He didn't deny it, didn't say anything for a while. Finally he frowned and said: "Well, I reckon I do have some explainin'."

"I'd say so. What did you do? Get drunk and forget about it, forget to open it? I came a thousand miles. . . ."

"You came a thousand miles with no guarantee, Tyrell, no invitation, no nothin', so don't take that tone with me." I backed away a few steps, scared by the blaze in his eyes, and realized he was like a cat backed into a corner and no longer scared of a dog.

"The truth is that letter wouldn't do me any good now or a month ago or a year ago. The letters your ma wrote to me, I had to get someone to read to me. I would have got someone to read me yours, but visitors have been a mite scarce these past months. Only person I see much is a Mexican farmer down the road a spell, and he can't read no English."

"The letters you wrote Mama?"

"Cowboys, strumpets mostly. Doug Simpson's daughter. I'd tell 'em what to say, and they'd put it down, tell Martha my writin' was just chicken scratch, which is the truth, so she would think better of me."

"All lies," I said, "about the ranch, the drives, everything?"

He shrugged. "Well, this is my land, my place, least of all

till the Yanks run me off. And there was a lot of truth about what I had wrote in them letters to Martha. But lies? Nah, I'd say them letters probably got more truth in 'em than them Eastern novels and such. Truth be known, I was a right good trail boss."

"What happened?"

He smiled then and jerked a thumb toward the coffee pot.

"Supper time, nephew. Hot coffee, cold tomatoes. Let's eat."

Chapter Four

As I choked down my first sip of cowboy coffee, Uncle Cliff laughed. "You gotta chew that stuff first, nephew, else use a knife and fork." He drank some and sighed. "Ah, hell, this stuff's too weak."

"Weak!" I exclaimed. "This could sink an ironclad."

Other than Uncle Cliff's snickers when I watered down my coffee, we ate in silence. I was famished, and thought I could eat the coffee and drink the tomatoes, but, surprisingly, the supper seemed to satisfy my stomach, although I wouldn't rank it with she-crab soup from Charleston. After supper, we retired to the porch and watched the sun set. Again, the sky turned brilliant red.

It amazed me to see two glorious sunsets in a row. Colorful settings were common in South Carolina, and I had witnessed a wonderful sunset during a thunderstorm in Memphis, but in this arid, rugged countryside, so desolate, there was a clearness to the colors that seemed to say God was here, after all.

I remarked about the beauty to Uncle Cliff, and he just shrugged. "I took a few herds to Californy in the 'Fifties," he said, "through Arizona Territory. Now them sunsets was something to behold. Or maybe we was just glad to see the sun go down after bakin' all day. Not that it did any good, 'cause we near froze to death at night. Then we'd fry again next mornin', eatin' dust for breakfast. It'd get so hot, so dry out there, it would blind the cattle, then they'd stampede when they smelled water . . . iffen they ever smelled water. Bad water. Apaches, too. I quickly got my fill of drivin' to Californy."

He shook his head and sighed, then continued. I was amazed he was so talkative this night. "We contracted out to the Confederates in the war, drivin' cattle to Louisiana. Gettin' Johnny Reb currency . . . no profit in that. Up to Missouri after the war, fightin' border gangs, damned sodbusters, thievin' Cherokees. Then laws pushed us west. So we hit Abilene, Ellsworth, Newton, Wichita. Same fights, different trails. Stampedes, locusts, drought, flash floods. There was always somethin', it don't matter if it's Californy, Missouri, or Kansas. Herdin' cattle is like bettin' on drawin' into an inside straight in a crooked poker game. It's a sucker's bet."

"Why do you keep at it?" I asked. "You've done it, what, twenty years?"

"To see the elephant, Tyrell. Besides, I'm too old to do anything else. I figure they'll bury my bones on the Chisholm Trail. There will always be folks wantin' beef, so there will always be drives to Kansas."

I shook my head, watching the colorful sky fade to gray. Clifford Rynders was in his mid-to-late forties, and I couldn't see him as long in tooth. And I thought about my father's advice, to look toward the future. Railroads had started into Texas toward Dallas and Fort Worth before the Panic stopped the track laying. When the money returned, so would the railroad workers. And when the rails criss-crossed the nation—and as a businessman's son I could see that happening—the days of the trail drovers would be over.

"Nothing lasts forever," I said, quoting my late father.

"It'll last through my lifetime," he said. "But, hell, I ain't goin' up the trail any more, least not as a boss. Sometimes I think I'd love to go up again, tie one on in Newton, Ellsworth, even hire on as a damned wrangler. But, hell, I ain't foolin' nobody. No one would trust me, even on drag. . . . Right now, I'd kill for some hooch."

Turning, I saw Uncle Cliff leaning against the wall, his arms folded tightly across his chest. He was shivering and looked pale in the dusk. "Uncle Cliff?" I said softly.

"Son, I bet you wouldn't have any tobacco on you, smokin' or chawin'?" I shook my head. "That'd take the edge off a bit, but what I really need is some whisky." He turned sharply and went into his shack, and I heard his meager furnishings being strewn about, trashing the inside we, or rather I, had cleaned up earlier in the day. I slowly went inside and saw him on the floor, frantically pulling reeking clothes and empty bottles from underneath his bunk.

"How about some more coffee?" I meekly asked.

He turned suddenly, and I saw the same fierce, wild look carved into his face that I had seen when I confronted him about my letter. He swore angrily at me, and I stepped back. "What I need, Tyrell, is a damned drink!" His right hand fell on a pewter flask and he unscrewed the top, shook the flask, and flung it at me, missing by several feet. He scrambled to his feet, dashed for a leather trunk, and began viciously going through the contents.

For some reason, I picked up the flask and noticed the engraving. "Seth Hannen," I read aloud, "Abilene, Kansas, Eighteen Sixty-Nine." The words stopped my uncle, who turned around and sat on the floor, his back against the trunk. At first, I thought Uncle Cliff had stolen the flask, but the name suddenly struck a cord, and I thought about it for a minute. "You mentioned a Seth Hannen in some of your letters," I said.

Uncle Cliff put his hands over his mouth, fingertips touching each other. After a couple of deep breaths, he lowered his hands and said: "Seth was a man to ride the river with. For a damn' long time, there was me, Seth Hannen, and Doug Simpson. Seth was the best man around, never did a damned fool thing till he went and got himself killed." He lowered his eyes, looked in a corner, then suddenly crawled across the dirt floor like a baby and grabbed a brown clay jug. He pulled out the stopper and lifted the jug to his mouth.

"Glory to Texas!" he yelled, and took a long pull.

I frowned, and walked outside.

There really wasn't much liquor in the jug, undoubtedly left over and forgotten from one of his benders, so he couldn't get roaring drunk. And maybe, I thought, it was good he had found something, because he seemed to relax instantly and was soon in his bunk, snoring. I also returned after feeding the horses, cleaned the shack a bit, and dropped to the pad on the floor we had fixed that afternoon. In minutes I, too, was asleep.

Barking dogs woke me late the next morning, and I heard a squeaking sound in the distance. I rose, and Uncle Cliff kicked the empty jug across the floor as he made his way toward his holstered revolver.

As the irritating, grinding squeaks drew nearer, I recognized it as a wagon wheel, one badly needing grease. Then Uncle Cliff and I walked into the morning light, spotted the dust, and saw a buckboard approaching from the east. The dogs kept barking, and we watched intently, and, although his eyes were red from liquor, Uncle Cliff managed to notice the most important thing about our visitor first.

"He's alone," he said, still holding the revolver. "Don't reckon he's a law dog, either. Not travelin' that noisy."

For a moment, I was scared. What if it really was a law man, and what if he was actually after me, for stealing the clothes in San Antonio. But I quickly dismissed the thought, and then I saw Uncle Cliff relax and shove the gun into his waistband.

"I'll be damned," he said softly as the squeaking buckboard pulled into the yard.

The driver wore a brown suit, caked with dust, and a faded Stetson. His hair was gray, close cropped, but his thick, drooping mustache matched his dark brown eyes. At first glance, he looked ancient, but his facial features were rock hard and bronze, and his giant fingers dwarfed the leather reins he held.

A wooden crutch leaned on the seat beside him, and I noticed his right pants leg pinned up below his hip. A casualty of the late war, I guessed, because one-armed, one-legged, and one-eyed veterans were common. Especially, it seemed, Confederate veterans.

Beside the crutch, I saw a rifle, for protection, I thought, until the man spoke. From his commanding tone, I realized this man wouldn't need a rifle to protect him. Crippled or not, this man with a booming voice seemed tougher than Texas.

"Clifford, I must speak to you."

Even the dogs quit barking when he spoke.

Uncle Cliff rubbed his stubble. "Doug," he said dryly.

They were quiet for a few minutes, sizing each other up, I guess, neither one knowing what to do. It was inappropriate for the man in the wagon to light down without being asked; it was also rude for Uncle Cliff to let him bake in the morning sun. Even I knew that, but neither man seemed willing to budge.

Finally I spoke: "Should I put some coffee on?"

Both men looked at me sharply, stunned that I had broken the silence. Neither man said anything, though, so I went inside. I got the fire going in the stove and soon heard the buckboard creak as the visitor stepped down. I found the Arbuckle's coffee, opened a canister of sugar, and dropped a few cubes into the pot of water. However, I located no grinder, so I followed Uncle Cliff's example and wrapped some beans in my still-wet bandanna.

I took three empty cups outside and found both men sitting on the porch. The man named Doug was sitting, the crutch and rifle at his side. For a second, I wondered if the two men planned to shoot it out there, for Uncle Cliff's revolver remained in his waistband and his right hand never strayed too far from the butt. He even used his left hand to pick up the coffee cup.

I went back inside and returned with the pot and poured three cups and sat on a crate near the two men.

"I'm Tyrell Breen," I said, again breaking the awkward silence.

"Douglas Simpson," the man boomed, and my eyes widened. He blew on his steaming cup, took a sip, then set the cup down to cool some more.

Both men stared across the porch at each other for a few minutes, then Simpson finally spoke, his voice still strong and demanding. "I have a contract to deliver two thousand beeves to Wichita by the first week of May," he said.

"Jesse Trace told me," my uncle said.

"I know he did."

"You're drivin' them out early this year."

"I ain't got much choice, not this year."

Uncle Cliff cringed at the remark. "Well, they probably won't freeze to death waitin' for a better price."

Now Simpson stiffened, and his face darkened in embarrassment or anger.

Silence resumed, and I stared at both men, slowly realizing they were probably about the same age, only Simpson looked ten to twenty years older. The man reminded me of my father as he seemed to be carrying some awful burden on his shoulders, which suddenly relaxed and slumped. He let out a heavy sigh and reached for the coffee.

Then Uncle Cliff softly cursed to himself. "I withdraw that remark, Doug," he said, and picked up his cup, this time using his right hand.

"Cliff, I'm about to be gutted like a catfish," Simpson said, his voice soft now, almost cracking. "I gotta make this drive, I gotta get that herd to Wichita by May just to get them Yankee tax men off my backside. It ain't to make a profit, it's just to break even this year. Else, I'm gonna lose my ranch, everything to them damned carpetbaggers."

The giant man fought back tears, as he fumbled with his cup, staring at the dark liquid rather than looking at my uncle or me. Uncle Cliff sighed and tossed his coffee out. He slumped forward a bit, resting his elbows on the crate we used as a table, his head in his hands.

"Jesse Trace said you had Jonas Taylor as ramrod. He can get you to Wichita sure enough."

Simpson shook his head and spoke, still not looking up. "Jonas got his head stoved in by a mule in Pleasanton. He's deader'n hell."

Uncle Cliff sat back as if he had been punched. He shook his head in disbelief, then suggested: "Well, there's others. I ain't never heard tell of a shortage of trail bosses, 'specially with the Panic tightenin' things up."

But Simpson shook his head again. "Ain't nobody wanting to go up with the jinxed outfit. That's what they're calling me now, from Brownsville to Chicago. . . . Couldn't raise money to make a drive last year . . . had to sell a bunch for hides and tallow for a lousy three dollars a head just to pay some damned bankers . . . frozed out waiting for the prices to go up some in 'Seventy-One and 'Seventy-Two. . . ." He trailed off, looking up apologetically at Uncle Cliff, who bowed his head for a moment.

"How 'bout Emmitt Fain?" Uncle Cliff suggested.

"Humph," Simpson said. "He's a good hand, but he is no trail boss."

"Ah, hell," Uncle Cliff argued. "He's got a lot of oats to sow, but he's a fine point man, and the hands usually like him well enough."

"They like him, but they'd string him up if he was their boss. Hell, he's gonna get strung up sometime anyhow. You know it, and I know it. And I wouldn't trust him with my herd, especially with everything, the ranch, Mattie, everything riding on this one." Simpson looked up at Uncle Cliff then, eyes pleading. "Cliff, I need you to boss my herd."

Uncle Cliff stood up suddenly, almost upsetting the crate. He backed up, half laughing, shaking his head. "No, Doug. I . . . I couldn't. N-not . . . I j-just couldn't."

"Cliff, you're my only chance, my only hope."

"No!" he shouted. "Hell, if anyone's jinxed, it's me. I lost that damned herd of yourn in 'Seventy-Two. Me! Let a bunch of thieves take it! I got Seth Hannen killed! No! You get Emmitt Fain, hell, let Jesse Trace try it. Or go your own damned self!"

"I can't fork a damned saddle, Cliff! Fain and Trace can't do it! And there ain't a trail boss this side of New Mexico that would take one of my herds . . . at least take it and get it done right! I lose money if the herd arrives past the deadline, and I can't afford to pay any penalty. Damn it, Cliff, I need you!"

"No, sir! I gotta stay here, look after my nephew. I got too much to do here."

Suddenly Douglas Simpson overturned the makeshift table, and I jumped back as the man boomed. "All right, damn your yeller hide! You want to wallow around in a pigpen, you wanna swamp out saloons and spittoons for your bug juice, go ahead! I'm offering you a job, a chance to do what you're good at! I'm not crazy about the idea myself, but damned if I see another choice!"

Using the rifle instead of the crutch, he stood up, raising himself as tall and as straight as he could. "We've known each other for many a year, Clifford. You saved my life once, and I'd like to think that's what I'm doing for you, offering you this chance." He slammed the rifle's stock down so hard it sounded like a pistol shot. "But," he bellowed, "I'll be damned if I'm gonna beg to a drunkard!"

Uncle Cliff swallowed, then whispered—"I can't, Doug."—and he stormed off the porch, kicking at one of the hounds as he hurried away. Slowly Simpson sank onto the keg he was using as a chair and leaned the rifle next to his crutch.

After a few minutes passed, Simpson looked up at me. "You make fine coffee, son. You're from . . . Carolina, right?"

"Yes, sir," I said.

"Came to Texas to be a cowman." He smiled, but I knew it was a false front for the rest of his face was sad. "Well, Cliff Rynders is the best. Was the best."

I shook my head. "I don't understand it," I said softly. "Last night, he was almost begging for a chance to go on a drive. And now. . . ."

"Whisky," Simpson said, "nerves. He took my herd up in

'Seventy-Two. Made it to Kansas but got jumped by thieves. They stole the whole herd, killed Seth Hannen, who took a bullet meant for Cliff. He and Seth went way back. Fact is, all three of us did. Cliff's been on a high lonesome since." He sighed. "And he was my only hope."

"What will you do?"

Simpson shook his head. "I have to try, even if I use Fain or go up in a wagon myself. For my sake, for my daughter's sake. I'm short-handed as it is." He looked at me. "Interested in going to Wichita?"

"As trail boss?" I said, smiling, hoping my joke would help his mood.

"Maybe," he said as he grabbed the crutch and stood. "If you can talk your uncle into it, tell him the job's his. And if you think you can eat trail dust and work till you're almost dead for thirty a month, like I said, I'm short-handed. Besides, I'd need you to look after him," and he motioned toward Uncle Cliff, who was still walking away from us, by now a speck in the distance.

And the giant one-legged man, who had seemed so big and so tough when he first arrived, picked up his rifle and slowly limped to the wagon, crawled aboard, and rode away, his head held down, the squeaking wheel crying in the stillness of the morning.

Chapter Five

It was dark when Uncle Cliff returned, caked with dried blood, and smelling of liquor and pig manure. He smiled when he entered the shack, then flopped on his bunk, holding an almost empty bottle in his right hand.

"Lucked out, nephew. Old man Juárez needed help killin' hogs, and I got a half-bottle of mescal." He offered me some, and I shook my head. Shrugging, Uncle Cliff took a drink and sighed. "Mescal ain't rye, but, by God, it does the job."

Disgusted, I turned away from him. I had piddled around the ranch all day, feeding the horses, cleaning up what I could, and later helped myself to an old can of potatoes. I had thought about feeding the dogs, but, when I went outside, I found them fighting over a jack rabbit. "You boys are eating better than me," I had said out loud, and forked another potato. As I had waited for my uncle, I had wondered what I was going to do, and now he was back, drunk on a Mexican farmer's rotgut.

"Mister Simpson offered me a job on his trail herd," I said, not looking at him.

"Humph," he grunted. "Doug Simpson is a luckless bastard. He ain't got a chance in hell of makin' that drive to Wichita by May."

I savagely turned on him, shouting so loud that the dogs began to bark: "What the hell's with you? The man's your friend, and he needs your help! Last night, you were begging for a chance to go on the trail, and he gives you that chance and you run away to kill hogs for one night's drunk!"

He started to scream back at me. "You don't understand! I got Seth Hannen killed! He was my best friend, and you don't know how. . . ." He was trying to stand, but I jumped forward, pushed him back into his bunk and sent the bottle crashing against a wall. I exploded, tears streaming down my face as my uncle cowered drunkenly in his smelly bed.

"Don't tell me I don't know how it feels! My mama died in childbirth! My father took a revolver and killed himself because he was losing his business. You don't think I hurt? You think I don't draw a breath without thinking about my father, hating him for being such a coward? You're pathetic. You're worse than he was. You'd be better off dead!" I pointed around the roughshod shack. "Your dogs won't even live in this filth. My dad was yellow because he killed himself, but at least he had the guts to pull the trigger. You're so gutless you can't even do that! You can't help yourself, you can't help your friends, and you sure as hell can't help me!"

Choking and sobbing, I stormed outside, leaving him alone with his broken bottle of mescal. I walked around for hours, kicking up dust, slamming my fist against the corral and startling the horses, cursing myself for ever leaving South Carolina, vowing that I would find Doug Simpson's ranch and help him on his drive, if for no other reason than to get away from my uncle. My mother had thought so much of her brother, and I was glad she hadn't lived to see him as he really was, a drunk, a coward, a man a snake wouldn't claim for a son.

Exhausted, I found my way to the porch and crawled up

against the wall, out of the wind, determined not to go inside with my uncle. Later, I felt Uncle Cliff put a blanket over me, heard him in the corral, working around the house, washing the pig smell from his body. But I was too tired to rise, too scared and mad to face him. I drifted back to sleep.

"Tyrell."

I forced my eyes open as Uncle Cliff lightly kicked my boots. When my vision focused, I realized he was clean-shaven for the first time since I had arrived. I sat up slowly and saw he was wearing a relatively clean muslin shirt, tan duck trousers, leather leggings, and a brown woolen vest. His dust-colored slouch hat was firmly on his head, and a green bandanna flapped in the wind. I almost didn't recognize him.

"Can you sit a horse?" he asked. After I nodded, he continued: "I don't mean ride around Florence with some school gal. I mean sit in a saddle, eighteen, maybe twenty-four hours a day?"

"I can try."

"It ain't no nickel romance, son. There's damn' little glory and hell's share of hardships, a lot of work and little pay. And you got a fair chance of gettin' killed. Snakebit, drowned, Injuns, stampedes, fever, herd thieves."

I nodded again.

"You're a boy," he said. "Remember that, and forget that nonsense about cow*boys*. It's cow*men* that you'll be workin' with, and they won't have much use for a green kid who don't pull his weight. You'll be on drag all the way to Kansas, eatin' dust from two thousand beeves."

He offered me his hand, and I took it. Buckling on his gun belt, he jerked his thumb inside the shack. "Get your possibles together and shove 'em in that war bag I put on your pallet. And polish off that coffee."

I looked around and saw the horses had been saddled, the leather shining from saddle soap and elbow grease. After shoving down a cup of miserable coffee and packing my meager belongings into a canvas sack, I stepped back outside and shut the shack's door.

"One other thing," Uncle Cliff said, handing me a piece of paper and a pencil. "Write a note for me." He told me what to write, which I did in big letters, and handed him the paper. He nailed the note to the door, using his revolver as a hammer. After holstering his gun, he swung into the saddle of his buckskin with ease while I tied my sack, what Uncle Cliff called a war bag, on the saddle horn, and mounted a skittish brown mare named Lizzie.

"Let's ride," my uncle said, and he took off down the road, pulling the third horse, a strawberry roan, behind him. The dogs followed, and I kicked my horse into a trot, then glanced back at the note on the door.

**GONE UP
THE CHISHOLM TRAIL
BACK THIS FALL
MAKE YOURSELF AT HOME**

We hit the main road and headed south for several miles, skirting around Floresville, which was the first town I had seen since San Antonio. Moving east, we crossed the San Antonio River and picked our way through the thick mesquite and heavy brush that covered the land like quills on a porcupine.

Eventually we came to a clearing and stopped near an overgrown cornfield. Uncle Cliff stared at the dead stalks from last year and spit. "Farm work," he said with disgust, kicking his horse forward.

The sound of cattle, horses, and men greeted us as we cleared the field. Douglas Simpson's ranch came into view, but it was not what I expected. Directly in front of us stood a solid corral and barn, both in good condition, but the rest of the outfit looked as old as dirt. A lean-to that needed a new roof was to the left of the barn. To the right stood a dog-trot adobe cabin, chipped, battered, and run-down, with a piecemeal sod roof. I had seen slaves' quarters in South Carolina that were built better. A ramshackle chuck house and bunkhouse were farther off, along with a few shabby privies seemingly held together by old rawhide.

There were no European-style structures, no white plantation mansion, not even a San Antonio façade. It was just another hardscrabble outfit in South Texas, smelling of dust, cattle, and . . . food.

"Sonofabitch stew," Uncle Cliff said. "We made good time."

As we eased forward to the corral, the bunkhouse door opened, and two men, one black, one white, walked toward us. Then Simpson's voice boomed, and I turned and saw him approach us from the main house. I also saw a girl behind him, a slender, dark-haired figure in faded red calico who waited on the porch.

"Light down, men," the one-legged man said, and I followed my uncle's lead. Only I kept staring at the girl on the porch and paid for my rudeness. My boot hit something slick and wet and sent me sprawling into the dust. An oath slipped from my mouth as I landed in the dung.

"Well," a familiar voice drawled, "if you knowed what it was, how come you stepped in it?"

My face flamed in embarrassment as Uncle Cliff, Douglas Simpson, and the black cowhand laughed loudly at Jesse Trace's comment. Trace helped me to my feet. A door closed, and I looked toward the main house, but the girl had vanished inside, and I frowned.

"You'll do us the honor of eating dinner with us," Simpson said, glanced at me, and added, "after washing up."

Uncle Cliff nodded and handed his reins to Trace. "Unsaddle her, will you?" he said, and Trace smiled and took the reins. I offered my mount to Jesse, but Uncle Cliff snapped—"Unsaddle your own damned horse!"—and walked toward the main house with Simpson.

Trace introduced me to the black cowboy, a slender teen-ager with a small face dwarfed by the almost colorless sugarloaf sombrero he wore. His name was Les Slaughter, and, although he was only seventeen, he had been cowboying for five years. I was amazed, or rather envious. Five years ago, I had been in the Widow Langston's class in Florence, learning arithmetic, reading MOBY DICK, and singing "The Flying Trapeze" while Les Slaughter was pushing twenty-five hundred longhorns from South Texas to Abilene.

They showed me how to rub down the horses, after which we talked some while I washed quickly behind the chuck house.

"You're more than welcome, Ty, to eat with us in the bunkhouse. Sonofabitch stew and coffee," Trace said, and Slaughter added: "Mister Bibberman is a mighty fine cook. Even better than Miz Mattie."

But I glanced at the main house and declined. "I'd better eat with Uncle Cliff."

Trace and Slaughter grinned. "Yeah," Trace said, "Les and me figgered as much."

The inside of the ranch house was as barren as the outside, a cracked Chippendale mirror in the hallway the only semblance of civilization. The rest of the furniture was rough-hewn, which seemed to fit Doug Simpson's manner. But it was out of place when you considered his daughter.

Her name was Mattie Simpson. She was a year younger than me, had a round face, and easy smile, and I was mesmerized by her—just like a sixteen-year-old boy. It was too warm inside, so we ate beans, bacon, and sourdough biscuits on the porch, washing them down with bitter coffee. Afterward, Uncle Cliff and Simpson fired up yellow cigarettes and walked to the corral, leaving us alone.

For a few minutes, we stood like fence posts. Finally she asked a question, and I answered, and we began an unassuming conversation, but I sensed she felt a need to talk, especially to someone my age. Plenty of the cowhands were young, but her father, one leg or not, was not a man to be trifled with—and he sure wouldn't let a common cowhand talk to his daughter. Even though any one of those common cowhands had more money to his name than me.

"You're from Charleston?" Mattie asked.

If you're from South Carolina, people assume you're from Charleston. I frowned and told her I was from Florence, an old railroad town far from the landed gentry of Lowcountry.

My uncle's hounds had found a cool spot on the porch, so we talked about them for a half minute before that topic was exhausted. After chit-chatting about Carolina and Texas, the war and cattle, school and Dickens, Charleston and Floresville, she asked why I had come West.

"My parents died," I finally said, and I realized I also wanted to talk to someone my own age. "I had dreamed about riding the range . . . that sounds pretty silly, doesn't it? . . . and I had no ties to Florence any more."

"I'm sorry about your parents," she said. "My mother took consumption and crossed the river three years ago. But do I miss her terribly!"

"I miss them both," I said, feeling my eyes tear up.

If we had not already struck a bond, we did then. The easy conversation ended, and she spoke freely, glancing at her father. "It's been hard on me, but I think it was worse for him. That's about when his luck went bad, if you believe in such. Sometimes I think he would have quit were it not for me." She shivered and blinked back tears. "Sometimes I wish he would quit, sell out, move anywhere, some place with people and boys and girls my age. I do miss that. But I think that would kill him, and this is home, and I really do love this place."

She turned to me. "This can really be a fine place, Tyrell. Daddy just needs one break. He got a letter from a man with a firm in Kansas City this winter, with a contract and all. I guess that's good. I mean he doesn't have to worry about finding a buyer. But he has to make this drive on time."

"He'll make it," I said, and immediately felt stupid.

But Mattie smiled. "I've talked too much, but thanks for listening."

Uncle Cliff and her father were walking toward us, and she said: "I like talking to you, Tyrell. I hope you'll see me before you leave for Wichita."

"I will," I promised. "I enjoy listening to you."

The two men stopped in front of us. "What else will you need?" Simpson asked.

"What I really need is one more cowhand. Even with my ambitious nephew, we're short at least a man."

Simpson shook his head. "Maybe you can hire somebody in Austin, Waco. Pedro O'Donnell's two brothers are supposed to be here in a day or so, to look after the ranch, but Consuela O'Donnell isn't about to let her two youngest boys go on a trail drive. It was hard enough to convince her to let Pedro be wrangler. What else?"

"Tobacco," Uncle Cliff said, "and a good slicker. I had to sell mine a few months back. Compass, if you got one, letter of introduction to that buyer, Ferguson, in case we beat you to Wichita, and a letter of credit."

"I'm low on tobacco, but I'll scrounge up enough to get you to San Antone. Been using dried corn husks for my papers."

"Yeah, I noticed your damned farm while riding in, you sorry sodbuster."

Douglas Simpson guffawed, and Mattie smiled. "I figgered you'd frown upon that, but we need the corn. For bread, grain, and"—he held out the remainder of his cigarette—"smoking papers."

"Leaves a peculiar taste in your mouth."

Simpson laughed again. "I'm sure most of the boys will have tobacco, maybe some store-bought papers. You can have my slicker, and I'll find that old compass we bought in Baxter Springs . . . remember?"

Uncle Cliff smiled.

"Letter of introduction is no problem. Letter of credit, I dunno. The banks don't like me much, and I don't know if any stores up the trail will honor it anyhow. Money's still tight. And not to sound like some old skinflint, Cliff, but I'm flat busted."

Uncle Cliff nodded. "Guess I'll have to tell Emmitt Fain that he's no longer trail boss, just point man." He tipped his hat to Mattie, then looked at me. "Let's see what kind of outfit I'm bossin', nephew," he said, walking toward the bunkhouse.

I quickly said good bye to Mattie and her father, and followed Uncle Cliff. He stopped in front of the building, waiting for me to catch up, and turned. Eyes burning, voice low, he said: "Ty, I've been shot twice, trampled, bucked, beaten, hooked. But I ain't about to be hazed by a bunch of damned waddies all the way up the trail to Wichita. From here on out, it's Cliff, Clifford, Mister Rynders, Boss Rynders, Capt'n, sir, even President Ulysses S. Grant. But you call me uncle and, son, you will rue the day."

Smiling, I opened the door and followed him inside.

The cowboys were sitting around a long, wooden table, polishing off their dinner, laughing at some ditty Trace was singing. They looked at us and fell silent. I stared at a collection of Western hats and faces, and locked on a black Boss of the Plains at the end of the table.

"My God," I whispered, "it's the outlaw, Rip Ford."

My uncle followed my gaze to the handsome man in black, then shook his head.

"No," he said, "it's my point man, Emmitt Fain."

Chapter Six

"My name is Clifford Rynders," he told the cowboys, "and I'm bossin' this outfit. Some of you have been up the trail with me before, so you're familiar with my methods. That's good. But for those of you that ain't, I'll keep this short. There's only one rule . . . do your job. Do that, and you get paid off in Wichita. Don't do it, and I'll feed your guts to the buzzards." He was silent for a minute, letting his words sink in, then added in a quieter voice: "One other rule is n-no whisky on the drive, 'cept for maybe a beer or a shot when we stop for supplies in Fort Worth, maybe Saint Jo . . . and I'll tree any of y'all who try to tree the town. Otherwise, we're dry till Wichita."

"Glad to see ya ag'in, Boss Rynders," a voice said. Another similar greeting was sounded, and the chatter in the bunkhouse picked up again. Uncle Cliff turned to leave, glanced at me, and said softly: "Ty, we're short-handed, so try not to kill Fain until we get to Wichita."

The door closed behind him, and slowly I turned, my eyes avoiding Emmitt Fain, alias Rip Ford. Jesse Trace walked to me, slapped my shoulder, and said: "Tyrell, let me introduce you to the boys." He rolled off some names, but I knew I would never remember them all—Charley Murphy, John Dalton, Ian Cochrane—then he came to a boyish-looking, blue-eyed cowboy in white cotton pants and a gray hat.

"This is Brazos Billy," Jesse said, and I realized there was at least one name I would recall. "At least for this year. He goes through names faster than beer through a tap."

Brazos Billy stood up, and I was amazed at how thin he was, even more by his bowlegs. "My pleasure, pilgrim," he said. "I've seen the elephant with Boss Rynders many a time and am glad to be goin' up the trail with him ag'in. If ya need a thing, just holler."

"Thanks, Billy," I said.

"Brazos Billy," he corrected. "I was Just Plain Billy in 'Seventy. Don't wanna run outta names."

I smiled, though uncomprehending, and we moved on as Trace explained. "Names don't mean a whole lot out here, sonny. It's how a feller handles himself. And Brazos Billy is one of the best. Besides, it's kinda interestin' to see what name he'll come up with next."

"Seems it would get confusing," I said.

"Not with the whores," the next man said, raising his voice. "The whores call him one thing no matter what's his handle." The room fell silent, and the red-headed cowhand waited. "Billy the Bulge."

The cowboys wailed like Comanches, and a few more offered names.

"Beddin' Down Billy!"

"Boomerang Stallion Billy!"

"No, it's Big Sugar Billy."

"Brothel Billy."

"Ya waddies just wish ya knowed," Brazos Billy replied.

The laughter was still thick, so noisy we passed the cowhand who had started the ruckus without introductions. "And this here is our top hand, I guess," Trace was saying, and my smile vanished as I came face to face with my robber, "Emmitt Fain."

"We've met," I finally said.

"Yeah," Trace said, "I kinda figured you had." Surprised, I glanced at him, eventually remembering how he had seemed to recognize my description of the robber on the road from San Antonio. "Y'all probably got some catchin' up to do. Let me know if you need me."

Trace turned and shouted to the other cowhands. "Let's hit the saddle, boys, so we can start this fandango *pronto!*"

The cowboys filed out of the bunkhouse, except Emmitt Fain and me. Fain slowly stood up, towering above me, but still smiling. He extended his hand, which I ignored.

"Glad to see you, pard. Fate deals some funny hands, don't she?"

I remained silent.

"Oh," he said, eyes dancing, "don't think so bad of me, Ty. I told you I just needed a stake. There was a big card game in Floresville, and I found myself in a somewhat embarrassing state of finances. I'll pay you back when we hit Wichita."

"You're a low-down thief," I said.

He leaned his head back and laughed. "Well, that's pretty good coming from a guy wearing a stolen bandanna and pair of boots." My right hand immediately reached for the piece of cotton tied around my neck. "C'mon, Ty, let's step outside."

I surprised myself by trailing him to the corral, but he obviously was an easy man to follow. "I reckon I should have asked you for a loan, but seeing how we just met, I figured you would not be inclined . . . and last fall's Panic back East still has a grip out here . . . so I just went with my instincts."

He was saddling his horse while he spoke, and I just stood dumbly and listened. I knew he would never really apologize, which flabbergasted me.

"I saw Jesse Trace in The Clipper, figured he would pick

you up on the road and take you to Boss Rynders's place, and I was gonna pay you back, plus interest, when I met up with you again."

Another lie—I wasn't that green—and I called him on it. "I'm here," I said. "Pay up."

He stopped, reformed his battle lines, and tightened his saddle cinch. "I would, Ty," he said, "but damned if my luck didn't turn sour in Floresville. I mean, I had aces and kings and lost to three fours. It was an unbelievable run of bad breaks." He laughed, shaking his head. "The embarrassin' truth of the matter is I let them folks in Floresville clean me out."

My mind went numb because somehow I believed him. It would explain why he was ready to join a cattle drive again. "All of my money?" I asked.

He sighed. " 'Fraid so. I figure it to be fifty dollars, and I'm good for it, pard."

My math totaled it to more like sixty-five, but I let that slide. "And the money belt?"

"Lost it, too," he said. "Plus that roan I let you ride, and that was a good swimmin' horse."

"There was a letter in that belt," I must have said. I don't remember saying it, but I do recall Fain's reply.

"Aw, I do remember that. I ain't one to read a letter that ain't mine, so I left it in the belt. When I put the belt in the pot at the card game, I just plumb forgot it was there."

I hit him then, surprising myself. My fist caught him solid—another shock—and Fain reeled back and bounced off his horse. My blow stunned him, and this was the first fight I had been in since I was ten years old, but my glory was short-lived because Fain's reflexes took over.

The first blow caught my jaw, snapping my head back and sending me crashing against the corral. Another fist slammed into my cheek and sent me rolling across the rails. A flurry of punches found my head, nose, and face, and I stumbled, then felt a terrific uppercut jar my stomach that sent the air rushing from my lungs. As I gasped for breath and dropped to my knees, through blurred vision I saw Fain rear back and send a solid punch to my head that toppled me to the dirt.

Blood, warm and salty, dripped into my mouth as I lay there, aching all over, unable to see straight, praying that I would loose consciousness. In a moment, my prayers were answered.

My eyes opened, and I stared at a tintype of a naked woman. I gathered my bearings, finally realizing I was in the bunkhouse and some cowboy had placed the faded picture above his bed. The aroma of coffee soon perked my senses, and I tested my mouth. Pain shot through my face and body, but eventually I sat up in the bunk. Salve had been put on a cut on my forehead, and someone had cleaned me up, moved me into the bunkhouse. Uncle Cliff, I thought, or maybe Jesse Trace.

After a minute, I noticed the giant of a man sitting on a chair by the bed. In his massive black hands he held a cup of steaming coffee, which he offered to me without speaking. I shook my head and stared at him, intimidated by his size.

He was a man of color, seemingly larger than many horses. He wore tall, black boots and Union blue britches almost busting out of the seams. A red flannel shirt was unbuttoned over a muscular bare chest covered by black tufts of hair and a faded blue bandanna. His face was covered with beard stubble and, of all things, flour. He wore no hat, and the top of his head was bald, black, and shiny. I felt like David, staring for the first time at Goliath.

When he spoke, though, I was amazed. This Negro giant

had a high-pitched voice, woman-like, with an unmistakable Boston accent.

"I am Amos Obadiah Jonah Micah Bibberman, the cook. You may call me Bibberman."

"Tyrell Breen," I said.

He nodded. "My father figured if he gave me enough names from the Good Book, I would be more inclined to be a good Christian." He smiled, revealing a largely toothless mouth. "I'm afraid he failed miserably."

"Thanks for cleaning me up, taking care of me."

Bibberman shook his head. "Don't thank me. I will doctor snakebite, broken bones, gunshots, all sorts of injuries on the trail. But not those from ranch fisticuffs. You may thank Emmitt Fain."

"Fain!" I said, and immediately regretted my outburst as pain shot forth again. "He's the one who beat me up."

"He says you hit him first," Bibberman said. "He also says you're his pard, a boy with sand and one to ride the river with. I have to get back to supper now. If you feel up to it, I could use some firewood. It's out back."

The chair squeaked in relief as he rose and left the bunkhouse. I tried contemplating what the cook had told me, then stood up. Paper crinkled in my shirt pocket, and I reached inside and pulled out a note written in careless scrawl.

TyRel Bren I ow U
50 dolers 2 B payd
eN witchataw
E Fain

I shook my head clear, returned the note, and went outside. Bibberman was in the chuck house, singing an old gospel song in his high voice, and I found the woodpile and axe out back, tested my arms and shoulder, and tried chopping. Eventually I found a steady groove, and the pain in my face and head subsided.

Several minutes later, I gathered an armful of wood and took the load to Bibberman, who was outside with Uncle Cliff, writing out a list.

"Dried apples," the cook said, and wrote it down, "and a bottle of whisky. That should do it."

Uncle Cliff swallowed. "I said this is a dry drive, Bibberman. No whisky till Wichita."

"Clifford," Bibberman said, and I was surprised by his familiar tone, "I can't treat snakebite, colic, or fever with coffee, nor my brew. I'll keep the whisky in the wagon, and anyone who wants to get roostered on Doug Simpson's time will have to go through me. Including you."

"All right," he said, taking the note. "I'll see what we can get in Floresville." He glanced at me and sighed. "Tyrell," he said, "I thought I told you to wait until Wichita before you killed Fain." He laughed at his joke, and Bibberman joined him. Uncle Cliff was still cackling as he disappeared inside the main house.

Later that day, Uncle Cliff and I hitched up a buckboard for the Simpsons. "You'll eat with the hands," he told me, "and sleep in the bunkhouse. Doug, Mattie, and I are headin' into Floresville for supplies, won't be back till late. Fain'll be goin' with us, so you won't have to whup him no more."

Afterward, I helped Bibberman prepare supper and was quite relieved to be chopping more wood when the Simpsons rode off with Uncle Cliff. With my battered face, I was in no hurry to see Mattie again, or rather, have her see me.

For supper, Bibberman served leftover sonofabitch stew, more sourdough biscuits, and red bean pie. We filed past the chuck house, with Bibberman shoveling food on deep-dish plates, and walked to the bunkhouse, where a pot of strong coffee, tin cups, and utensils sat on the long table. The cowboys dug into the meal with little comment.

I hungrily attacked the food, savoring the stew, my first taste of fresh meat in weeks. Trace and Slaughter had been right; Bibberman was a better cook than Mattie Simpson. Finally, I asked Trace: "What exactly is sonofabitch stew?"

Trace smiled. "Beef. Sweetbreads. Calf heart and liver. Marrow gut." He took a sip of coffee. "Oh, and calf brains."

For the rest of the meal, I was less enthusiastic about supper. We finished eating, dropped our dishes into a nearby washbasin under Bibberman's watchful eye, and returned to the table. Talk and cigarettes flared up, while Trace strummed his guitar and sang.

Now Abilene and old Newton
Made us Texas cowboys shine
With whisky and women
Where nothin' is a crime.
It's the glory we live for.
We raise a little hell
To forget the pain
Of that damned Chisholm Trail.

After a while, Brazos Billy turned to me, noticing my cut and bruised face, and said: "Pilgrim, looks like ya got yerself dusted. Ya oughten to stay off them mean bronc's."

Immediately I was self-conscious of my battered face. I forced a smile and said: "It wasn't a horse, Brazos Billy, it was Emmitt Fain."

That got a whoop from the bowlegged cowhand. "Ya fit Emmitt Fain! I thought he was sportin' a small shiner today. Well, I swan!"

"I only got one punch in," I said. "It wasn't much of a fight."

The bunkhouse had gone silent. Even Trace had stopped playing his guitar, and every pair of eyes was turned on me.

"Boy," Brazos Billy said, "I sure hate to miss a fight. Next time ya fit Fain or anybody else, ya needs to get an audience. Fights is a whole lot more excitin' than roundin' up doggies."

"I don't think there will be a next time."

Suddenly Brazos Billy leaped from his chair and turned to the cook. "Mister Bibberman, I'd say this is cause for a round of Bibberman's Brew. At least, Tyrell Breen oughten to have a sip."

"You heard what Clifford said about no liquor," Bibberman replied. "Besides, I have just one or two fingers of my brew left."

"The drive ain't started yet, you belly-cheater!" another cowhand chimed in, and soon most of the cowhands were arguing that I deserved a victory drink, although I had been pummeled. Only Jesse Trace remained silent, and even he smiled.

"Don't let 'em push you into somethin' that might get you fired, Amos," Slaughter warned, but Bibberman grinned and left the bunkhouse amid cheers. In a few minutes he returned with a brown jug to louder applause and howls. He grabbed a tin cup, placed it in front of me, and poured a shot of an amber, reeking concoction. Bibberman quickly stepped back as if his brew were about to explode.

"Here's how!" Brazos Billy said, reaching for the cup. But Bibberman moved like a cougar and pinned his hand against the table. Brazos Billy cried out in pain.

"The drink is for Mister Breen," Bibberman said, releasing his grip, and Brazos Billy stepped back.

I turned to Trace, who smiled and nodded, and picked up

the cup. And then I swallowed the most wretched, foul-smelling drink that had ever found my mouth.

"Good God!" I cried after coughing and gagging, which prompted more wailing and hoots from the cowhands. Brazos Billy quickly took the cup from my hand, drained it, and ya-hooed. This time, Bibberman just laughed.

"What's in that . . . that brew?" I asked.

Trace finally spoke. "Grain alcohol for kick, tobacco juice for color, gyp water for taste, Louisiana hot sauce for flavor." He turned to Bibberman, who gave the final ingredient.

"And a pinch of strychnine to get your heart started again."

Trace slapped me on the shoulder. "One thing's for certain, Tyrell . . . you'll sleep good tonight."

He was right.

Chapter Seven

My sleep, deep and dark as a bottomless well, was rudely interrupted by Amos Obadiah Jonah Micah Bibberman's shrill greeting: "Top of the morning to you, you miserable waddies. Now come get this slop or I'll eat it myself!"

No one doubted that he couldn't, so we groped for our clothes in the predawn light and followed the bull-size Bostonian to the chuck house. By sunrise, we had wolfed down bacon, hot cakes, and coffee and were saddling horses in the corral. I expected some rough treatment because of my inexperience, but most of the cowhands were eager to give me pointers and answer my questions.

"Pull that cinch as tight as you can, else you might find yourself under that hoss' belly."

"Jes' foller Brazos Billy, pilgrim, and I'll help ya today."

"Let the horse do all the work, Tyrell. Just follow her lead."

"If you need anything, ask me."

Uncle Cliff rode up, and Bibberman handed him a cup of coffee. He took a sip and started barking out orders.

"O'Donnell, help Bibberman get the supplies on the chuck wagon, then check that remuda. Fain, I want that claybank and other horses trail broke by today. Trace, show

Tyrell around and get the Gen'ral ready to lead, then let Tyrell help Fain. Santee, scout ahead, and we'll map out somethin' tonight. Brazos Billy, I want a tally by supper time. The rest of you waddies, get them doggies out of the brush, branded, and ready to go. I want this herd movin' by first light tomorrow." He took another sip of coffee and poured the rest at Bibberman's feet.

"Bibberman," he said, tossing the empty cup to the cook, "someday you'll learn how to make coffee."

Bibberman smiled and pitched the cup back at my uncle, who caught it with his right hand. "Clifford," he said, "someday you'll learn where the dirty dishes go."

Laughing, Uncle Cliff kicked his horse forward a few yards and threw the cup into the washtub by the chuck house. "Let's move it!" he shouted. "We're burnin' daylight." Spurring his horse, he headed for the herd.

It was breathtaking, my first sight of Douglas Simpson's herd: a valley seemingly covered by cattle. Trace and I reined in our horses at the top of a small rise, stood in our stirrups, and surveyed the longhorns, grazing lazily in the coolness of early morning. Far to the right, smoke rose from a small fire as cowboys prepared to road-brand the rest of the herd. But mostly we watched the cattle, a collection of brown or black steers and several multicolored misfits, all with massive spans of horns glistening in the sunlight. It looked as if there were enough beef below us to feed the entire United States.

"Ever seen anything like it?" Trace asked.

"Not at all. It's really beautiful."

Trace laughed. "Enjoy it while you can, pilgrim. You'll be sick of this sight in about a week." And he spurred his horse forward to the longhorns.

We dismounted a few yards from the center of the herd,

and Trace reached into his saddlebags and pulled out—of all things—a triangular dinner bell and a small brown sack, which he tossed to me. I opened it and pulled out a handful of sugar cubes while Trace drew his revolver from his holster and used the barrel to ring the bell.

"It's time you met the Gen'ral," Trace said, and no sooner had the words left his mouth than a massive steer charged out of the herd and toward us. I took a few quick steps back, but Trace laughed and said: "Hold still, Tyrell. He ain't gonna hurt you."

I held out the sugar cubes as the muscular sway-backed animal stopped in front of me, and his coarse, huge tongue swept the sweets from my hand. Timidly I patted the steer's face and finally I laughed.

"I didn't know cows liked sugar," I said, as Gen'ral Houston chewed his cud, then attacked some grass at my feet.

"He makes sweet milk, too," Trace said.

Nodding, I patted the Gen'ral while avoiding his sharp horns before Trace's comment sank in. "It's a steer!" I shouted. "He can't give milk."

Trace laughed at his joke. "He's almost pet-like now," he said, "but take a close look at him."

Gen'ral Houston had a brown face and forelegs, but the rest of his body was dun-colored and spotted, with a huge Bar DS Bar brand burned into his flank. Assorted scars covered his body and face, including a relatively recent injury that had cut open his right ear. And when he looked up, I noticed he was blind in his left eye. His longhorns, scarred and wrinkled, stretched a good seven feet from tip to tip—considerable for even a Texas cow and probably as dangerous as any Comanche spear I had read about in my half-dime novels.

"Gen'ral earned his name," Trace said, mounting his

horse. "I watched him fight it out with a young steer a couple of years back. Fought all day long and half the night . . . a bunch of us gathered and watched it all, making bets, had a good moon that night . . . and Gen'ral finally just wore that youngster out."

I swung into my saddle, and we slowly began pushing the old, battle-scarred animal toward the northern end of the herd. "Gen'ral Houston has pointed Mister Simpson's herds north for at least eight, nine years and has earned his salt more than any waddie I've knowed. He's friendly enough with us when we've got sugar or salt for him, but he's heller in a fight with another mossy horn."

We left the Gen'ral in his lead position, then returned to the branding, and the stench of burning hide was enough to gag anyone. We watched as Les Slaughter brought in a steer toward the fire. Charley Murphy, who looked smaller than the longhorn, managed to toss the steer to the ground and sat on him while John Dalton, who looked out of place with his brown bowler, slapped on a brand. The steer bellowed in pain as smoke and a God-awful smell rose from the hide. Murphy unhooked Slaughter's lariat and let the longhorn up, which wasted no time in running to the main herd.

"How's it goin'?" Trace asked.

"Slow as Christmas," Slaughter replied, reeling in his lariat.

Trace frowned. "I was afraid you might say that." He turned to me and asked if I could find my way back to the main ranch. I told him I could, and he eased off his horse and walked to the branding fire.

"All right, you waddies, let me show you how it's done by a real cowboy."

Smiling, I left the cowboys and the stench of branding and rode back to the Simpson ranch.

A crowd was gathered at the corral when I rode in, watching Emmitt Fain ride hell for leather on a bucking horse. I reined in by the corral, and Mattie Simpson turned around and smiled. Then, staring at my still-bruised face, her eyes widened. And she laughed.

It wasn't the reaction I expected, and my face reddened as Douglas Simpson and Pedro O'Donnell turned their attention from Fain to me. I slowly dismounted, politely greeted everyone, and led the horse to the barn. Simpson and O'Donnell looked back at the horse-breaking show, offering cheers to Fain, but Mattie ran after me.

"Oh, Tyrell," she said, "I'm sorry. I didn't mean to embarrass you. But. . . ." She laughed again.

I unsaddled my mount, rubbed her down while Mattie tried to stop her giggles, unsuccessfully, and after a few minutes I laughed, too.

"I guess I do look a mess," I said, and she nodded before laughing some more.

"What happened?" she finally asked.

Sighing, I told her about my run-in with Fain, about him robbing me on the road, even about stealing the clothes in San Antonio. When I was finished, she wasn't laughing any more.

"My father doesn't think too much of Emmitt Fain, except as a cowhand, and neither do I," she said.

"I reckon he's not all bad. He did give me an IOU for the money, and he can charm anyone . . . I've seen that. I'm surprised you don't like him."

She let out an unlady-like snort and said bitterly: "Charming, I'm sure. I wouldn't trust him, Tyrell, and I'm sorry I laughed." She was smiling again. "C'mon," she said, "let's go watch Fain break those horses. Maybe he'll break his neck."

We climbed on the corral rails and watched Fain at work, and I had to admit I was impressed. The horse was bucking in a circle, but Fain rolled with its every turn, raking it with his spurs, smiling through every hard bounce and cloud of dust. Finally the horse gave up the fight, and Fain rode it around the corral to the cheers of O'Donnell and Simpson—even Mattie and me.

"*Señor* Fain *es* a *caballero muy grande,* no?" O'Donnell said.

"Heck, Pedro," Simpson said, "I could do that."

Pedro laughed and entered the corral, taking the halter as Fain dismounted and headed for a canteen hanging on the nearest post. Uncle Cliff rode up, then shouted at Fain.

"I'll have these widow-makers ready, Boss Rynders," Fain said before emptying the canteen over his head.

"All right, O'Donnell get up to the herd and help with the branding. Tyrell, you take over here." He turned toward the chuck house. "Hey, Bibberman! The ramrod is here, and he would like some coffee!"

A muffled voice replied: "Well, Clifford, you can come and get it yourself."

"I am too damned tired to get off my horse!"

"I'll get you some," Mattie said, and she ran toward the chuck house.

"Rider comin'," Fain said, dripping wet and walking toward us, and we turned as a lone man on a chestnut gelding rode in. The hounds by the porch growled for a minute before Uncle Cliff snapped at them to be quiet. The stranger reined to a stop, looked us over, and spoke to Uncle Cliff, apparently deciding that he was the man in charge.

"Name's Richard Hamilton. Understand you're putting together a drive to Kansas and might need a hand."

Uncle Cliff nodded. "You been up the trail before?"

"Time or two," Hamilton said in his Southern accent. He

was a tall man in a red flannel shirt, shotgun chaps, and a battered Confederate slouch hat similar to the one I wore. His hair was black, streaked with gray and shoulder length, and he also donned a slick mustache and underlip beard. But it was his eyes that I really noticed, a tired, colorless blue that added ten years to his appearance.

"No doubt you've heard what all they're saying about this outfit," Douglas Simpson said.

Hamilton smiled, but it was without humor. "Let's say I'm used to lost causes."

Uncle Cliff asked: "Who all have you worked with?"

"Rode swing for Shanghai Pierce last year. I was supposed to work for the Lazy P this spring, but I quit 'em when I found out they have a nigger bossin' the drive."

"A darky trail boss!" Fain shouted. "That's the damnedest thing I ever heard!"

Hamilton nodded. "I ain't takin' no orders from no nigger."

Uncle Cliff gestured to the chuck house, where Bibberman stood outside holding a coffee pot. Hamilton turned as the giant, black cook filled a cup for Mattie, who slowly brought it to Uncle Cliff.

"Will you eat one's cookin'?" my uncle asked, taking the cup from Mattie.

"He the cook," Hamilton asked, "or the chuck wagon?"

"He's the cook," Uncle Cliff said. "And there's another Negro on this drive. You have a problem with that?"

"Nope," Hamilton said. "I'll eat their slop and work with 'em. I just ain't about to take one's orders."

Uncle Cliff took a sip of coffee, glanced at Douglas Simpson, who shrugged, and turned back to Hamilton. "Pay's thirty a month and found, plus a ten dollar bonus if we get top price in Wichita."

"That's fair."

"You can store your gear in the bunkhouse, but we hope to be on the trail at first light tomorrow. You can ride out with O'Donnell after you store your possibles and cut out a fresh horse."

Hamilton nodded, tipped his hat to Mattie, then walked his horse to the barn.

We were silent for a few minutes as Uncle Cliff drained his coffee and Bibberman disappeared into the chuck house.

"Man's worked with Shanghai Pierce, he must be a pretty good hand," Fain said.

"Man's a fool," Uncle Cliff replied, tossing me the empty cup. "Any cowhand who pisses off the cook before the drive begins is just plain stupid. Now let's get to work."

We picked our horses that afternoon, pointing them out to O'Donnell, who must have memorized which cowboy wanted which horse for he never wrote anything down; he just nodded. Of course, I didn't pick my mounts, being last in seniority, although Uncle Cliff told me to use his brown mare, Lizzie, as a night horse. In addition, my string included two chestnuts, a claybank, black, buckskin with three stocking feet, and a white dun.

"Don't ride the dun at night," Uncle Cliff warned. "It's the surest way to get struck by lightnin'."

I was half worried how I would be able to catch my mounts for these animals were still half-wild and my skills with a rope were nonexistent, but my uncle smiled. "You ain't touchin' a lariat, Ty. Only ones I want ropin' a horse are Pedro, Slaughter, and Trace."

After supper, we sat around the table and listened to Fain's lies about cattle drives and wild horses. Uncle Cliff, Trace, and the red-bearded Red Santee had ridden out to the herd, and Bibberman was checking the chuck wagon.

"Tyrell can tell you," Fain said. "I barely tasted gravel all day. I guaran-damn-tee you those bronc's knew I was boss."

The door opened and in walked Bibberman, who took a seat beside Slaughter. Fain turned to the cook and said: "Bibberman, you tell these waddies that I was pure hell on them horses today. Why, I'd bet there ain't a creature I can't ride."

Bibberman laughed, and we all turned to him. There was a gleam in his eye, and, when he finally spoke, he slurred his words. "Mi-mister Fain, I got a three-cent nickel and one-dollar gold piece that says I know a critter you can't ride to a standstill."

We were silent for a minute, shocked at Bibberman's challenge.

"Amos," Slaughter said, "you're drunk."

"Drive ain't started yet," Bibberman said, "and I had a bit of brew left. But the bet stands, for all of you waddies."

"A dollar and three cents ain't hardly worth the effort," Fain said. "Besides, we'll be on the trail tomorrow."

"Right now," Bibberman said, and he stood up and pulled off his shirt. He walked to his bunk, then shed his boots and pants until he was wearing only his dirty long johns, well-worn socks, and battered bandanna. "Outside. One dollar and three cents says you can't ride me to a standstill."

"You!" Fain said, and laughed. "That's a damnedest thing I ever heard."

"No, the damnedest thing you ever heard is of a man of color bossing a cattle drive. I'm betting you . . . and any one of you . . . that I can buck you off my back."

Brazos Billy busted out laughing. "Hell's fire, boys, I'll see a little of that action!" He pulled off his boots and walked outside. Bibberman smiled and followed, despite Slaughter's pleas, and, amid guffaws and complaints, the rest of us joined them in the moonlight.

We formed a loose circle around Bibberman and Brazos Billy. The drunk cook got on his hands and knees, and Brazos Billy climbed on his back, put his right hand around Bibberman's bandanna, and removed his hat with his left and slapped Bibberman's bulky buttocks.

"Let 'er rip," Brazos Billy hollered, and in one quick motion Amos Bibberman sent the arrogant cowhand flying head over heels, still holding the cook's bandanna as he hit the ground with a thud and a groan.

The ranch yard exploded in laughter as Brazos Billy sat up, slowly shook his head, and said: "What a fart-knocker."

Bibberman laughed, but Fain yelled: "Hold your horses, cookie, and let me show you how a real bronc' peeler sits your saddle." He knelt and quickly unfastened his spurs, took his position on Bibberman's back, and got a good grip on the bandanna.

"Turn him loose!" Fain yelled, and the cook began bouncing around the yard to our cheers and jeers.

"Stay with him!"

"Show him who's boss!"

"Fain, you're about to dirty your shirt!"

It should have been a pathetic sight, a grown man riding the back of an overweight, balding, and almost-naked cook, but it was the most entertainment we had had in ages. Side bets sprang up as Bibberman bucked and Fain screamed with childish delight, and the circle of cowhands widened as rider and man-horse demanded more room.

Both men were sweating now, as Bibberman crawled toward a hitching post to try to knock Fain off.

"Hell, that ain't rightly fair!" Charley Murphy shouted.

"Sure it is," Brazos Billy argued. "I seen horses do it many a time."

Emmitt Fain was laughing as Bibberman tried to pin him against the rail, but the veteran cowhand pulled on the cook's bandanna, then kicked his stomach with his boots, and Bibberman veered away, took a deep breath, and reared backward, whinnying like a horse and sending an unsuspecting Emmitt Fain to the ground.

"Emmitt," Brazos Billy said, "you've been dusted."

Fain laughed and wiped sweat from his brow. "Charley, how 'bout bringin' me a canteen. And Brazos Billy, I think I out-rode you by several minutes."

"There ain't no horse that can't be rode," Les Slaughter said, "and there ain't no cowhand that can't be throwed."

Fain smiled as Charley Murphy handed him a canteen. He took a deep pull, then passed the water to Bibberman, who also drank greedily. "Ain't no horse that can't be rode," Fain said, "but I dare say there is one cook."

"I disagree," Richard Hamilton said, stepping toward the cook. "I'm about to iron out the humps on this nigger horse."

Bibberman was still panting as he put the stopper in the canteen and tossed it to Murphy.

"Give Amos a minute to catch his breath!" Slaughter shouted.

"I'm all right," the cook said, dropping to his arms and knees again.

Hamilton grinned as he took a seat on the cook's back, and I noticed he was still wearing spurs.

"Take off your spurs," I said, and the crowd immediately went silent.

"Yeah," Slaughter said, "that ain't fair."

"Uhn-uh," the new hand said. "That wasn't in the bet." And he bent his knees until his huge, sharp rowels were against Amos Bibberman's stomach. "All right, you pot walloper," he said, "let's ride over to the water trough. That's where horses and niggers should drink."

"Shed them spurs, Hamilton," Fain said, but Bibberman motioned him back.

"It's all right. There wasn't anything in the bet about spurs."

A dangerous quiet filled the night as Bibberman slowly crawled toward the nearest trough, carrying a grinning Hamilton on his back. We followed closely, not speaking, the previous fun forgotten. Hamilton wore Mexican-style spurs, big, mean, and capable of gutting Bibberman like a well-honed knife. After a couple of minutes, man and rider were beside the water trough near the corral.

Hamilton laughed. "Well, cookie, take a drink. You've earned it."

Bibberman's scream cut through the night like a scythe as he quickly rose to his knees, clamping giant hands around Hamilton's boots and pulling the spurs away from his stomach as Hamilton's head hit the dirt. With a mighty grunt, Bibberman stood, lifting a screaming Hamilton by his boots as if he were a flour sack, turned, and dumped the new cowhand headfirst in the water trough. Bibberman, suddenly sober and exhausted, staggered back against the corral as Slaughter rushed to his side.

Hamilton emerged from the trough, spitting out water and hurling oaths in every direction. He climbed out of the trough and was heading for Bibberman when Fain and Brazos Billy stopped him, pinning his arms back.

"Let me go! I'm gonna kill that Jim Crow."

"Ease off, Hamilton. Ya had that comin'."

"I'd rule it a fair ride and say you lose, Hamilton," a voice sounded behind us, and we turned to face Uncle Cliff, sitting in his saddle, rolling a corn-husk cigarette by the moonlight. How long he had been there was anyone's guess.

Fain and Brazos Billy released their grip, and Hamilton wiped the water from his face. He was still fuming, but my uncle's presence had ended any present danger, and Hamilton rapidly walked to the bunkhouse.

"Hope you waddies had fun," Uncle Cliff said. "Because from now on, it's all work till we reach Wichita."

Slowly, silently we filed back into the bunkhouse.

Chapter Eight

Bibberman shrieked at us that pitch-black morning, and someone struck a match and lit a lantern. "We're burning daylight!" Bibberman said, laughing at his joke as he walked toward the chuck house.

Slowly I rose, swung my legs out of the bed, and grabbed my boots. Something jingled, and, after blinking the sleep out of my eyes, I noticed someone had strapped a pair of spurs to my cowboy boots. They were plain black steel with seven-point brass rowels and undecorated tan leather straps. Scratched on the sides of the spurs were the initials **E.F.**

Emmitt Fain was smiling when I looked at him. He pulled on his boots, picked up a pair of leather chaps, and tossed them to me. "I won this pair in a faro game in Floresville the other night," he said. "And we'll be headin' through some rough country. Leggin's and spurs will do you proper."

"Besides," Jesse Trace said as he walked by, "the key to bein' a cowboy is lookin' the part."

We dressed, then filed by the chuck house for coffee, bacon, and biscuits, ate in a hurry, and began saddling our mounts, still relying on lantern light.

"Tyrell!"

I turned, and Uncle Cliff motioned me over as he tightened his saddle cinch.

"Ty," he whispered when I arrived. "Mister Simpson will need some help with the ranch after we pull out. Those O'Donnell boys still haven't showed up . . . they'll probably get here today or tomorrow . . . but no one's gonna think bad of you if you stay on."

My stomach almost turned over. I knew what Uncle Cliff was trying to do, but I had no intention of being robbed of my chance to go on a cattle drive and, as Jesse Trace and others had said, "see the elephant."

"You'd be short-handed," I argued.

"I'll hire me someone in San Antone or Austin . . . jinxed herd or not."

"I'm going with you," I said.

"This ain't no picnic, Tyrell."

"I'm going, damn it!" I said, and walked back to my horse.

Uncle Cliff grunted and led his horse out of the corral.

"All right!" he hollered. "Fain and Santee will take the point, Cochrane and Trace at swing! Hamilton and Slaughter will ride flank. That puts Tyrell, Charley, and Dalton at drag. And you too, Brazos Billy."

"Aw, hell, Boss Rynders," Brazos Billy said. "I gotta ride drag ag'in?"

"Only way I know to shut you up," Uncle Cliff said as he mounted his horse and rode off.

We finished saddling our horses, then tossed our bedrolls and war bags into the chuck wagon, a red Studebaker with the Simpson brand burned into its sides. Jesse Trace handed Bibberman his guitar and said: "Amos, take real good care of this."

The cook grunted. "I'll try not to cut it up for firewood."

Gray light began appearing in the east as we rode away,

but I reined in my horse when someone called my name. I turned in the saddle and saw Mattie on her porch. Jesse Trace stopped beside me, looked back, then turned to me, and grinned. "I'll wait for you here, pilgrim."

I spurred my horse forward and rode to the Simpsons' house.

"I just wanted to say good bye, Tyrell, and good luck. And here. . . ." She handed me some paper and a pencil. "Maybe you'd like to write a letter or something."

"I'd like that," I replied, accepting the gifts.

There was an awkward silence as I looked into her eyes, unsure of what to say or do. I stayed in the saddle and tried to find my voice.

"Daddy's going to take me to Wichita with him. I've never been to Wichita, but he says, if the herd brings a good price, we'll splurge and stay at the Munger House. He says it costs a whole two dollars a day but that we deserve it. He says Wichita even has a three-story hotel. I can hardly imagine that."

I smiled, as silent as my saddle, when her expression changed and she reached out and touched my left arm that was hanging at my side. "Tyrell, please be careful. I don't want anything to happen to you."

Suddenly, overcome by my Beadle's half-dime imagination, I swept my father's hat off my head and leaned over and kissed her. Her lips were sweet, my heart pounded, and blood rushed to my head, and although I was half-expecting a scream or a slap—or to fall off my horse—to my disbelief she kissed back.

Then I straightened in the saddle and looked down at her, and realized that this mental picture of her, standing on her porch in a calico dress, her face warmed by the lantern light, would be with me all the way to Kansas.

"I'll be careful, Mattie," I said. "And I'll see you in Wichita."

Kicking my horse forward, I, Tyrell Breen, a cowboy in full regalia and love-struck schoolboy, rode to join Jesse Trace. We rode side by side to the herd, silently, both of us smiling, when after a while Trace broke out in another verse of "The Lonesome Chisholm Trail."

Now the long nights get lonely
On this lonesome Chisholm Trail.
I'm far from my true love,
And that cold north wind wails.
Oh Mattie, my sweet Mattie,
I'll be dreamin' of you.
To you and Texas
You know I shall be true.

I took my position at the end of the herd with Charley Murphy, Brazos Billy, and John Dalton, and, as the cattle slowly got to their feet, we began chanting and yipping.

"Ho ho ho ho cattle."

"Get up you doggies."

"Yip yip yip yip."

The longhorns looked at us stubbornly, then grudgingly took the first steps north to Kansas. It was slow going at first, but gradually the longhorns formed a line, about five abreast, and, as we cleared a rise, I realized the herd must have stretched more than a mile, maybe two, a long stream of brown rolling north.

"Push 'em hard!" Dalton shouted as he pulled up his bandanna to block out the rising dust.

Suddenly a black steer bolted out of the herd and tried to turn south, and I was amazed as my horse sprang after him, cut him off, and forced him back to the herd. I rode back to my position and saw Murphy's eyes dancing. He lowered his bandanna and shouted over the bawling cattle: "See, Tyrell, it's true! The horse does all the work!"

We kept them at a tiring clip, stopping only for a noon break to change horses and have a meal—eating in two shifts—of coffee, biscuits, beans, and bacon by the chuck wagon.

A few longhorns tried to turn back, breaking up the monotony of riding drag, and the afternoon heat pounded us unmercifully. My legs grew stiff in the saddle, my throat turned as dry as a lime-burner's hat, and it didn't take long to realize I had about two more months of this to look forward to.

The black longhorn made another bolt south, but again my horse and I cut him off and nursed him along. Before dusk, we slowed the herd and allowed them to drink from a small creek, then bedded them down in a circle and slowly rode to the chuck wagon.

It took a lot of effort for me to dismount, and Pedro O'Donnell smiled as he took my horse and led it to the remuda. I beat the dust off my clothes with my hat, took a long drink of water from the barrel on the chuck wagon, then stood in line as Bibberman dished out supper.

"Beans, biscuits, and bacon," Brazos Billy said. "Nothing like a little variety."

Bibberman handed him a plate and cup without comment, and Brazos Billy took a step back, stared at the bulge in the cook's cheek, and said: "Amos Bibberman. I never knowed ya to chaw tobaccy."

The cook sent a stream of brown juice onto Brazos Billy's boots and reached for another cup and plate. Brazos Billy laughed and found a spot to eat.

"Dish it up," Richard Hamilton said, and Bibberman

handed him a full cup and plate, saying: "Enjoy."

John Dalton silently said grace before he ate, but the rest of us dug in immediately and forgot our upbringing and manners. A casual banter sprang up as we polished off the food and helped ourselves to more coffee while Bibberman and O'Donnell washed the dishes.

"Hey, Dick," Red Santee said, "I hear tell you took a bath last night while wearing your clothes."

"I wanted to get the black stench off me," Hamilton said dryly. "And the name, mister, is Richard."

"Why do we have to drive 'em to Kansas?" an exhausted Charley Murphy asked.

"Why don't we just drive 'em to San Antone and say we went to Kansas?"

"The whores look better in Wichita," Santee offered, to which young John Dalton simply shook his head and sipped coffee.

"Nah, the best-lookin' ones work in Abilene," Brazos Billy said.

Santee cackled. "Hell, Brazos Billy, you was in the cattle yard, not the Devil's Addition," he said, and most of the cowhands, Brazos Billy included, joined him in laughing.

Uncle Cliff rode up and took his customary coffee cup in the saddle before firing out orders. "For the first few days, we'll split the night watch half and half until we tire them doggies out a bit. First watch is Murphy, Slaughter, Brazos Billy, Ty, and Trace. Fain and Cochrane are out with the herd now. Murphy, you and Slaughter go spell 'em so they can get some chow. And if you let them cattle stampede while I'm sleepin', all of you will rue the day."

Less than an hour after almost falling off my horse to eat supper, I found myself back in the hard saddle, riding around the longhorns in a star-filled night. The moonlight cast an eerie glow on the cattle that milled lazily and grazed or dropped to sleep. Voices, low and soothing but for the most part not very musical, carried through the night. The cowboys sang to keep the cattle calm, but I was too tired to sing. I heard Trace's baritone as he rode toward me.

I'm a poor lonesome cowboy.
You know I was just bound to die
Somewhere on this wide prairie
On a drive by and by.
Now we're at that Red River,
How I wish she were dry.
If the Red takes me under
Who'll tell her good bye?
She was just a poor farm girl
Who I've known all my life,
A red-headed young beauty
Said I'd make her my wife,
But if the Red takes me under
As I ride this big dun,
Pard, tell her I'm sorry
For the wrong things I done.

He reined in beside me and held out a plug of chewing tobacco, which I declined.

"Nasty habit," he said, and spit. "I'd prefer my Bull Durham to smoke, but don't wanna strike a match and scare the herd."

I thought he was joshing me, but he shook his head solemnly and said: "Longhorns are tough bastards, Ty, but they scare as easy as a school gal. They smell a wolf or panther, match strikes, twig breaks, pot falls, and they might be up and running. Hell, I seen 'em run when a cowhand sneezed."

"You think they might stampede?"

"First few days are usually the worst. That's one of the reasons we push 'em hard. Keep 'em tired and they're less likely to bolt for home or parts unknown. If they run, Ty, just stay in front of 'em, and we'll try to turn them into a circle. But I'd sing to 'em now. They like music." He kicked his horse ahead and continued his lament.

Red River, you're a killer.
Ain't you got any shame
For all those young cowboys
Whose deaths you're to blame?
You're wide, deep, and muddy
But your banks would not hold
All the tears of young farm girls
When the tally's been told.

In a few minutes, I began humming a few bars to "Lorena," and studied the ground I was traveling, trying to avoid any twigs that might snap.

I was spelled around midnight, rode back to camp, slid off my horse, unsaddled it, and turned it into the rope corral. Dragging my feet, I found my way to the Studebaker chuck wagon, where Bibberman was busy setting batter for the morning's breakfast.

After grabbing my bedroll, what the cowhands called a sugan, from the wagon bed, I found a spot and was asleep before I could take off my boots and spurs. It seemed only a minute later—and it was still dark as coal—that Uncle Cliff was kicking my feet and Bibberman was yelling to come and get it. I washed my face, even combed my hair, and took my spot in the line for breakfast.

"I'll take oysters," Brazos Billy said. "I do love those oysters. And a slice of peach pie, your best white wine, and a two-bit cigar afterward."

Bibberman looked at him silently, handed him a plate of beans, bacon, and biscuits and a cup of black coffee, and turned to pour another cup and fill another plate. We ate in silence, too tired to talk, and afterward had Slaughter and O'Donnell catch our horses in the remuda. Emmitt Fain and Red Santee, who had been with the herd while the rest of us ate breakfast, rode in while I was saddling my claybank.

"Problems?" Uncle Cliff asked.

"I think we got one coaster," Fain said, "a little black bastard hell-bent on startin' trouble."

Uncle Cliff nodded. "We'll take care of that if he keeps it up." He turned toward us and yelled: "Let's get a move on, boys!"

Dawn was breaking as we got the longhorns up and on the trail, pushing them at another hard clip. For hours we stayed in the saddle, eating dust, shouting at the cattle, intercepting the occasional beeves that tried to break from the herd. My already stiff legs hardened some more, and the black longhorn twice tried to turn back. Once he prodded a cow in front of him with his horns, but John Dalton rode in and hit him twice with his lariat to stop him.

By noon, we halted the herd and let them graze, then rode in two shifts to the chuck wagon where I eagerly awaited more beans, biscuits, bacon, and coffee. We took our dinner from the tobacco-chewing Bibberman, ate quickly, and put our dishes in the washtub, what the cowhands called the wreck pan, and walked to the rope corral where O'Donnell lassoed fresh mounts.

I was slipping on a bridle when Uncle Cliff loped in. He took a cup of coffee from Bibberman and stopped me as I prepared to ride back to the cattle.

"Fain's bringin' in that coaster," he told me. "I want you to wait till we get the herd a mile or so away, then take care of it. Bibberman will show you how. Then get back to drag."

"Pedro and I can take care of it, Clifford," Bibberman said, but Uncle Cliff shook his head.

"I want Tyrell to do it." He gave me a hard look, tossed the empty cup into the wreck pan, and stared at Bibberman. "Make sure he does it," he ordered, before raking his horse with spurs and galloping away.

Slowly I dismounted, wrapped my reins around the wagon tongue, looked at Bibberman, and waited. In a few minutes, Emmitt Fain rode in with the second shift, leading the black longhorn with his lariat. He tied the cow to a wagon spoke, and, as I helped Bibberman load the chuck wagon, Fain and the others threw down coffee and food before getting fresh horses from O'Donnell and galloping toward the cattle. We waited a while after they had gone, and Bibberman gave O'Donnell an axe and sent him off for firewood. He looked at me and jerked a thumb toward the cow as he walked to the chuck wagon's boot. I was pretty sure what was coming as he opened a drawer.

When Bibberman withdrew a revolver, I felt sick. We stood in silence, waiting, as the longhorn moaned. My throat was parched as Bibberman handed me the heavy Colt Dragoon.

"It's time, young Breen," he said. "Kill him."

I took a few awkward steps toward the scared longhorn, the giant horse pistol hanging at my side.

"Tyrell," Bibberman said, "he's a troublemaker, bent on causing a stampede or something. We can't sacrifice the herd for one cow. He won't go to waste. We'll have fresh beef tonight, but you have to do this."

"Why me?" I said.

"Clifford knows what he's doing. Aim for his head. He won't feel a thing."

My eyes filled with tears as I pointed the pistol and thumbed back the hammer, but the longhorn stared at me with child-like eyes, and the Colt long barrel shook violently. I steadied the pistol with both hands but still couldn't shoot.

"Damn you, Tyrell!" Bibberman screamed. "Pull the blasted trigger!"

The gun exploded, and the black longhorn dropped with a sickening thud. I bit my lip, tossed the smoking gun to the black cook, quickly mounted my horse, and rode away.

Uncle Cliff was waiting near the herd, and I stopped beside him but did not speak.

"This ain't no storybook, son," he said softly. "I've tried to tell you that. It ain't all fun and games. It's cruel, and it'll get worse." He moved his horse in front of me and waited until I looked up at him, revealing my tear-streaked face.

"You wanted to be a cowboy, well killin' coasters is part of the job. So is shootin' your horse when he breaks a leg. And lickin' horse sweat when we run out of salt, puttin' tobacco juice in your eyes to keep from fallin' asleep, ridin' all night in a thunderstorm to keep the beeves from runnin'. You wanna turn back and ride to the Simpsons, it's fine with me."

"No," I said.

"Good," he said. "Now ride it out. Get back to drag and be thankful you have fresh meat to eat."

I pulled up my bandanna as I took my position, letting Uncle Cliff's words sink in. He was right, I knew, and I felt weak for crying over a cow, but after a while I settled into a groove of pushing the cattle and choking back dust, joining Dalton and Murphy in shouting encouragement.

"Ho cattle ho ho ho ho."

"Hiya he-e-e. Keep movin'!"

"Yip yip yip, you beeves. You got a date with the Leavenworth slaughterhouse!"

At last I smiled, wondering what Brazos Billy would complain about at supper when he found out we were having fresh beef.

Chapter Nine

"Hell, Amos," Brazos Billy said as Bibberman filled his plate with a pan-fried steak, sourdough biscuits, and vinegar pie, "I had my heart set on bacon and beans."

Tobacco juice splattered on the cowboy's boots, and Bibberman snorted. "Mouth off again and I'll spit into your eyes." Brazos Billy glanced at his soiled boot, laughed, and walked off as the giant cook wiped his mouth with his shirtsleeve and reached for another plate.

I found a spot near Jesse Trace and attacked the food. The steak was pretty much burned, the way most of the hands liked, but it was a relief from the monotony of beans and bacon. Washing the food down with strong coffee, I noticed the rest of the hands filing by the chuck wagon to grab their plates.

Amos Bibberman handed Richard Hamilton a plate, grabbed a tin cup, knelt by the coffee pot, and poured—discretely adding a stream of tobacco juice. The huge cook rose, handing the former Confederate soldier the coffee while adding his customary: "Enjoy."

Jesse Trace, who also had seen Bibberman's trick, snickered, but the smile vanished as Hamilton sat beside us. We watched as he ate his food, and I held my breath when he took his first sip of coffee.

"How's the grub?" Trace asked, glancing at me with mischievous, dancing eyes.

"Fair," Hamilton said, taking another sip.

I finished eating, leaving the rest of my coffee untouched, and Trace and I headed to the wreck pan to dump our dishes. Trace smiled at Bibberman and softly asked: "How long you been sweetenin' Hamilton's coffee?"

Tobacco juice spanged against the side of the wreck pan as Bibberman scowled, then grinned. I recalled Uncle Cliff's statement that only a fool would anger a cook, and now I had to agree with him.

"I'll say one thing about the Rebel bastard," Bibberman said. "He has a cast-iron stomach."

Uncle Cliff rode in and issued the watch assignments, grabbed a cup of coffee—*sans* tobacco juice—and rode out again to check the herd. The rest of us settled into our bedrolls as Jesse Trace brought out his guitar and began playing "Listen to the Mockingbird." Conversations started about saddles, moved to cigars, and finally settled on food.

I would have imagined the favorite dish to be steaks, buffalo, or some wild game, but to my surprise the sentiment was for a slimy seafood that I had long despised.

"In 'Seventy-One I went to the Drovers Cottage in Abilene," Brazos Billy said, "and I was in hog heaven. I started out with oyster soup, had some turkey with oyster sauce. Then for the entree, I had some escalloped oysters . . . and that was the best eatin' I ever had."

"Oyster pie in Newton was pretty good, too," Red Santee added.

"Yep," Brazos Billy said, "but them escalloped oysters was the best meal I ever et. When I die, I hope to come back as an oyster. Hey, Tyrell, you bein' from Carolina and all, I bet you got to et oysters regular as clockwork."

I was laying back, eyes closed, enjoying the banter. I laughed at Brazos Billy's suggestion, and said: "Heck, no, I think oysters are the most repulsive food in the world."

The silence that followed was eerie—even Jesse Trace's guitar strumming had stopped. I opened my eyes and pushed myself up to find almost every eye in camp trained on me.

Red Santee spoke: "You're joshin' us, ain't you boy?"

After stifling a laugh, my mouth fluttered as I realized my comment had flattened these men. "No," I said, shaking my head, "I can't stand oysters. I'd rather eat . . . er . . . mud."

Silence resumed. Then Brazos Billy said: "You musta had a careless upbringin', not likin' oysters. That's the craziest thing I ever heard."

Charley Murphy added. "Mud ain't so bad, if you season it with enough salt."

A couple of cowhands laughed at the lame joke, and Trace began playing the guitar again. Red Santee looked at Brazos Billy and shook his head, and I closed my eyes and fell back.

"Ever et squash pie?" Brazos Billy asked.

"Nah," Red said, "but my ma used to fix us a mighty fine plum pudding."

We rolled and tied our bedrolls, then hurriedly ate breakfast the next morning before getting the herd up and moving before the sun was high. Uncle Cliff asked how I was feeling, but I had pretty much put the dead cow behind me. He put his hand on my shoulder, gripping it hard for a second, and smiled. "I knew you would be all right," he said, turning to find his horse.

The sun pounded us relentlessly that day and all the next, but Uncle Cliff shortened the night watches so I started to get a little more sleep, but not a whole lot. "A cowboy catches up on his sleep come winter," my uncle told me over breakfast one morning.

I fell into a certain routine: a quick breakfast, several hours on horseback, choking on dust while shouting at bawling longhorns, a short break around noon for coffee and beans and a change of mounts, several more hours at drag before welcome relief at the day's end for supper and sleep, often broken up by watch duty. The one thing I usually enjoyed was the gatherings around the chuck wagon for dinner and supper, not only because of Bibberman's grub, but also for the conversation among the cowboys, their tall tales and peculiar topics.

It was during one of those times that I got into my second fight with Emmitt Fain.

We had watered the herd and crossed a narrow river—the Guadalupe, John Dalton had said—that afternoon. After eating supper—Bibberman had returned to the staples of beans, bacon, and coffee—we stretched out as the conversation turned to women.

By their names—Newton Nancy, Abigail Delight, The Occidental's Oriental—I knew these were not the kind of women my mother would want me to be associated with, but as Brazos Billy bragged about his daring escapades, my thoughts turned to another girl. I remembered Mattie, her smile, her eyes, our good bye kiss, and I longed to see her again. Wichita and the Simpson ranch both seemed so far away now. Saddened, I went to pour another cup of coffee.

"Hey, Tyrell, you got a sweetie back in South Carolina?" Brazos Billy hollered. At that moment, Fain rode into camp, dismounted, handed the reins to Pedro, and joined me by the coffee pot as Bibberman put away the dishes and the cowhands waited for my reply.

Jesse Trace smiled. "I think he's got a sweetheart, only he ain't been told yet. And I dare say she's a lot closer than South Carolina."

"Yeah?" Brazos Billy asked Jesse. "Who?"

Trace lowered his head and concentrated on tuning his guitar. Brazos Billy turned back to me with pleading eyes, but I didn't feel like discussing Mattie Simpson with anyone. At last it dawned on Brazos Billy, and he hooted. "Not Mattie!" he yelled.

"Saints alive!" Red Santee chimed in. "If Doug Simpson finds out, he'll peel your hide!"

I drained my coffee and tossed the cup into the wreck pan. Fain looked at me, grinning, and asked: "You really sweet on Mattie?"

Shrugging, I turned to leave, but Fain yelled to the others. "Son-of-a-bitch, it's true." I was walking away, but Fain came at my heels. "Rein up, Ty, and tell us about it. I've stolen a kiss or two from Mattie myself, but I ain't. . . ."

I turned savagely and lunged at him, but Fain simply side-stepped me, and I harmlessly sailed past, almost stumbling to the dirt. Then I was at him again, swinging wildly, blindly, as Fain ducked. Someone yelled: "Fight!" But no one was offering encouragement for either of us, nor was anyone trying to stop the fight. I swung again, and Fain blocked my punch and connected a right to my jaw. My teeth rattled, and I dropped like a bag of oats, landing on my hind end, legs in front of me.

"Ease up, Ty," Fain said, offering a hand. I slapped it away and rose on my own power.

My face reddened in anger and embarrassment as I realized everyone's stares were locked on me. Maybe I was jealous because I expected he hadn't been kidding when he said he had kissed Mattie; it explained why she had acted so bitter about him. Or perhaps I was shamed to have lost a fight—if you could call it that—in front of everyone.

"I've got first watch," I said. "I'd better get to it."

"No," a voice said from behind me, and I turned to see Uncle Cliff, still mounted, frowning. "I don't want you watchin' the herd while you're still smartin'. Charley Murphy, you take first watch. Ty, you take second. Maybe you'll be cooled off by then."

"Hell, Mister Rynders," Murphy said, but Uncle Cliff glared at him, and Murphy cowered and went to the remuda to pick out a horse.

Uncle Cliff's stare fell on Fain. "I was just joshin' the boy, Boss. I didn't mean no harm. We're just a long ways from women and. . . ."

"Shut up, Emmitt. I'd say a cow camp ain't the proper place to discuss a teen-age girl or lady, and Mattie Simpson is both." He looked over the rest of the cowhands and raised his voice. "And the next pair I catch fightin' will be walkin' back to Floresville!"

As we slithered off to our bedrolls, Uncle Cliff swung from his horse, letting the reins fall to the ground and waited as Bibberman fixed his plate. "Actin' like a bunch of boys," he said when the cook handed him his supper.

"Clifford," Bibberman said, "they *are* boys."

I stewed that night and all next day and was picking at my supper when Fain sat beside me. He held out his hand. "I'm awful sorry about last night. We still pards?"

"Yeah, sure," I said without conviction and ignoring his peace offering.

Fain sighed. "It was at a Christmas dance, Ty. All I did was kiss her. It didn't mean nothin'. I'm a thirty-a-month-and-found cowhand. I ain't one for a proper lady."

"Emmitt," I said, raising my voice, "I don't want to hear. . . ."

"Hell's fire if I don't always make you mad," he said, clamping his right hand on my thigh. "If you was wearin' a gun, we'd probably wind up killin' each other. . . . Aw, hell." He released his grip and ate a bit, then sat his plate down, and turned to me again. "How about I make it up to you?"

"You don't have to make anything up to me, Emmitt."

"No sir, I got to make things right between us. I did that about the money I borrowed"—to which I laughed—"and I'm bound and determined to do it again."

"Just do whatever you want," I said, and couldn't help smiling as I watched him pick at his supper, his brain working, trying to think of something.

"I'll teach you everything I know about cowboyin'," he said suddenly, as if he had been thunderstruck with the idea. "You want to be a top hand, probably a rancher someday, well, it's time to start your schoolin'. That sound fair?"

"I don't care," I lied. But he had grabbed my interest, and, after he pleaded a few more times, I relented, trying to hide my enthusiasm.

We finished our supper, and he took my plate to the chuck wagon and brought back two fresh cups of steaming coffee. After sitting down beside me, he looked over the camp and asked: "Who's the best cowboy here?"

"You?" I replied sarcastically.

"Naw, Ty, be serious. Look them over and tell me who you think is the best."

I glanced at my saddlemates quickly, then found myself studying them harder, trying to analyze their weaknesses and strengths. After several minutes, I offered: "Jesse Trace?"

Fain shook his head. He lowered his voice, saying: "That's a fairly good guess, but there's something about cowboyin' that makes a good one special. Jesse knows his business, but he sings in saloons . . . for wages sometimes even . . . and a cowboy, a real cowboy, won't do nothing that ain't done a-horseback. Besides, fiddlin' and the banjo's mighty fine, but a guitar's for women."

He settled back, crossing his legs and sipping his coffee as he continued. "Look at their hats. I got a Stetson, you and that sum-bitch Hamilton wear those Johnny Reb slouch hats, Slaughter has that big ass sugarloaf sombrero, Red Santee has that porkpie number, Cochrane wears that Hardee thing, John Dalton wears that silly lookin' bowler. But you can't tell a cowboy by his hat. But you can by his saddle."

"Why?"

"Cowboy keeps his saddle clean, if he's worth a damn. Clothes may be moth-eaten, boots might be well-ventilated, but if he's worth his wages, his saddle will be well taken care of."

"How about Slaughter?" I asked. "He's been cowboying a long time."

"He is as good as they come when they come colored," Fain said, so I frowned and didn't even suggest Pedro O'Donnell or Amos Bibberman. It was apparent that only white cowboys mattered to my new teacher.

"Brazos Billy?"

Fain laughed. "You know better than that. Brazos Billy talks too much. Hell, he talks more than an old widder woman. And all Charley Murphy does is complain. Johnny Dalton won't ever curse, and he carries his mama's Bible in his war bag. Now there ain't nothin' wrong with the Good Book, but I ain't never known a good cowhand who hasn't uttered an oath now and then. Them old mossy horns will drive a preacher to cussin'."

So I looked at the remaining cowhands, keeping in mind

that, according to Fain's law, a good cowboy had a shiny saddle, didn't complain or talk too much but when he did speak was sure to swear a time or two. My eyes lighted on Ian Cochrane, a taciturn Scotsman who rode swing, kept to himself, and spent most of his nights reading a book by camp light before turning in. I couldn't recall him saying ten words to me since I joined the ranch.

He wore high black cavalry boots, brown wool britches with a leather saddle seat, heavy blue bib-front shirt, and a yellow scarf. His hat was the military Hardee style, black with the right side pinned up by what appeared to be a pewter thistle. The hat had a dark plume and red hat cord, which represented the artillery if I remembered correctly.

"How about him?" I said, pointing with my chin toward Cochrane as he tugged on his reddish-brown Vandyke beard while reading his book.

"Heavens no," Fain said. "You ever watched him closely?"

I shook my head.

"He sleeps with a pistol under his head," Fain said, and my eyes widened in surprise. "He joined up just a few days before you and Boss Rynders arrived. Now he does his job well enough, I'll give him that, but mark my words, Ty, he ain't no cowboy."

By the process of elimination, I guessed Red Santee.

"The old man's good," Fain said, and I looked again at Santee, who appeared to be in his thirties—not what I would call an old man. "Brought in that wood, though, for Bibberman yesterday . . . tryin' to get on Amos's good side. But Red's a man to ride the river with for damn sure. But, Ty, the best cowboy here is your uncle. I figured you would have guessed him right off."

"He's not in camp," I said.

"Well, he's the best. Take how he got those cattle watered at the Guadalupe. Gets them spaced right, drives the leaders in downstream so they don't muddy up the water for the others. Makes sure they get enough grass before beddin' them down on level ground. And watch how he forks a saddle. He's got a ramrod back, knows exactly how to handle his men and his cows. That takes experience and good cow savvy."

He stood up and drained the rest of his coffee. "Well that's enough of school for tonight. Get some sleep, pard." He took my empty cup and walked away.

Chapter Ten

Richard Hamilton dropped to his knees the next morning, bent over, and retched in front of us while we ate breakfast. He groaned, his face suddenly white, long hair hanging over his eyes, and sent forth another river of reddish-brown vomit. Slowly he straightened, breathing heavily, and wiped his brow, knocking off his hat.

"Christ," he said dryly before leaning over again, gagging spastically, but there was nothing left in his stomach.

"Lordy," said a pale Charley Murphy, who almost heaved himself.

Bibberman spit out tobacco juice, and Trace and I looked at each other, realizing the massive cook had finally exacted his revenge. But neither of us was smiling, for Hamilton's sickness was not funny. In fact, nobody was eating, our appetites soured.

"Bring him over here," Bibberman said, turning toward the chuck wagon and opening a drawer. Red Santee and Emmitt Fain helped the sick cowboy to his feet and eased him to the wagon as Bibberman mixed an assortment of powders and liquids into a bowl. He stirred it, then brought out a bottle of whisky, and added a couple of shots.

"Hey, Amos," Fain said, licking his lips, "I'm feelin' a mite ill myself."

The cook ignored him, poured the concoction into a cup, and handed the strange liquid to Hamilton. The ex-Confederate took the cup with both hands, brought it to his nose, then almost dropped it. "That smells God-awful," he said.

"Drink it all down," the cook ordered, and slowly Hamilton responded, gagging, stepping back, and shaking his head. But he was standing on his on two feet.

"Better?" Bibberman asked.

Hamilton nodded, and John Dalton, carefully stepping around the vomit, picked up Hamilton's hat and handed it to him. The weak cowhand slowly placed it on his head, but no one was sure if he wouldn't keel over at any second.

Uncle Cliff rode in, stared at Hamilton, who was still as colorless as his eyes, and asked: "You fit to work or you wanna ride in the chuck wagon today?"

"I'll do my job, Capt'n," he said firmly, but softly, and walked toward the horse herd.

"Hold up," Bibberman said, turning to the chuck wagon, where he found an empty canteen and filled it with the rest of his remedy. He corked it and handed it to Fain, who passed it to Hamilton. "You might need some more. It reeks, but it'll help your stomach." The cook looked up at Uncle Cliff and, as soon as Hamilton was out of earshot, said: "Reckon he must have took hold of some bad water the other day."

"No doubt," Uncle Cliff said sarcastically, turned to face the rest of us and barked: "We're burnin' daylight. Let's ride!"

Bibberman stared as Hamilton slowly mounted his horse, missing the stirrup on his first two attempts, and rode toward his flank position. I think he might have earned some of the cook's respect as he went to do his job, too sick really to be in a saddle. Slowly the cook reached into his mouth and tossed his plug of tobacco to the ground. He fumbled in the chuck wagon again and threw Santee a small pouch.

"Red," he said, "be my guest. Chewing tobacco is a nasty habit, and I'm quitting."

We crossed the San Marcos River without incident and kept driving the herd north. I still choked on dust, but my legs were getting used to the demands, no longer as stiff at nights, although my backside still felt chafed and my feet were swollen so much that it became a chore to pull off my boots.

I tried one night after a hard day, groaning as I made no progress and muttering: "Son-of-a-bitch." Fain looked at me and laughed. I tried again, but the boots were welded to my heavy legs, and I dropped to my bedroll with a thud and moan. "Son-of-a-bitch," I whispered, closing my eyes.

"You're gettin' to be a cowboy, Ty," Fain said in a faraway voice. There would be no lessons tonight.

"River crossings are the most dangerous happenings on a drive," Fain told me the next day as we nooned. He took a sip of coffee and added: "Next to stompedes, of course. But I don't like talkin' about no stompedes. It's bad luck."

"We haven't had any troubles at rivers so far," I said, recalling our swims across the Guadalupe, San Marcos, and a few creeks.

"We ain't crossed no real rivers, Ty. The Colorado usually isn't that bad, but the Brazos can be, and the Red is a holy terror, 'specially when she's flooded. The farther north we get, the worse the rivers are. South Texas ain't got no real rivers."

"Yeah," I said, thought of something, and laughed. "I guess in South Carolina we'd call those ditches, not rivers."

Fain smiled. "The danger is if the cattle start millin' in

midstream," he said as the smile vanished. "You don't want them to panic, else they might drown. So if they start to mill, you got to beat 'em, break 'em up, and keep 'em pointed north. And if you happen to lose your seat, grab your horse's tail, or grab a cow's tail. With luck you'll get pulled ashore with only a quick bath and a mouth full of river water.

"The other concern is quicksand, mostly at the Red and in the Nations. They get bogged in and there's not much you can do for them, except shoot the poor bastards." He laughed suddenly. "I remember ridin' up to the Canadian in the Nations one year. There was this darky waddie standin' on a sandbar in the middle of the river. So I hollers at him . . . 'That firm ground where you're at?' And he says . . . 'Lordy no, massah, I's on quicksand.' And I says . . . 'Well if you're standin' on quicksand, how come you ain't sinkin'?' And he says . . . ' 'Cuz I's standin' on my hoss.' " He cackled, pulled my hat down over my eyes, and walked to the remuda to pick out a fresh horse.

At the Colorado River, I found out just how dangerous crossings could be, but it was like nothing Fain or I had imagined. It was an easy ford a few miles below Austin, near a place Uncle Cliff called Montopolis. This was some of the prettiest country I had seen in Texas, full of green hills to the west and plenty of shade trees.

Gen'ral Houston led the herd into the river late one cool afternoon—"The Gen'ral takes to water like a skinny dipper," Jesse Trace had said.—and the rest of the longhorns followed, easing up along the far bank and moving on as we yipped and yahooed at the lean beasts.

Still half blinded by the dust from the day's drive, Charley Murphy, John Dalton, Brazos Billy, and I swam our animals across the river behind the last of the longhorns as Fain and Uncle Cliff watched from the bank. Charley made it across first, then bolted after a stubborn longhorn that was climbing the bank under a tree—a small cedar, I think—rather than following the other cattle along an easier path. Murphy raised his quirt and struck. "No!" Uncle Cliff yelled, but he was too late, because the leather quirt caught a tree limb and a white, papery cone dropped to the ground and seemed to explode, sending forth brown shrapnel and a loud humming.

"A-i-y-e-e-e!" Charley screamed as his horse threw him and took off after the suddenly fast-running longhorn steer.

"Cripes!" Uncle Cliff yelled, spurring his horse hard as he turned around and retreated north at a fast lope with Brazos Billy right behind him. Fain tried to follow, but his mount slipped on the muddy banks, sending him sprawling to the earth and galloping off alone after Uncle Cliff, leaving Fain afoot.

A panicking Charley was running toward the river, followed by a flying brown streak, wailing like an Indian and diving into the Colorado. And as I blinked away the dust and grime, I knew why.

"Hornets!" I cried as the swarm veered from a submerged Charley Murphy and flew toward Dalton and me. My horse reared in the shallow water of the near bank, and I swiped at the angry insects on my face and arms as I slipped from the saddle and splashed into the river, swallowing a healthy portion. I came up quickly for air, took a deep breath, and swore as one stung my neck. In an instant, I saw that Dalton was also in the water, and, as I dived under, I heard Emmitt Fain screaming and caught a glimpse of him running—his knees hardly bending—heading for the safety of the Colorado.

"Shit!" Emmitt Fain cried as Bibberman pulled a stinger from the back of his neck and rubbed it with salve. The cook smiled—I think he took pleasure in tormenting Emmitt—and applied the medicine on another swollen bite.

Charley Murphy had been stung the most. His face was swollen, his right arm pockmarked with hives, but he wasn't seriously injured. And for once, he wasn't complaining, because it hurt to open his mouth. I had received a couple of painful lumps on my neck, face, and arm, and Dalton had a welt above his left eye, but for the most part we were fine. Just sore, wet, and embarrassed.

"Hey!" Fain cried again when Bibberman removed another stinger. "That smarts, you fat belly-cheater!"

Uncle Cliff suddenly howled, slapping his knee, his eyes bright and laughing as he watched the spectacle. Trace, Santee, and a few other cowhands laughed with him, while Fain, Dalton, and I responded with glares. Murphy simply moaned from beneath his bedroll.

"Boys," Uncle Cliff said after catching his breath, "that was one funny sight, seein' y'all take to that river. I'd pay good money to see that at an opery house."

"How the hell would you know?" Fain said. "You turned tail and showed nothin' but your yellow back when them hornets hit the ground."

"Now I ain't paid to drive hornets to Kansas. We dodged that nest all evenin', and I thought about helpin'," Uncle Cliff said in jest, "but my mount was too lame to get you fellers out of that mess."

"I don't know, Boss," Santee said, clucking like a hen. "Fast as you passed me, I reckon you could be in the Nations by now."

Even Dalton and I joined the laughter this time, and Fain was smiling as Bibberman found the last stinger.

"Shit, Amos!"

Charley Murphy, whom Red Santee and a few others took

to calling "Hornet Herder," rode in the back of the chuck wagon for two days, until the swelling went down. He might have stayed longer, but Amos Bibberman was threatening to throw him out because he kept complaining about being jostled about in the springless Studebaker. We crossed the San Gabriel River with little trouble, other than annoying mosquitoes, but I found those bloodsuckers much less painful than a nest of angry hornets.

The countryside slowly changed as we moved north, leaving behind the brush country near San Antonio and verdant hills around Austin and discovering rolling prairie. I even noticed rich cotton fields that reminded me of South Carolina. And the sunsets faded from a brilliant orange to a mellow jaundice that seemed to soothe us, our horses, and the steers. I still choked often on dust, but, as we pushed northward, I took pleasure in watching the herd, stretched out like a long, brown river in front of me, horns glistening in the sunlight. I felt as if I were a part of history, and, although the work was demanding, a far cry from the glory I had originally expected, I was enjoying myself.

And then it rained.

A hard wind whipped in from the west—"That's a sure sign of rain," Uncle Cliff said at noon. "Better grab your slickers."—and clouds soon appeared, slowly heading our way, darkening the sky as they moved along. Long before sundown, we felt the first cold drops of water, so we donned our yellow pommel slickers and black-rubberized ponchos, fastening our hats down with latigo strings or bandannas.

"This ought to settle the dust," John Dalton hollered. Charley Murphy's reply was drowned out as the clouds burst and a cold stream of water poured over us. There was no lightning, a welcome relief, but the rain beat down without mercy, soaking my slouch hat through, and I shivered beneath my poncho.

At supper, Bibberman's coffee failed to warm my bones, and to my surprise I learned that the chuck wagon contained no tents to keep us out of bad weather. I looked for shelter, but found none. Beneath the chuck wagon was a sea of mud, so I simply pulled my waterlogged hat down tight and braced myself against the wind and rain.

Uncle Cliff splashed in on his horse and slid from the saddle with a sneeze. He shook it off and stepped under a small lean-to Bibberman had set up to keep the rain off his cook fire. I was refilling my cup, but handed it to my uncle instead, who downed it as if he were drinking water.

"Rain's set in," he said to no one in particular. "Better double the watch just to be safe."

"How long will it last?" I asked, but my uncle just shrugged and turned to Bibberman.

"No stars tonight. Use the compass to point north."

"Already done, Clifford."

"Damn, it's cold." And I noticed he was shaking. So did Amos Bibberman, because he threw a gray, wool blanket over his shoulders and pulled a sack of Bull Durham from a chuck wagon drawer. Slowly he rolled a cigarette, lit it, and handed the smoke to my uncle, who took a long drag and relaxed.

"That'll take the edge off, Clifford," Bibberman said. "Get some sleep."

I realized it wasn't only rain tormenting my uncle. It had been almost two weeks since he had drunk whisky, and he was longing for a stiff shot. As the rain pounded down, I looked at the other wet, miserable cowhands and knew every mother's son of them would want to join him.

As Fain and I rode out to relieve Les Slaughter, who was watching the cattle before we took over as the first night herders, I asked about the use of compasses. Fain laughed. "How do you know we're headin' north?" he asked. "We could be drivin' to Mexico."

"I know what a compass does," I said, "but Uncle . . . er . . . Boss Rynders said something about stars. And what happens if you lose your compass in a stampede?"

"Don't mention no stompedes, Ty. Amos Bibberman and Boss Rynders probably don't need a compass or stars, they've been up the trail so much. They know most of the landmarks. You know about the North Star, don't you?" Without looking for my nod, he continued. "When Bibberman sets up camp, he finds the North Star or uses a compass and points the wagon tongue north. That way, next morn all he has to do is get a fix on a landmark in the direction of the wagon tongue, and he's set.

"To be a cowhand, you have to read the stars. You can tell time by lookin' at the Big Dipper. That's how you know when you're supposed to be spelled since ain't many of us owns a good pocket watch. 'Course, tonight, we ain't gonna have the luxury of usin' the stars."

"So how will Red and Charley know when it's their watch?"

Fain laughed. "Knowin' Red and Murphy, I warrant we'll have to tell them."

Suddenly he reined in. In the fading light we saw Les Slaughter galloping toward us. His mount slid in the mud, almost spilling him, as he stopped, eyes wild underneath his Mexican hat, and shouted: "We got big problems!"

I looked ahead at the steers. Instead of bedding down for the night, the longhorns were walking on their own, bunched together, moving determinedly to parts unknown. Only there were no cowboys driving them.

Emmitt Fain swore underneath his breath. "Son-of-a-bitch. They're driftin'!"

Chapter Eleven

All night we followed the herd, trying to keep the steers from scattering, fighting off the wind and rain that pounded us without pity. The cattle weren't running, just walking, keeping the wind at their backs. But they were moving east, away from the trail—and there was nothing we could do to stop them.

"When they get to driftin' and the weather's like this, ain't no way to hold 'em, short of shootin' 'em!" Charley Murphy shouted over the wind. "I'd druther 'em stampede!"

We rode in the wet, dark night, over a few small hills, eventually struggling through farmland, leaving some luckless farmer's ruined cornfield in our wake.

Hours later the wind changed direction, and the herd veered northward, a giant turn of luck for us, although we were still off course. I heard muffled shouts ahead, but could see little in the blackness before dawn. A distant light appeared, fast approaching, and horse hoofs sounded, followed by Jesse Trace's "Hallooo, drag riders!" Brazos Billy yelled back, coaxing the rider our way.

Trace jerked his mount to a stop when he found us. He held a dimly lit lantern, steaming in the rain and casting an eerie, yellow glow on his face. "The Lampasas River's up ahead, and them doggies ain't stoppin'!" he shouted.

"What are we gonna do?" Murphy hollered.

"Ain't got no choice but to follow 'em in! Swim 'em 'cross and don't let 'em mill! And Murphy. . . ." Trace paused. "Keep away from the hornets' nest this time." Laughing, he turned his mount and loped off toward the river.

As we neared the river, now high and swirling, I saw four lanterns hanging from tree limbs on both banks. But, in the storm, they gave off little light, serving as only a beacon for man and beast.

The longhorns hit the river with sheer determination, but the Lampasas was swift, and the current pushed us downstream, filling my boots with water. In midstream, a steer bawled and lunged near me. My horse panicked, splashing and screaming in the darkness, and I grabbed the saddle horn and held my breath, waiting to be thrown into the Lampasas, but as we neared the north bank, the horse regained its footing, and we sloshed ashore with the last of the cattle and followed the herd, still moving—showing no signs of stopping.

We were a rough-hewn crew at daybreak. The rain and wind eased up, allowing us to push the longhorns back toward the trail, where we let them graze and relax while we waited for Bibberman and O'Donnell to arrive with the chuck wagon and horse herd. Soaked, cold, exhausted, and hungry, we found shelter underneath a few cottonwoods, gnawing on jerky or chewing tobacco.

My slouch hat had soaked through, the brim bent over my ears and face, dripping water. But my headgear was in better shape than some. Ian Cochrane had lost the ostrich plume of his battered Hardee hat, and even Emmitt Fain's sturdy Stetson was showing wear. Poor John Dalton's bowler had blown into the Lampasas. "At least something good came out of the night," Red Santee told Dalton. "I won't have to see that stupid hat."

O'Donnell didn't show up with the remuda until mid-morning, and it was a half hour later before the chuck wagon appeared. Bibberman quickly set up the lean-to and ordered: "Fetch that cooney." Slaughter brought a hide out of the chuck wagon and dumped dried cow chips onto the ground and struck a Lucifer. In seconds, the dung was ablaze, and Bibberman soon had us plied with hot coffee.

Uncle Cliff rode in from the herd and immediately barked orders. "Trace, that was a good idea to bring them lanterns along. Now ride back to the Lampasas and fetch 'em. Brazos Billy, we'll let the herd graze today to rest up and put on some weight, but I want a tally. If we're short, we'll round up any strays we can find." He filled a cup with coffee, drank a sip, then turned to Santee.

"Red," he said, "get a fresh mount and scout Kimball Crossin'. If it ain't flooded, we'll cross the Brazos there. Else, it's Waco at Goode and Norris fords."

Santee drained his coffee. "We won't be able to cross at Waco, Boss. I can guaran-damn-tee you that. She'll be way too high, and them sum-bitches at the Bridge Company done started shorin' up the banks with cedar pilings. Only way to cross at Waco is over that damned suspension bridge."

Frowning, Uncle Cliff finished the coffee as Santee walked to the remuda.

"Anybody know what the toll is at that bridge?"

"I crossed it coming to San Antonio," I found myself saying. "They charged me five cents."

"That's highway robbery!" Richard Hamilton said.

"Better than drowning," Charley Murphy added.

Brazos Bill laughed. "Ain't no hornet nests on that bridge, though," he said, and elbowed a frowning Murphy in the side.

Uncle Cliff grunted. "Five cents for a foot passenger,

probably a dime for horse and rider. Add that up with a toll for each loose cow and horse. Now how in the hell can Simpson or us afford that?"

"It's either pay or wait for the river to go down, Clifford," Bibberman said, "if Kimball Crossing's flooded."

The weather broke later that afternoon, and, as the sun finally appeared, we stripped to our long johns and let our clothes dry, trying to enjoy our day of rest. My nose was running, and I heard a couple of other cowboys sneeze. A few hands played cards, others slept, Bibberman started supper, and Trace, after returning from the Lampasas, brought out his guitar and sang.

Now we get rained on and bucked off
On that lonesome Chisholm Trail.
Shot at and stampeded
Through months of livin' hell,
Then we're ripped off in Kansas
Of our money or life.
No fun'ral, preacher
No widow, drum, nor fife.

Brazos Billy rode in from the herd, frowning, looked at Uncle Cliff, and said dryly: "I count us thirty-five head short. Could been a lot worse."

"Thirty-five head!" Uncle Cliff spat. "That's more money than you'd make in three years, Billy, if they fetch top dollar. Mount up, you waddies, and let's get to work!"

With our clothes still drying, we saddled our horses and rode off in hats, boots, and long johns—with Dalton wearing a bandanna like a bonnet in lieu of his bowler—and I might have laughed at the sight if I weren't bone tired, fighting off the sniffles, and, for the moment, sick of cowboying. We split up: half working the north side of the Lampasas, the others fording the flooded river again and backtracking, looking for stray Simpson beeves.

I paired up with Fain and was fortunate to work north of the river, because I had no desire to cross it again. Fain and I combed the brush and bogs for cattle, but only found two beeves, one grazing underneath an elm, the other in—of all places—the middle of a cotton field.

It was dusk before we returned to camp with our two strays, but others had been luckier. Of the thirty-five Brazos Billy had counted missing, we rounded up twenty-eight.

"Maybe this outfit ain't so jinxed, after all," Fain said, " 'cause that's a miracle. Missin' only seven beeves! We'll pick that many up before we're out of Texas."

"Pick them up?" I asked.

Fain grinned. "Oh, Tyrell, cattle herds have a tendency to grow as we push north. A few strays from other herds join in, maybe one wanders in off the range or some farm. Matter of fact, I'd venture to guess some of them twenty-eight we brought in didn't start with us at the ranch."

Not our two, I knew, because I had checked the brands. "That's rustling," I said.

"Careful with that word, pard," Fain said. "It ain't really rustlin', just the law of the open range. Besides, I'd warrant that, early on, Doug Simpson increased his herd more from a wide loop and hot runnin' iron than good seed cows."

"You wouldn't say that to his face," I said.

Fain cackled. "Not by a long shot."

We wolfed down bacon and beans for supper, and let the herd graze most of the next morning before putting them on the trail. My cold had worsened by then, and a number of others were sneezing and coughing over breakfast.

"Great," said Uncle Cliff, his voice dry and sore. "What

we really need is for the whole damned outfit to come down with pneumony."

"Don't worry, Clifford," Bibberman said. "I have just the remedy in my possibles drawer. Line up, you waddies!"

Slowly, unsurely, we filed by the chuck wagon as Bibberman pulled out a spoon and a small bottle of yellowish liquid. First in line was Charley Murphy, who held his nose and swallowed the spoonful, then gagged. "That's castor oil!" he yelled.

Les Slaughter dashed out of the line, but Trace tripped him and sent him sprawling into the mud. Before he could rise, Fain and Trace had firmly gripped his shoulders and brought the struggling black cowboy to Bibberman while the rest of us laughed.

"Open wide, Lester," Bibberman said softly, but Slaughter, his face tight with frustration, sealed his lips. "Les," Bibberman pleaded, and, when Slaughter set his jaw firmer and closed his eyes, the heavy cook slammed a boot heel on the unsuspecting cowhand's foot.

Slaughter screamed, and Bibberman shoved the spoon in and out, clamping the cowboy's mouth shut with both hands and waiting until he swallowed. The cowhand grimaced and limped to the horse herd, swearing under his breath, while the rest of us took our dosage—without protest.

I was last, and, when I coughed down the bad medicine, Uncle Cliff laughed, slapping his knees.

"Boys!" he shouted after catching his breath. "Between hornets, castor oil, and you fellers chasin' strays in your long johns, this has been a drive to remember. I might get my nephew to write it up and send it to *Frank Leslie's Illustrated*." He hooted and howled, then suddenly sneezed.

Bibberman revealed his almost toothless grin, filling another spoon with castor oil, and the rest of us beamed as the smile on Uncle Cliff's face vanished.

"Your turn, Clifford," Amos Bibberman said.

We drove the cattle northward, pausing for our noon break of coffee, biscuits, and beans, and continued until dusk. It was cloudy to the west, but the sky remained clear above us, and the recent rain kept the dust settled. We were eating supper when Red Santee returned, but his heavy frown told us what he saw at Kimball Crossing long before he spoke.

"The crossin' looks like a lake, Boss Rynders," Santee said. "Not only that, but D.C. Pearson had his herd camped nearby, waiting to ford, and he said there was another herd not far behind. We'd have to wait for them to cross first."

Uncle Cliff frowned, removed his hat, and slapped it against a wagon wheel. "I'd like to get to the Red before the hard rains come, and, if we wait, we'll be so far behind schedule, we'd never make it to Wichita in time for Doug Simpson to collect on that bonus. At least, not with any beeves fat enough to sell!"

"The bridge?" Jesse Trace suggested.

"I don't see another choice," Uncle Cliff said, "if they have the crossings at Waco blocked off. We'll have to wire Doug back in Floresville, see if he can come up with the toll money."

"That'll set us back, too," Trace said.

"You got a better idea?" my uncle snapped.

"Drive 'em cross the bridge and don't pay no damnyankee toll," Richard Hamilton suddenly said.

Uncle Cliff shook his head. "The Bridge Company would have the McLennan County sheriff after us in a second. You fancy spendin' all spring in the Waco jail?"

The camp was silent for a few minutes, the only sound the lowing of the cattle and a distant humming from Les

Slaughter as he circled the beeves.

"I might could get us across for free."

All eyes turned to Emmitt Fain, who stood at my side, smiling as he sipped coffee.

Jesse Trace shook his head. "Last I heard, the Bridge Company don't charge for peace officers, reporters, and preachers, and I don't think even you could convince the toll keeper that you're any of 'em. And that still don't take into account the cattle and remuda."

Fain smiled. "Your confidence in me, Jesse, is inspiring. But I think me and my pard could charm our way across." His grin widened, and he slapped my back. "Ain't that right, pard?"

My stomach knotted.

Fain kicked my boots, and I awakened with a yawn, balled my fists, and rubbed sleep from my eyes. He pointed to the stars, and slowly I made out the North Star, almost parallel with the end of the Big Dipper. "Two o'clock," he whispered. "Our watch. Best get at it before Cochrane and Hamilton come in raisin' hell."

We saddled our horses and rode to the herd. Fain was still grinning, even though he had never explained his idea to cross the Waco bridge free of charge. When I asked him about it, Fain simply laughed.

"Hell, Tyrell," he said, "it'll be a day or two before we're in Waco. I'm sure to have thought of somethin' by then."

The knot in my stomach tightened some more.

Chapter Twelve

Waco was a major city and uncivilized cowtown. It had gas streetlights, brick buildings in an expansive business district, and a sizable population—and shotgun shacks, stucco saloons, rawhide brothels, and the unseemly characters cattle towns attracted. They called it "Six-Shooter Junction."

Emmitt Fain and I rode in late one night, herding four steers into an abandoned, run-down livery. I didn't know Fain's plan—I even doubted at times if he had one—but somehow he had convinced Uncle Cliff to give him a chance. "If you don't hear from Ty by dawn, Boss, you're on your own," he told my uncle. We culled four steers from the herd and left the others camped an easy ride from town.

We eased through the deserted business district and made our way for the lights of the saloons and dance halls. It was Saturday night, and the red-light district was anything but deserted. Frowning, Fain studied each saloon before reining in at a rawhide-looking, dimly lit bar. He quickly told me his plan, swung down, and disappeared through the batwing doors before I could protest.

I had a clear view of him. He fished out a gold piece, flipped it, and said: "Two bottles of rye, gents. I'm in a hurry to get roostered!"

"Two bottles of that bug juice will shore do the job, friend," said a tall cowboy with a high-crowned Texas hat.

Fain smiled, flipping his coin again as the bartender placed two bottles on a warped pine plank that served as the bar. "Join me in a smoke?" Fain asked the Texan, who happily accepted. Fain ordered two nickel cigars, and he, the Texan, and the bartender—the only people in the saloon—walked toward the end of the bar where the cigars were stored.

That was my cue. I entered the saloon smiling, trying to hide my fear, but the bartender just glanced my way and quickly turned back to Fain, who was flipping his gold piece with mesmerizing effect. "Be with you in a minute, sonny," the bartender said, clipped a cigar, and handed it to Fain.

As he was lighting the cigar, I picked up the bottles and headed outside, but just as I reached the swinging doors, I heard Fain scream. I turned suddenly and was shocked to see him pointing his freshly lit cigar at me.

"Stop you damned thief!" he screamed, and drew his Colt.

I was through the doors in a second, almost dropping the bottles as I mounted my horse, and spurred down the road, awkwardly holding the rye and reins, half-expecting my hat to fly off at any second. A bullet sang past me, and my throat went dry. I looked back and saw Fain, the Texan, and the bartender standing in front of the saloon, and heard their shouts. My eyes widened as Fain aimed his revolver again, and I gulped at the gun's report.

"You crazy son-of-a-bitch! You could have killed me!"

Emmitt Fain was sitting on the top rail of the corral, laughing hysterically and smoking his cigar. I was pacing back and forth, kicking up dust, and annoying the four steers we had left penned. The rushing blood warmed my face, and

Fain's hoots made my ears burn with anger.

"Ty," Fain said, slipping off the rail and pulling another cigar from his vest pocket. "Relax, pard." He placed the rank tobacco in my mouth, then lit it with his own cigar. "You're gonna blow up like a engine boiler, but, if you coulda seen that look on your face back at the saloon. . . ." He laughed some more. "Besides, it worked out fine. I didn't have to pay for the rye. 'Course, I had to buy Milt a beer and thank him for offerin' to help track you down and get that whisky back."

"Who the hell is Milt?"

"Milt? Milt's the Texican in the saloon with me. You got to admit, I planned this pretty good."

I took a drag on the cigar, gagged, and threw it on the ground. "Yeah," I said, "well, what would have happened if Milt had decided to take a shot at me, instead of you? What if Milt had killed me?"

Fain withdrew his cigar, flipped the ashes away, and exhaled a chimney-full of foul smoke. "By jingo," he said, "that would have been a tragedy."

We herded the cattle toward the bridge, halting them when we were in sight of the bridgekeeper's cottage. Fain asked for a bottle, and I reached into my war bag and handed him one. He took a short pull, swallowed, and said: "Somethin' just came to me. If this guy's a temperance man, we're in trouble." He corked the bottle.

I had crossed the Waco Suspension Bridge before, on my way to San Antonio, but the nation's longest suspension bridge was even more impressive in the dark. Spaced across the bridge were gaslights that cast an eerie glow about the massive iron structure and bounced off the rippling river. The bridgekeeper's house was brick—complete with running water inside, I had heard—and a stone fountain sat outside for watering horses and persons crossing the toll bridge.

The bridgekeeper, on our side of the Brazos, was in his cottage by a window, drinking coffee to stay awake and reading a newspaper. There was no traffic at that time of night, but, if someone wanted to cross, he was ready to collect money.

My horse snorted, and the keeper was outside in an instant, smiling as he folded his *Waco Daily Advance* and tucked it beneath his left arm. He was a portly man, bald, in a homespun shirt, striped woolen britches, and brogans.

" 'Evenin'," he said, "y'all crossin' the bridge?"

We halted in front of him, and Fain took a sip of rye, then passed me the bottle. I coughed down a bit and handed back the liquor. Both of us noticed the keeper's eyes following the rye's passage.

After another pull, Fain smiled and said: "Sure would like, too, if we can afford it."

The keeper frowned. "Ten cents for each horse an' rider an' five cents for each cow," he drawled. "That comes to, uh, forty cents. Ain't too bad, now, is it?"

"Well," Fain said, then took another pull, watching the bridgekeeper's Adam's apple bob. "I'm sorry, mister. Care for a snort?"

The keeper licked his lips, swallowed, and said: "I better not, but much obliged. My boss frowns upon that."

"You mean you ain't the boss?"

"No sir, I'm the assistant keeper. The boss takes off on Saturday nights for . . . er . . . well you know. 'Course, he lets me stay in the cottage while he's gone."

"The dickens you say. Well, if he's gone to . . . er . . . well you know, I reckon you deserve some rye. It's prime stuff. Pard, hand him the extra bottle."

Prime, hell! I thought as I removed the second bottle of

rotgut from my war bag and gave it to the keeper, who took it awkwardly and eyed us suspiciously.

"As I said," the keeper said firmly, "it be forty cents to cross the bridge."

Fain frowned. The keeper's accent was deep South, so I took a chance and thickened my own Southern dialect. "Where ya from?"

Fain and the keeper looked at me. "Selma."

"Selma, Alabama! I'll be damned. I'm from Florence, South Carolina, and my daddy used to do a lot of business in Selma. An' he rode with Bedford Forrest durin' the late War of Northern Aggression."

Actually, my father had ridden with Wade Hampton and, as far as I knew, had never been south of Atlanta, Georgia. But the keeper bought my story and slowly took a sip of whisky.

"I met Gen'ral Forrest once, in 'Sixty-Four," the keeper said, taking another swig. "Damned Yankees never whupped him, by Gawd."

We introduced ourselves, using our real names, and he called himself Bane Jackson. The conversation continued about Forrest, the war, and Selma while Fain and I took extended pulls on our bottles but swallowed little whisky. After a several minutes, our bottle was still almost full, but the keeper's was halfway finished. He didn't seem to notice the difference, though.

"Forty cents, eh?" Fain finally asked.

"Forty cents," the keeper responded, slurring his words. "I'd like to let you go free, bein' Alabama boys and all, but my boss would tar my feathers."

"I understand," I said, wondering when the keeper had started to think of us as Alabamans.

"Well," Fain said, "the truth of the matter is we got whipsawed at a faro table. We got a little bit of money left, but not no forty cents."

"You can try swimmin' 'cross," the keeper said, "but she's high, and you'd probably all drown. I seen forty beeves drown at one time down by the crossin' last year." He laughed at the recollection.

"I reckon so," Fain said, turning to me. "Well, pard, I reckon it's back to Kimball's. Get the bottle from Mister Jackson." I moved my horse toward the keeper and plucked the bottle from his hand. His laughter stopped.

" 'Evenin', Bane," I said. "See ya around."

" 'Bye," he said sadly.

"Aw, hell," Fain finally blurted. "How about we work out some kind of deal? A swap instead of hard cash."

"Boss wants cash only, so does"—he belched—"the Bridge Company."

"We pay you twenty cents, for each horse and rider, and you keep this bottle."

"Well," he said, his eyes trained on the bottle I now held. "I reckons it is . . . might be all right. It late . . . river's high."

"Better make it all legit," Fain said. "Ty, write out a contract." I gave the bottle to Jackson, then took a pencil and paper from my war bag, writing as Fain dictated and the keeper drank. "I, Bane Jackson, employed by the Waco Bridge Company, grant permission for Tyrell Breen to take his herd across the Brazos bridge for only a twenty cents toll. Signed Bane Jackson, Bridgekeeper's Helper." I finished the note and handed it to the keeper, who dropped his newspaper, but not the rye, as he scribbled his signature and handed the paper to Fain.

Fain smiled at me. "Ty, go get the cows and cross the Brazos. I think I'll have a few more drinks with Bane, here."

"This will never work," I told him, turned my horse

around, and galloped for Uncle Cliff's camp.

The herd was moving by first light, faster than we would normally push them, and we drove them down Bridge Street and onto the mighty Waco Suspension Bridge as bells from the churches and pistols from the saloons rang in the distance.

It was quite a sight, some two thousand cattle crossing a modern bridge, and it attracted more than a few spectators. That, I was certain, wouldn't please Uncle Cliff or Emmitt Fain. I tried to focus on my task at drag but couldn't help but feel overwhelmed as I watched the thin line of longhorns move underneath the bridge's arches, clopping over the yellow pine plankings, balling and lowing while crossing the swirling Brazos below, then disappear into East Waco, past the brick manufacturers and homes and on toward Kansas.

By the time I reached the bridgekeeper's cottage, Uncle Cliff and Fain were mounted, and Fain kept grinning smugly. Reining up as Murphy, Brazos Billy, and Dalton herded the last of our beeves across the bridge, I looked inside the shack and saw Bane Jackson passed out in his chair by the window. Uncle Cliff folded up the paper the bridgekeeper had signed and tucked it in a vest pocket.

"That's just insurance, Boss Rynders. I'm hopin' Bane won't remember any of this, and we're home free."

"He might not remember anything," my uncle said, nodding toward the spectators lined down Bridge Street, "but they sure as hell will."

Fain's grin vanished. "I hadn't expected an audience. Figured on everybody heading to church or still in the saloons."

Uncle Cliff grunted something. "Well let's keep 'em movin' and get the hell out of here."

★★★★★

There was no noon meal that day as we drove on, only stopping to change horses. Uncle Cliff was determined to put McLennan County, Waco, and the bridge as far behind us as possible, but he knew we couldn't keep up the pace forever. He bedded the herd down earlier than usual, mainly because we were all about to fall out of our saddles and the longhorns were about to drop. I was certain of one thing, though—the exhausted cattle wouldn't stampede tonight.

Most of the hands got a good laugh when Fain told them how we had hoodwinked the bridgekeeper, and I joined them, although I wondered what Fain had done with the extra bottle of rye, a detail he conveniently omitted.

Cochrane and Slaughter were with the herd as Bibberman prepared supper, and Uncle Cliff sent Trace to watch our back trail. We were laughing at Fain's second telling of what he called "The Rye Thief Shootout," much to my discomfort, when Jesse Trace rode in.

"Riders comin'," he said. "Buggy and a horseman."

Chapter Thirteen

The riders hit camp while we were eating our beans, biscuits, and bacon in silence. Uncle Cliff stood up slowly, hot cup of coffee in his hand, and waited as the buggy driver set his brake and jumped to the ground. A tall man with slick black hair and a neatly trimmed mustache, wearing a gray business suit and black bowler, he seemed ill-prepared for traveling across Texas on a Sunday afternoon. The man on horseback, however, looked as if he had been born in a saddle. His clothes were stamped cowboy from the stovepipe boots to his high-crowned Texas hat. He was also wearing a six-point brass star, engraved **Deputy Sheriff**.

" 'Evenin', gents," Uncle Cliff said casually. "Care for some supper?"

The buggy driver ignored the invitation. "That's them, Deputy. I want this herd impounded and all of these saddle tramps arrested. The Bridge Company won't stand for this kind of swindle."

His accent was fast and hard, something I had never heard, but I was sure of one thing: it was Yankee.

Arresting an entire trail crew by himself made the deputy look a bit uncomfortable, but suddenly he smiled, walked toward Uncle Cliff, and extended his hand. "Boss Rynders!"

Uncle Cliff was taken aback, but gradually he placed the deputy's face. "Cam Montgomery," he said, and they shook hands. "Last man I ever thought to see leading a posse. Running from a posse maybe."

"Well," the deputy said softly, "it ain't much of a posse. . . ."

"Deputy!" the Bridge Company official barked.

"Oh," Montgomery said, "this is Mister Van Arnsdale, vice president of the Bridge Company. Mister Van Arnsdale, this is Clifford Rynders, one of the best trail bosses in Texas. I been up the trail two or three times with him before."

"Fine. Now arrest these outlaws!"

The deputy frowned. "Boss, Mister Van Arnsdale says you got the bridgekeeper's assistant so drunk he passed out early this mornin', then crossed over without shuckin' out with the toll."

"That's exactly what I say! And the charge for these four thousand cows alone is two hundred dollars."

Montgomery, my uncle, and a few cowhands snickered at the vice president's estimate. "Sir," the deputy said, "this herd sure ain't no four thousand." He turned back to Uncle Cliff. "But, Boss Rynders, he's right about owin' a toll."

Reaching into his vest pocket, Uncle Cliff smiled as he withdrew our so-called contract. "We paid a toll," he said, handing the note to Montgomery. "I'm told this explains the entire deal we made with the keeper. We cut a bargain."

Montgomery read the paper and smiled, then passed it to Van Arnsdale.

"Tyrell Breen?" Montgomery asked as the fuming bridge official read on.

"That's me," I said, slowly standing.

"This your herd?"

"More or less, I reckon."

"Well, Mister Van Arnsdale, this looks pretty legal to me."

"Legal, hell!" he shouted, wadded the note, and tossed it to the ground. "If you think a lousy piece of paper will get you out of paying the toll, you are sadly mistaken. This will never hold up in court, and I intend to prosecute you tramps to the fullest extent of the law!"

He was red in the face, talking so rapidly we could hardly understand him. "The Bridge Company is a duly chartered corporation, and we will not be swindled by a bunch of Texas ruffians, lowlife outlaws the lot of you. You trail drivers think you are so high and mighty, but you are nothing but dollar-a-day trash. And I'll have you jailed for larceny. The law is on my side!"

Cam Montgomery, ears burning for he had once been a trail driver, stooped and picked up the "contract," which he stuck in his coat pocket. "Well, Mister Van Arnsdale, right now, I'm the law, and I'm sayin' this contract is legit, and this herd is free to move on."

"Deputy Montgomery! I'll have your badge and your ass in a sling! And I'll take this to the state police, Governor Coke, the United States marshal, if need be."

"Maybe," the deputy said, "but if I was you, I'd think some first. Like, knowin' how much folks in Waco hate payin' your damned toll, you think a jury will convict Mister Rynders and his crew? And think 'bout them lawyer fees. Right now, only you, me, Mister Jackson, and this crew knows what happened. Word gets out, and a lot of other folks might try the same thing. With the rains and all, you'll have a lot more herds passin' through Waco . . . and payin' the toll. If I was you, I'd concentrate on that, and let these men go about their business."

The official slammed his bowler to the dirt. "We'll see about this, Montgomery! We'll see what the sheriff says!" He picked up his hat and briskly climbed into his buggy, whipping the horse out of camp. I never saw Van Arnsdale again, although for the next few days we kept looking over our shoulders, expecting to see him coming with a large posse. And it took years before I had nerve enough to cross the Waco bridge. When I did, I paid my ten cents for horse and rider without complaint.

Montgomery smiled as soon as Van Arnsdale was gone, and soon the entire camp was laughing.

"Cam," Uncle Cliff said, "I owe you."

"Forget it, Boss. You ain't scotfree, yet. That Yankee son-of-a-bitch is greedy and mean enough, he might yet get me fired and y'all arrested."

"Think so?"

The deputy shrugged. Uncle Cliff turned toward Fain and said: "Fain, why don't you fetch that bottle of rye from your saddlebags and give it to Cam here. He and Van Arnsdale have a long ride back to Waco and might need it to cut the dust."

"What bottle, Boss?" Fain said.

"You know damned well what bottle, Emmitt. Now get off your sorry ass and get it!"

Fain did as he was told, as Bibberman brought the deputy a cup of coffee.

"Amos Bibberman," the deputy said, "this is just like old times."

"Now, Cam," Uncle Cliff said, "explain to us how you got to be a law dog?"

"Aw, hell, Boss. Last summer, I got to thinkin'. Saw how the railroad was in Dallas, pushin' on to Fort Worth and all. Hell, the Katy's even got a spur to Denison City these days. So I just said to myself there ain't much of a future for cowboyin', at least, trail drivin' to Kansas. So I figured I'd better look into another line of work." He took a sip of coffee. "That, of course, was before the Panic hit last fall. They stopped layin' track outside of Dallas, and the herds are still movin'. And most of 'em to Kansas, not Denison City."

"Kansas freight's cheaper," Uncle Cliff said.

The deputy shook his head and tapped his star. "So here I is. Well, deputyin' ain't so bad."

By then Fain was back with the rye, which he gave to Montgomery. "Well, I'd best try catchin' up with Van Arnsdale. Mad as he is, he'll have kilt his horse or hisself before I can offer him a shot of this rye. Much obliged, Boss."

"We're obliged, Cam."

He finished his coffee and turned toward his horse, but suddenly stopped. "I reckon I ought to do some official business while I'm here. We got a wire from down in Brownsville askin' us to check all trail herds for a wanted murderer."

Our camp went silent as Montgomery pulled a poster from his coat pocket and handed it to Uncle Cliff. "He's a Scotsman, like my family was. Forbes MacNab. Soldier boy killed an officer over some strumpet."

"Trail herd ain't the fastest way to make a getaway, 'specially with Mexico spittin' distance from Brownsville," Uncle Cliff said, and handed the poster back.

"That was my thinkin', but they say this is a peculiar fella, asked around about some herds. Professional soldier, they says, served in the French Foreign Legion, then came over to fight for the Yanks. You ain't seen him?"

"No Forbes MacNab here, Cam."

"I figured as much. That man's in Mexico." He extended his hand. "Boss, best of luck to y'all. Thanks for the coffee and red-eye. And, oh, I'd be inclined to steer clear of the Waco bridge for a spell."

As soon as the deputy left, Uncle Cliff turned to Trace.

"Fetch Cochrane. Tell him I want to see him."

"Cochrane?"

"Cochrane. Forbes MacNab."

Ian Cochrane slowly walked into camp, dropping his saddle by the chuck wagon, ignoring every pair of eyes trained on him. He removed his battered Hardee hat and ran his fingers through his reddish-brown hair, searched out Uncle Cliff, and walked over.

"Ye needed me, sir?" he said in his thick Scottish accent.

Uncle Cliff was squatting by his bedroll, enjoying a smoke. He took a long drag, then flicked the cigarette away, and stood. "We had a visit from the McLennan County deputy sheriff," he said.

"Aye."

"He asked about a wanted murderer named Forbes MacNab. Showed me a dodger that looked a lot like you. Scotsman. Green eyes. Mustache and Vandyke."

"Aye." This time it was a heavy sigh, and Cochrane pulled on his pointed beard. "Where might this deputy be, sir?"

"I sent him back to Waco."

The Scotsman stopped stroking his Vandyke, staring at my uncle, uncomprehending. "Sir, d'ye want me to leave camp?"

Placing his hands on his hips, my uncle took a deep breath, let it out, and said: "Cochrane, MacNab, whatever your name is, I want to know if you plan on finishin' this drive."

"I dunna understand."

"Here's all there is to understand. I don't give a tinker's damn how many Yankee soldiers you killed in Brownsville. All I care about is gettin' this herd to Wichita. And I don't want to find myself short-handed in the Indian Nations because you took off in the night. Now I'll ask you again. You hired on to for a drive to Wichita. Do you plan on finishin' it?"

Smiling, Ian Cochrane replied: "Aye, sir, it is my intention to finish this drive. And I appreciate ye lying to the law."

"I didn't lie. I told him there was no Forbes MacNab here."

"Aye. Then me name is still Ian Cochrane."

"Then, Cochrane, get back to the herd."

As the Scotsman made his way back to the remuda, Emmitt Fain elbowed me in the ribs.

"See," he whispered. "I told you that man was no cowboy."

"Damnation," Red Santee added, "if this drive don't get more an' more interestin' each day."

Actually, for the most part, life on the trail was anything but interesting. It was a daily grind of ungodly hours in the saddle, a diet of beans, bacon, and coffee, eating the dust caused by two thousand smelling, balling longhorn steers, and falling asleep bone tired, grimy from sweat and dirt.

The first few mornings I had combed my hair before breakfast, but that soon stopped, and now my brown hair was knotted and unkempt, and I dared not think what Mattie Simpson would say if she saw me. I felt whiskers beginning to sprout on my chin, but didn't bother to shave as most of the other cowboys found time to do. Instead, I would force down supper and listen to Fain's lectures on being a cowboy and Trace's songs.

There was no glory in cowboying, and little excitement. I had expected adventure at every milepost, but had seen mostly dust. No fantastic stampedes, no wild Indians, no violent gun play. Just miles and miles of Texas cattle—and coffee—and biscuits—and beans.

We shuffled into camp at dusk, finished supper, and were resting one night when Trace brought out his guitar and played a few cords of "The Lonesome Chisholm Trail." He was humming some bars, slowing strumming while Cochrane read his book and John Dalton read his Bible. Fain and Hamilton were shaving by the chuck wagon, Bibberman and Slaughter were sipping leftover coffee, and Brazos Billy was darning a sock.

"For God's sake," Red Santee finally said, "Trace, can't you play anything besides that gol-durned song?"

Trace stopped and looked up.

"Yeah," Brazos Billy chimed in. "How about a ditty or somethin' livelier. Somethin' about a woman, by God."

"Something dirty!" someone yelled.

"Hell, yeah," Santee said. "A woman. We ain't seen a woman in a coon's age."

"Hell, you two wouldn't know what to do with a woman," Trace said. "But here. . . ." He played a cord and sang slowly.

I was up in E-Town
In the spring of 'Seventy-One
Minin' for the yellow iron
Went to town to have some fun.
I met up with young Molly
In a saloon owned by Abe Meeks.
I asked her if she liked romance
And the words she said were these.

Jesse Trace smiled, picking up the tempo, and continued:

If you wanna poke, it'll cost a poke
Of that gold dust in your vest.
I ain't one to brag, but I ain't no hag.

You might say I'm one of the best
Lovers that you'll ever have.
And, honey, this ain't no joke.
If you wanna poke, it'll cost a poke
The next thing I knew I was broke.

Santee and Brazos Billy howled at the song, and most of us joined in. John Dalton, however, slammed his Bible shut and said—"That's obscene."—which had us laughing harder.

"Again!" Brazos Billy shouted, and Trace began picking the tune once more, much to Dalton's displeasure.

That night, however, as Dalton and I were night herding, I heard him humming the ditty. I couldn't blame him; it was a catchy little tune.

Chapter Fourteen

As we were about to arrive in Fort Worth, I decided to mail Mattie a letter. The thought of visiting the rambunctious cowtown titillated the cowhands—especially me, recalling my excitement in San Antonio and Waco. But, mostly, I was thinking about Mattie Simpson—and had been since leaving the ranch. The last two nights, I had pulled out the paper and pencils she had given me and stared blankly at them. All that I had been able to write were two words: **Dear Mattie**.

I was near the campfire one evening, holding the paper and pencil, trying to think of something to say, when Ian Cochrane knelt beside me. His presence chilled me. We had all, more or less, avoided Cochrane since we learned of the Army officer he had killed in Brownsville, but the former soldier didn't seem to mind. Nor was he bothered by the obviously frightened boy in front of him now.

"Aye, laddie," he said, "are ye writing your lass back at the ranch?"

"Trying to," I replied nervously.

He patted my knee. "I was wondering, lad, might I borrow some paper to write a letter meself, then have ye mail it for me in Fort Worth? I'll pay the postage."

I fumbled around and handed him a piece of paper,

hoping he would leave quickly. He thanked me, then suddenly frowned. "Seems as if I've the consumption, eh?" All I could do was swallow. "I could say it was self-defense, but me doubts if ye'd believe me."

"Sure, I would," I lied.

The smile returned. "Well, thanks, lad. The Army wouldn't have agreed, but I thank ye the same."

Brazos Billy was at my side as soon as Cochrane had gone. "What did he want?" he whispered.

"Just some paper."

"Did he say anything 'bout, you know . . . ?"

"No."

Brazos Billy thought for a minute, then looked at the paper and pencil I held. "Whatcha doin'?"

"I'm trying to write a letter."

A smile brightened Brazos Billy's face, and he made himself comfortable by my bedroll. "Hey, Tyrell, would ya writ a letter fer me? Mail it and all? I can pay for the writin' and mailin'."

"Sure, Brazos Billy," I said, putting away my "Dear Mattie" paper. "What do you want to say?"

"Keno, boys!" he shouted. "Tyrell's gonna writ me a letter!"

Red Santee, Pedro O'Donnell, and Charley Murphy came over, kneeling or squatting beside us. Brazos Billy didn't mind the audience, he was so excited, rubbing his hands and bouncing around as if he were on a wild mustang.

"Who you writin' to, Brazos Billy?" Charley asked.

"I ain't decided yet. Maybe Squirrel-Tooth Alice. Nah. Laredo Lucy in Wichita, or is she in Ellsworth now? Hell's fire, boys, it's hard to decide."

"Well, hell, Brazos," Santee said, "come back when you can figger it out. Ty, think you could put down a note for my sister? I'll pay for the trouble and stamp."

"Sure, Red," I said.

He spit tobacco juice, thought a moment, and said: "It's for Caitlin Larue, General Delivery, Murfreesboro, Tennessee." He worked his tobacco in his cheek, spit again, and continued. "Dearest sister . . . I am on my way to Kansas again, with two thousand head of prime steers and the finest bunch of waddies a man would ever care to ride with."

"Hey, Red," Murphy said. "That's real kind of you."

"Hell, boy, I start all my letters like that."

Santee finished dictating, tossed some coins in my hat, and walked away. Charley Murphy looked at the still-fidgeting Brazos Billy, who told Murphy to go ahead as he hadn't decided yet.

Murphy also paid me for the short note to his mother. O'Donnell frowned at the sight of money, but Brazos Billy handed him a greenback. "You can owe me until we get paid off it Wichita, Pedro," he said. "And go ahead. I jes' can't make up my mind."

Pedro's was the toughest letter to write, a mixture of Spanish, which I didn't understand and he couldn't spell, and broken South Texas English. It was to his mother, sisters, and brothers. I'm sure my spelling was atrocious, but the Mexican wrangler was happy, nonetheless, with my patience. He proudly looked over the words, as if he could read them, thanked Brazos Billy and me profusely, then turned in.

Brazos Billy walked off, too, without ever deciding to whom he should write, leaving me alone with my pencil and paper and still only two words for my own letter. I looked around. Cochrane was leaning against the chuck wagon, writing his letter; Bibberman and Santee were drinking coffee; everyone else was either sleeping or tending to the herd. An owl hooted, and the longhorns lowed in the distance, and Jesse Trace's gentle baritone carried over the wind as he sang to the steers.

Slowly I began scratching at the paper, my hand cramped and fingers aching from writing letters for my three illiterate friends:

Dear Mattie:

I take pencil in hand and hope these humble words find you in good health. We have had no troubles so far and are nearing Fort Worth. I have just finished writing letters for Red, Charley, and Pedro and now find time to write you.

I can hear Jesse Trace's singing as he night herds. I have heard him singing "The Lonesome Chisholm Trail" for weeks and now I realize how lonely the cattle trails can be. I think I have friends in camp, but I truly miss your company and cannot wait until I get to see you in Wichita. I hope you feel the same.

There are plenty of stories I want to tell you, about Waco and crossing the Lampasas and poor Charley Murphy's attack of a hornet nest, but I fear I must close for now. I have been thinking of you a lot, and you will stay in my thoughts until I see you in person.

Until then, I will remain
Affectionately yours,
Tyrell Breen

I looked over my words with tired eyes, folded the letter carefully, and placed it in my war bag, along with the letters for Red Santee's sister, Charley Murphy's mother, and Pedro O'Donnell's family. Using my hat for a pillow, I closed my eyes and drifted off to sleep to Trace's faraway voice.

Now there are times I'm so lonesome
Down that lonesome Chisholm Trail.
When there's nothin' to hear
Except the lobo's wail.
So far from my true love
The fairest gal I've known.
Of her I'm dreamin'
Until I come back home.

We could taste Fort Worth, "The Paris of the Plains," long before the cattle ever smelled the Trinity River. The thoughts of a turn in a dance hall had most of the cowhands waltzing in their saddles, while I was more concerned about mailing the letters and maybe finding a bathhouse.

"We gots to take Tyrell to The Two Minnies," Brazos Billy said as we made our noon camp. That prompted a "Hell, yeah!" from Santee and Fain.

Brazos Billy smiled. "Place gots a glass ceilin'. And ya can see all them naked ladies upstairs! Ever heard of such a thing?"

"No," I honestly replied.

"Fort Worth's as happenin' a town as there is in Texas," Santee said.

Except nothing was happening in Fort Worth, when we drove through the center of town several days later. Two thousand steers kicked up dust down Rusk Street toward the north bluff overlooking the Trinity. But my high expectations of seeing "The Paris of the Plains" were quickly shattered.

Only a handful of sad-eyed merchants, gloomy prostitutes, and out-of-work railroaders greeted our arrival. We passed several decrepit buildings along Rusk Street, two abandoned wagon yards, vacant lots, a burned-out mercantile—even a dead mule. Scavengers, removing warped plankings from a saloon front and loading them in two wagons, stopped to watch us pass in silence.

The line of one-story saloons, dance halls, and shops still in business also looked dead. They were poorly built frame structures, some of the wood rotting, most of the gray paint fading. I wondered if Fort Worth even had a post office, for this wild cowtown looked as lively as a weedy cemetery.

We crossed the Trinity east of the high bluff without trouble and allowed the cattle to graze while we made camp early that afternoon. Biscuits, bacon, and coffee greeted us in camp, and, when we were finished, Bibberman hitched up the chuck wagon to go to town.

Uncle Cliff rode up beside him, staring at the expectant cowboys in camp. Fort Worth might not have been "The Paris of the Plains" any more, but she was still a town with all the comforts—namely, saloons, bathhouses, and brothels—a cowboy needed.

"Cochrane," my uncle said. "You're in charge while I'm gone. No one leaves camp." He searched us out, his face hard and unemotional—but I thought inside he must be laughing. Putting the killer Ian Cochrane in charge was bound to stop even Brazos Billy from trying to sneak into town.

"Damn it, Boss!" Fain shouted. "They ain't fair! We deserve a chance to hoorah a bit and drink a toddy."

"Yeah," Murphy said. "Ain't like we gonna tree the town!"

"This ain't no damned debatin' society!" my uncle roared. "You ain't gonna tree the town 'cause you ain't goin' in! I told you waddies this is a dry run till Wichita!"

He was still fuming when he turned to me. "Ty, get them letters and climb up with Bibberman."

That sent my self-appointed partner and tutor, Emmitt

Fain, into a froth. "Tyrell! Why the hell does he get to go in?"

"Because I said so. He's got letters to mail, and I need him to help Bibberman." Uncle Cliff was boiling. "You don't like the way I run things, Fain, you can draw your time! But all I can give you is an IOU."

Slowly Uncle Cliff let out a long sigh as his shoulders relaxed. "I can't let you boys into town," he said, softly now, " 'cause I can't advance y'all any pay. And I sure as hell can't go your bail."

I pulled the letters from my war bag and collected Cochrane's. As I walked toward the chuck wagon, Fain whispered to Trace: "That man can be a gen-u-ine son-of-a-bitch."

"Yep," Trace replied, smiling, "but he's our son-of-a-bitch."

We forded the Trinity, eased down Rusk Street into town, turned at Weatherford Street, and made our way to Main, stopping in front of the *Fort Worth Standard.* I longed to buy a newspaper. There was little in camp to read, except Cochrane's book—and I was too scared to ask to borrow it—and the cans, bottles, and boxes in the chuck wagon. **DR. PRICE'S CREAM BAKING POWDER: MOST PERFECT MADE. COLGATE & CO.'S HONEY SOAP, BROWN WINDSOR. DR. SWEET'S INFALLIBLE LINIMENT. CURES CUTS AND WOUNDS IMMEDIATELY, AND LEAVES NO SCAR.** I had them all memorized, but buying a paper was a luxury I knew we couldn't afford.

"We'll see if the Panther Hotel has any news from Doug," Uncle Cliff said. "And you can mail your letters there. Then we'll see if we can get any supplies at York and Draper's or Nash Hardware."

The Panther Hotel had closed down, but we mailed our letters from a general store between Main and First, then checked a few other places for any word from Douglas Simpson without luck. Despite my first impressions, I soon found Fort Worth to be anything but a ghost town. There were several businesses—even a Ladies Ice Cream Parlor—and some bathhouses and barber shops that I eyed longingly as we rode to York and Draper's store.

Doug Simpson's credit wasn't worth much, and I thought we were out of luck until a well-dressed, cigar-smoking man entered the store. He wore a dark suit and bell crown hat and carried a leather satchel. "Clifford Rynders!" the man shouted. My uncle turned and smiled. "Doc Burts," he said.

"Mayor Burts, if you please. Duly elected last year."

They exchanged handshakes, and the mayor told the clerk to put the supplies on his bill, that Douglas Simpson could owe him. Then they stepped outside while I helped the clerk load a few items in the chuck wagon, where Bibberman sat waiting.

"So the Panic back East scared everyone here, too, Clifford," Burts was saying when the last sack was loaded. "They stopped building the railroad at Eagle Ford a few miles east of here. Lots of folks just packed up, headed elsewhere, east to Dallas, Denison City, or moved west."

"But not you, eh, W.P.?" Uncle Cliff said.

"Not me, Clifford. I've been here since this was just a dirty, one-street town. And I can still see a good place here. A man's got to look to the future. That's what I'm doing."

My uncle smiled. "Reckon that's why they elected you mayor, W.P."

Burts laughed, shook hands, and left. I was amazed my uncle could be on a first-name basis with a mayor. Fort Worth might not be St. Louis or Charleston, but it was a major town on the Chisholm Trail—financial depression, notwithstanding. Uncle Cliff finished his cigarette and was moving to his horse when someone called his name.

An ancient, grizzled man crossed the dusty street toward us—the stink of bad whisky reaching us long before the rank smell of his body. The boots he wore were well-ventilated, his trousers three sizes too small, and his calico, moth-eaten shirt covered with dirt and grime. He held out his hand, which my uncle accepted skeptically.

"You don't remember me." The stranger's raw voice had the effect of a chair scraping against a hardwood floor. As my uncle slowly shook his head, the man said: "Lacy. Jack Lacy."

"Of course," my uncle said after a moment, but I heard the disbelief in his voice. "We joined herds in 'Sixty-Six on the way to Baxter Springs. And you helped us out when that stampede scattered our beeves all across the Nations in 'Seventy. How've you been?"

"Awe, I've had some poor luck lately. Ain't bossed a herd in a while, but I'm thinking next year, maybe. Got some folks interested down near the Nueces Strip."

An awkward pause stretched forever. The tiny man smiled and said he had best be going. Uncle Cliff quickly turned to Bibberman, who read his mind and tossed him a small leather purse.

"Jack," he said kindly, fishing out a coin and pressing it into Lacy's hand. "I've got to get back to my herd. But you'd do me an honor if you'd let me stand you to a drink."

Lacy clutched the coin, and I saw his eyes mist. "Thanks, Capt'n. I'd be proud to. And next year . . . maybe I'll see you on the trail."

Slowly the leathery old man drifted down the boardwalk and disappeared. "Jesus," my uncle said softly. "Jack Lacy."

"Cattle drive takes it out on a man," Bibberman said, glancing at my uncle. "Even the best of them sometimes."

I couldn't help but think how my uncle might have turned

out just like Jack Lacy. He had been well on his way when I first met him: unclean, dirt poor, and drunk, with absolutely nothing to live for.

And from the look in his eyes, I was certain Uncle Cliff was thinking the same thing.

Chapter Fifteen

My worn thighs and chafed backside were grateful for the chance to ride in the chuck wagon, even if the mammoth cook hogged the seat and the wagon jerked and pitched with every hole we hit.

Uncle Cliff had sent us back to camp while he went to the sheriff's to ask about any news from the Indian Nations. We were silent as we made our way through town, and I couldn't think of anything to say until we neared the river crossing.

"Old Emmitt and Charley were pretty sore about not getting to come into town," I said, trying to make conversation.

The cook grunted. "Charley's a crockhead and Fain's trash."

My jaw almost hit the wagon bed. I stuttered, groping for words, and finally offered: "They aren't so bad. I mean, Charley helps me out on drag, and Fain's my partner and is trying to teach me all about cowboying."

Amos Bibberman flicked the reins at the team, shaking his head. "You'd do better partnering up with someone else. Trace, maybe, or Cochrane."

"Cochrane! He's a killer."

"He's a professional soldier. A man of honor. I was in the war, Tyrell, with the Fifty-Fourth Massachusetts." I caught a gleam in his eye as he added: "Killed a passel of Johnny Rebs. So I know a little about soldiering." He looked at me, adding: "And I also know you don't need any lessons from the likes of Emmitt Fain."

We were on the banks of the Trinity, and Bibberman pulled on the reins until the wagon stopped, then set the brake. He turned his massive body toward me and placed his hand on my shoulder. The grip was firm, but there was a gentleness in his voice.

"I've seen you ride, son, and you got a natural-born instinct in a saddle. That must be the Rynders's blood in you. Only lesson you need is that the cook knows everything about a cattle drive. And this cook knows that Emmitt Fain is no good." I started to interrupt, but Bibberman hushed me, his high-pitched voice rising. "Take that . . . that bullshit at Waco. Did you try thinking that one through?" There was no chance to respond, because Bibberman shrieked: "Hell, no! If not for the Good Lord's doing, our herd would have been stopped, we'd all be in jail, and the Simpsons would be on their way to the poor house!"

"Well, Uncle Cliff let us. . . ."

"His mistake! Clifford's rusty. A few years back, he would have waited and forded the Brazos when the water went down, then made up for lost time. That's what we should have done."

"I guess so," I replied. "It all worked out, though."

"Yeah," Bibberman conceded, releasing the brake. "Well, we still got a long way to Wichita."

The chuck wagon rolled gently into the Trinity River, low despite the rains, and we eased north. "How long have you known Uncle Cliff?" I asked, and was pleased when the cook smiled.

"Since 'Sixty-Seven. That may not seem like long to you,

but it's a lot of miles on a cattle trail. First drive I was on was when Mister Simpson lost his leg."

My eyes widened. As we neared the Trinity's far bank, I told Bibberman I had assumed Simpson lost his leg during the war.

"No, Clifford and Mister Simpson didn't fight in the war. Mister Simpson got his leg smashed to pieces during a stampede in Kansas." The cook slowly shook his head. "We were gonna winter the herd in the Nations, but then we found out they were shipping cattle in Abilene, so we made a beeline. It was late fall, and a blue norther was whipping in, and the herd ran. We found Mister Simpson after, and Clifford, he orders me to strip down the wagon of everything, tells Seth Hannen to keep the herd moving to Abilene.

"Then we load Mister Simpson in the wagon and make off for Fort Harker, almost freeze to death the three of us and ruin a good team of mules, and, when we get to the fort, the Army surgeon says he won't have a thing to do with Mister Simpson, says the man is as good as dead. And Clifford, he pulls that big old Dance Forty-Four he still carries, and makes that surgeon amputate Mister Simpson's leg and patch him up at gunpoint."

That heroic story had never been in any of Uncle Cliff's letters to my mother. It was something straight out of one of the half-dime or Dumas novels I had read, something I would have imagined my uncle doing.

So far, my adventures had included everything but gun play, Indians, and outlaws—hardly the kind of story Beadle and Adams would publish—and mostly I had been worn down daily, my eyes stinging from dust, too tired even to dream about deeds of derring-do.

Brazos Billy greeted us in camp, asking if we had bought

any supplies. Bibberman grinned wickedly. "Oh," he said slowly, "I got some flour for some biscuits . . . and some coffee . . . and bacon . . . and beans."

The jovial cowhand shuffled off in silence, but he was happy that evening when Amos Bibberman surprised us with a deep-dish apple pie. But there was an edge in the air that night as we ate, probably because the hands were still sore about not getting to go into Fort Worth. I took my plate and found a seat.

"Boy, you gonna sit by me, you wash that stink off you first." It was Richard Hamilton, and the unreconstructed Rebel had lowered his plate and put his right palm on his pistol butt.

I attempted to ignore him and took a bite, but he was standing now, towering above me. "You got nigger smell all over you, boy, from ridin' in that wagon," he said. "This camp already stinks enough as it is with them two Jim Crows. Get to the river . . . now."

Bathing actually sounded good to me, but I was determined not to be bullied by the likes of Hamilton. From underneath my hat, I glanced toward Fain, hoping he would come to my aid, but he was sitting by a wagon wheel, watching silently. I guess he was right. This was my fight, if I wanted it.

"Aye, now, I dunna think the lad wishes to bathe yet. But maybe ye'd like to now that ye've finished supper."

Ian Cochrane was standing beside me. He wasn't wearing his Hardee hat, but an English-made double-action revolver was tucked in his waistband. And his right hand floated dangerously close to it. It chilled me as I watched Hamilton take a step back, his gun hand also ready. This was something from the pages of my half-dime novels, but it was all too real.

"I killed a chance of Yankee assassins like you in the war," Hamilton said.

"Commence at it and try again."

Deadly seconds passed. Slowly Hamilton backed off, his eyes flaming, and he turned and rapidly left camp. No one spoke for several minutes, then Cochrane knelt beside me.

"Thanks for mailing me letter, lad," he said. I could only nod, and the Scotsman patted my back and walked away.

I couldn't sleep that night, and was wide awake when Emmitt Fain crawled to my bedroll. "Hey, pard," he said, "Brazos Billy and me's sneakin' into town. Let's go."

"No," I said. "Uncle . . . er . . . Boss Rynders would fix our flints."

"He's snorin' like a razorback. He won't even know we went. C'mon, Ty. We'll have us a couple of toddies at the Dixie Bar and be back in camp before sunrise."

My head shook violently. I expected Fain to argue more, but someone snorted in his sleep, and Fain simply said—"Suit yourself."—and disappeared.

They were back—waking me and a few others—shortly before O'Donnell rose to bring in the remuda. By breakfast, their clothes were still wet from swimming the Trinity, eyes bloodshot, and faces pale. A small cut was bleeding above Fain's left eye, and Brazos Billy kept rubbing his temples and didn't wear his hat the entire day. Uncle Cliff glared at them over coffee but never said a word.

The plains northwest of Fort Worth rolled gently, and the trees thinned and gradually disappeared except along the creekbeds. A constant wind groaned as it whipped southward, but the weather warmed and the skies cleared—"a false spring," Trace called it.

Uncle Cliff was pleased, too, not only about the weather,

but also because the grass looked good and the longhorns could graze and fatten up for the country ahead. We still had many miles to go, but, all in all, things looked fine as we trailed north, past Decatur. I even found time to bathe, sort of, in Denton Creek—but only because my mount stumbled and sent me splashing into the cold water.

"Boys," Brazos Billy said after supper, "this is about as good a drive as it can gets. No stompedes, no real bad weather. Nothin's gone wrong."

"You turd!" Charley Murphy shouted. "Now you done jinxed us."

Slaughter and Trace also admonished Brazos Billy, but he just smiled, shaking his head, and said: "Nah, nah, nah. I ain't jinxed nothin'. See, they was callin' this the jinxed outfit before we even left the ranch. So if I says we're doin' fine and ain't had no stompedes or bad shit, it ain't jinxin' us 'cuz we was jinxed to begin with. Instead, this more or less jes' takes the jinx off us." He took a sip of coffee. "Now, was I ridin' up with D.C. Pearson or Shanghai Pierce and said that, then I would have jinxed 'em 'cuz them outfits ain't said to be jinxed. But 'cuz we was already jinxed, I can say that without jinxin' us. Savvy?"

Even John Dalton had closed his Bible and was staring at Brazos Billy along with every hand in camp. Fain's mouth was open, and Trace was scratching his head. I heard Santee snort and say—"I done got me a headache."—and I bit my lower lip and tried to decipher Brazos Billy's rambling logic.

"You mind," Fain said, "dealin' that hand again?"

"All I'm sayin'," Brazos Billy repeated, "is you can't jinx no jinxed outfit by sayin' somethin' that would jinx some herd that ain't jinxed. So I can say we ain't got nothin' to worry 'bout."

"My word," Fain finally said, "that makes sense."

And for the next few days, it looked as if Brazos Billy had been right. The weather held out and the creeks we crossed were clear and easy to ford. But the monotony of the work was hypnotic; once I even fell asleep in the saddle before Murphy punched me awake. Despite our good fortune, I was soon longing for a hornet attack or anything—short of gun play between Hamilton and Cochrane—to break up the dullness of North Texas.

But Brazos Billy's prediction was like the weather. And as we neared the broken country of the Red River, the "false spring" would end.

Chapter Sixteen

The sound of thunder was eerily absent as lightning flashed in the distance. And the wind, unrelenting since Fort Worth, died suddenly, leaving the air thick and heavy. I bit my lip while the steers in front of me balled fearfully, moving faster despite our best efforts to slow them. By late morning the approaching lightning streaked continuously through the dark skies; by noon it had turned into balls of heat and light that seemed to dance across the ground like tumbleweeds.

Sweat dotted my face as the sickening smell of sulphur and sticky heat made it feel as if the gates of Hades had opened. Electricity filled the air, and, when my horse's ears and saddle horn began glowing—an eerie bluish light settling on them like morning dew—I thought I was witnessing the beginning of Armageddon. Nor was I alone, because the constant cursing that filled our cattle camp had ceased as I rode in for the noon break; in fact, I saw Pedro O'Donnell clutching his crucifix and heard Amos Bibberman softly singing "Rock of Ages."

My throat was dry despite the coffee I drank, and my eyes burned. Others moved to the chuck wagon to prepare for the storm—removing gun belts and anything metal (even spurs!) and donning rain gear—but when I went to put on my poncho, I dropped my hat in shock. A phosphorescent light was dancing on the brim.

"Fox fire," Fain whispered. "If there's one thing I hate, it's fox fire."

St. Elmo's fire, fox fire, whatever you prefer, is a strange phenomenon during electrical storms. I can't explain it, although Trace allowed—"God uses it to bring religion to sailors and waddies."—but the first time you experience it—and the second, third, and so on—you can't help but think about your own mortality because for all you know, it's Judgment Day.

Ominous clouds now overhead quickly turned afternoon to midnight. The heat never lessened, nor did the cattle's cries, and every minute dragged on for eternity as we picked at our food, staring at our glowing hats and horses' ears. The air was so thick, so hot and humid, I could hardly breathe. Charley Murphy, smiling, seemingly oblivious to the foreboding we all felt, suddenly held out his quirt. "Hey, fellas, watch this." He popped the short whip in front of him, sending sparks from the woven-leather end, and laughed.

"Murphy! You fool!" Bibberman snatched the quirt from Murphy's hand and tossed it to the ground. "You want to start a stampede!" Charley mumbled an apology. No one spoke again until Uncle Cliff galloped into camp.

He was wearing a rain slicker, but the heat was so intense he was drenched in sweat. "Every man to the herd!" His eyes were wild—the first time I think I had ever seen him really scared—and he raked his spurs across his lathered gelding, whose ears also glowed, and was gone in a flash.

Pedro roped our best night horses, and we silently rode to the scariest sight I had ever witnessed. In the blackness, balls of blue light had formed on the tips of every horn. Most of the steers were still lying down, yet balling in terror. I sensed more than I saw, however, for blackness had enveloped everything except a hot ball of light—the glow from the longhorns—as we circled the herd. I hugged my horse's chest tightly with both legs and gripped the reins hard. Cattle and horses wailed at the hell surrounding us, accompanied by our strains of lullabies, ballads—and plenty of prayers.

"Please, God," I said out loud, holding the reins close to my mouth. "Please, God, don't let them run."

My answer was a sharp crash of lightning, followed by a thunderclap's cannonade and hard sheets of icy rain. The rumbling over the ground was instant, and my mount sprinted ahead on instinct before I realized what was happening or heard someone's terrified shriek: *"Stampede!"*

Every lecture I had been given about stampedes since the trail drive began—from Uncle Cliff, Jesse Trace, Amos Bibberman, and even my mentor, Emmitt Fain (when he would mention "stompedes" against his better judgment)—I forgot in that moment. My one motive during the beginning of every cowhand's worst nightmare was to stay on my horse.

The thundering hoofs of the frightened steers, crashes of thunder and lightning, bullet-like pellets of rain, cries of my comrades all seemed distant as I leaned low and stared into the night. I vaguely recall screaming at the cattle—or maybe in sheer terror—and at some point I felt my hat go whipping off my head.

My whole body was jarred as we galloped on, unable to see anything, but Lizzie, my night horse, stayed close to the stampeding cattle by sound, keen night vision, or maybe just instinct. I must have been in some sort of trance, but gradually I came out of it, although I had no idea how long the herd had been running. The rain was still pouring, lightning flashing, and I couldn't see a damned thing. Slowly I realized the rumbling of the longhorns seemed to be lessening, but on we ran, and it dawned upon me that the herd had split. There was nothing I could do about it, however, except ride it out—literally.

And then Lizzie screamed, trying to slide to a halt in the muddy ground. I loosened my boots from the stirrups, preparing to jump clear when I realized we were falling over a ledge. I leaped from the saddle and into a void of nothingness, hurling for what seemed to be an eternity before hitting the ground with a thud.

I lay spread-eagled for a while as my vision cleared and rain pelted my face. After sucking in a deep breath, I stumbled to my feet, called out for my horse in a weak voice, and groped around in the pitch black. The rain, wind, and thunder were all I heard; the rumbling of the herd and Lizzie's screams and snorts had been silenced. My feet carried me to the side of a wall, mound of earth, cliff, whatever we had fallen off, and I felt my way along it.

A limb scratched my face, and I looked up. Although my vision had adjusted to the darkness, there was still nothing to see—it was pitch black—but a streak of lightning served as a match, and I saw the tree. It was a massive cottonwood on the top of the cliff, and a wind-twisted limb stretched down into the cañon.

I summoned some reserve energy and pulled myself onto the limb, then crawled toward the top of the cliff, falling when I was halfway up and starting over. The second time I made it to the cliff top and walked along the edge, fruitlessly pleading for help. After traveling several yards, I knew it was hopeless. Drenched, cold, and alone, very much lost, I would have to wait until dawn before I could do—or see—anything, so I walked back toward the cottonwood. Its limbs would provide some shelter, I thought, from the storm.

A flash of light blinded me, and an explosion rocked me off

my feet as intense heat scalded my face and sucked the air from my lungs. My ears were ringing, and I felt myself falling again, only this time I did not recall hitting the ground.

Daylight brought a different perspective to my situation. I was caked in mud and soaked to the bone, hidden under a cutback in the cliff wall. At some point I must have regained consciousness and crawled out of the rain, which had stopped, although the overcast skies threatened to open up at any time. My face felt as if I had the worst case of sunburn, and there was a soft ringing in my ears, but I had survived the night. And as I crawled out of my wet bed and surveyed the countryside, I realized my being alive was a miracle.

The cliff that seemed so steep and forbidding was no higher than eighteen feet; in fact, it was just the wall of a deep arroyo. The rain had filled the creek, which was bubbling along peacefully in the quiet dawn. My makeshift ladder, however, the massive cottonwood, was no more. It had been splintered, literally torn apart by sharp lightning, and I realized had I been any closer to it when the bolt hit—let alone sleeping underneath the tree's limbs—I would be dead.

And then I saw Lizzie.

She was by the creekbed, on her side, forefeet at awkward angles. Two longhorn steers were nearby, their necks broken, and another was several yards away, partially submerged in the shallow creek. Lizzie, however, was alive.

I stumbled over toward her and begged her to get up, but she just snorted, blood dripping from her nostrils, eyes filled with pain, and I cried, stroking her neck and wishing there was something I could do. After my tears ran their course, I stripped the horse of saddle, blanket, and bridle, then looked around for a rock or something. I had to make my way back to the herd—somehow—but I couldn't leave Lizzie behind, suffering, slowing dying. But there was no rock big enough to do the grim task, and I wished I had my Barlow knife that I had left in the chuck wagon with my spurs, or carried a six-gun like most of the other cowhands.

Then I heard a soft voice, singing in the distance, from the top of the arroyo's banks. I yelled for help, half-expecting to see Jesse Trace or maybe Emmitt Fain, peer over the side, but it was Ian Cochrane, the murderer, who appeared a few minutes later, carrying his own saddle and bridle. He saw me and grinned.

My stomach turned over as he climbed down, and I have to admit I thought he was going to kill me, leave my bones for the buzzards, and move on. It was silly, I know, but I was terrified, speechless, even as he knelt by Lizzie and tried to soothe her by humming some Scottish ballad.

"Hopeless, laddie," he said to me after a minute.

"I know," I finally said. "I was trying to find a rock to bash her head in."

"Aye, it's for the best," he said. "I'd use me revolver, but it's caked with mud, and me hammer's jammed from a spill meself." Cochrane hadn't been in camp when we shunned our metal objects, and I doubted if he would have removed his arsenal anyway.

Slowly, he pulled a knife from a boot sheath and quickly slit Lizzie's throat. "Let's be gone," he said, and I picked up my saddle, blanket, and bridle and followed him, never looking back at the brown mare.

We walked across the wet North Texas ground for an hour without speaking, stopping to rest beside an abandoned, dilapidated wagon. I was thankful for the chance to catch my breath because my feet were becoming raw and my saddle and blanket had gained a thousand pounds since we started out.

"Ye'd make a good soldier," Cochrane suddenly said.

I looked up, surprised to see him smiling. "How's that?" I asked tiredly.

He shrugged. "Been marching along and not a complaint out of ye. I marched out this way and ye didn't question me direction. I dunna, lad, I've soldiered with many a man worse than ye. But ye look a mess. What happened to ye face?"

My hands instantly felt along my forehead and cheeks, and I cringed at the burning pain, slowly realizing the lightning had singed the beginning sprouts of beard, even eyebrows and eyelashes. I explained what had happened, and he shook his head and was lost in his own thoughts.

After several minutes, he blurted: "The man I killed, Master Breen, it was self-defense. I want ye to know that, and believe that."

I could have nodded, but I asked: "Then why did you run?"

"First sergeants," he finally said, "dunna kill second lieutenants, especially when the officer comes from a well-to-do family in Michigan. Especially in a fight over a camp laundress." He looked relaxed then, pleased to get his burden off his chest. "I do like soldiering, lad," he said, his eyes beaming, "much better than this shit."

Laughter rocked my aching body, and Ian Cochrane and I cackled until tears streamed down our face. "Now, laddie, dunna tell Capt'n Rynders I said that," he remarked between breaths.

"Only if you don't tell him I agreed with you," I replied, and we howled some more.

When we had finally calmed down, I asked: "What do you do after the drive?"

"I re-up in this man's army."

"You can't do that. They'll court-martial you, maybe hang you."

"Forbes MacNab can't. But Ian Cochrane, or whatever name I choose, now he could. There was an Irishman I rode with during the rebellion when fighting with Stoneman. Myles Keough, a temperamental sort as micks are prone to be. That's who I had ye mail me letter to. He's with the Seventh Cavalry. So I'll join his command and ride to glory again, barring another laundress or silly young officer."

He stood up then, hefted his horse tack, and held out his hand. He pulled me to my feet and slapped my back. "Ready to rejoin this . . . shit?"

I picked up my gear and followed him again, and we chatted as we walked another mile, then he started singing "Ball of Kerrymuir," an old bawdy tune I had heard a few times in upstate South Carolina, only Ian Cochrane had a few choruses I had never heard of—and would never repeat, even in a cattle camp.

"Smell that?"

I stopped and sniffed the air, but it was a while before I could place the aroma. "Coffee?"

Ian Cochrane laughed. "More that just coffee, laddie, that's Amos Bibberman's coffee. Let's move double-time." And off he was jogging toward the smell of freshly brewed Arbuckle's.

"Son-of-a-bitch! It's Tyrell! And Cochrane's with him!" Jesse Trace ran to meet us, slapped me on the back, and took my saddle. "Sonny," he said, "we thought you was dead for sure. Found Cochrane's horse lame, but didn't see no sign of you. You give us quite a start."

I surprised myself with my first question. "How's the herd?

"Scattered from here to Christmas. Got most of the men roundin' 'em up, but Fain and Santee are out searchin' for y'all."

We staggered into camp, and Bibberman brought us coffee that was as good as gold. And then I saw Uncle Cliff. He was leaning against a wagon wheel, holding my mud-caked, beaten slouch hat. Uncle Cliff had it by the brim, twisting it with his hands, his knuckles white, face ashen. I handed Bibberman my empty cup and walked toward him.

"Slaughter found the hat this morn," he said, slowly handing it to me. "Thought you went under the hoofs and was deader than hell." I took the ruined hat and placed it on my head because, after months of wearing it, it didn't seem right to go around hatless.

"I'm afraid Lizzie's dead," I said. "She broke two legs when we went into an arroyo."

Uncle Cliff nodded and took a deep breath as his face regained color. "That happens, Ty. She was a good horse, though, but don't fret over it." He gripped my shoulder and smiled. "I'm just glad you're all right."

"I'm fine."

"Good," he added, his voice rising. " 'Cause we've got a bunch of longhorns to round up and we're burnin' daylight."

And so my hero's welcome was short-lived. After downing some biscuits and another cup of coffee, Cochrane and I, bone-tired, wet, and dirty, got remounted and joined the roundup. That night, however, after Bibberman put salve on my burned face, I was forced to tell my adventures twice and enjoyed my celebrity status.

We were laughing about it, when I glanced at Ian Cochrane, silently reading his book, alone by the campfire, while the rest of the cowhands had gathered around me. A pang of regret hit my heart, for the Scotsman was more the hero than me—I would have never found the camp without him—but I didn't have too much time to consider it.

Because that night the herd stampeded again.

Chapter Seventeen

"Heave, heave, heave, you waddies, heave!" Bibberman grunted as we fought against the weight of the overturned chuck wagon. The Studebaker budged, and the cook, Cochrane, Hamilton, Dalton, Pedro, and I groaned, regripped, and forced the wagon up some more, gave a final shove, and watched. It uprighted, bounced a couple of times, then finally settled on its wheels on the damp Texas ground.

The camp was a mess. Torn bedrolls, pots and pans, and flour, sugar, and cornmeal were strewn everywhere. I removed my battered slouch hat and wiped my sweaty brow. Bibberman walked around the Studebaker, checking the wheels first before beginning to reorganize his cookware. "It'll be a spell, fellows," he said softly, "before I can cook up any breakfast or coffee."

We never knew what caused the herd to stampede, but run they did—straight through our camp. Luck was with us, though. We had just ridden in, and our mounts were nearby. Despite the trembling ground, I leaped into my saddle and joined the chase, while the cattle bulled their way through, overturning the chuck wagon and leaving a swath of destruction in their wake.

They ran for five miles before we turned them, forcing

them to mill until they forgot the terror—real or imagined—that had caused them to stampede. And for the rest of the night, we circled the herd, singing gentle ballads to soothe them, until I fell asleep in the saddle. Fain punched me awake, but it was dawn, so we rode back to what was left of camp.

After picking up the pieces of camp while Bibberman fixed coffee and soggy bacon, we parked our sore backsides on the ground and rested. Dalton fell asleep before breakfast was ready, and I was about to join him when Uncle Cliff and Fain rode in.

"Everybody accounted for?" Uncle Cliff asked.

"Yeah," Bibberman said without looking up from his cook fire. "But we're out of flour and sugar. Corn meal and bacon's practically ruined. Most of the coffee's gone."

"Wagon all right?

"Far as I can tell. How's the herd?"

Shaking his head, Uncle Cliff dropped from the saddle with a thud. Pedro O'Donnell instantly took the horse's reins and led the lathered animal away.

"Counted twenty head dead," Fain said, still mounted. "Then I stopped." He shook his head. "I'll get Brazos Billy and Murphy and see about roundin' up them strays we spotted near that blackjack grove." He weakly kicked his mount and trotted back toward the longhorns.

I was too tired to eat, but I swallowed some burned bacon and washed it down with coffee, then stretched out for a nap. The camp was quiet, except for Bibberman's and my uncle's whispers, and I drifted off to sleep.

Trace's voice woke me up. "My guitar's all right, ain't it?" he asked excitedly. After wiping the sleep from my eyes, I slowly rose. Jesse swung from his horse and trotted over to the chuck wagon. "It's fine," Bibberman said.

"Jesus!" Uncle Cliff's voice boomed, and he sent his coffee cup hurling across the camp, lifted himself from his seat by the wagon, and lashed out at the amicable Jesse Trace. "You son-of-a-bitchin' worthless little waddie! We got a herd scattered to the next county, more'n twenty dead beeves, and a deadline to get to Wichita . . . and all the hell you care about is your music box!"

Biting his lower lip, Jesse Trace backed away from the fast-striding trail boss. "Why the hell ain't you out with Fain and them?" my uncle barked.

"Easy, Clifford," Amos Bibberman said, and Uncle Cliff stopped his charge toward Trace and turned toward the giant cook. By now, the whole camp was awake, silently watching our trail boss, who turned his anger toward Bibberman.

"Don't tell me to ease up, belly-cheater!" He whipped his slouch hat off and sent it sailing toward Bibberman. "You ain't bossin' this outfit!" He was silent for a few long seconds, then swore several oaths. He glanced at the rest of us, toward the trembling Trace, and finally back at the unmoving, unblinking Amos Bibberman.

"Bibberman," Uncle Cliff said, "give me that bottle of liquor."

"No, sir."

Uncle Cliff cursed and walked toward Bibberman, who quickly blocked the possibles drawer in the rear compartment of the Studebaker. "That's an order, cookie! I aim to have me a drink!"

"No."

The slap sounded like a cannon shot in the early morning air as Uncle Cliff's backhand struck Amos Bibberman's cheek. I was on my feet—and so was just about everyone else. Uncle Cliff lunged at the cook, swearing at the top of his lungs. Suddenly he was on the ground, his upper lip bleeding after a solid right from Bibberman, who quickly turned to the drawer. In an instant, before Uncle Cliff could rise, Amos Bibberman held that massive Colt Dragoon and pointed it at the squatting trail boss.

"You ain't drinking," Bibberman said, cocking the six-gun.

"Amos, no!" I shouted, and took two steps toward the chuck wagon, when I heard another revolver cock behind me. I stopped and turned.

"You pull that trigger, nigger, and your brains, if you got any, will splatter against that wagon sheet." Richard Hamilton grinned. "Hell, I ought to kill you right now, just for hittin' a white man."

"Aye," said Ian Cochrane, who was on his bedroll a few yards to Hamilton's right. "Ye do that, and I'll send you straight to Hades." The Scotsman cocked his own revolver and aimed it at the unreconstructed Rebel.

"Christ All Mighty!" John Dalton said, the first time I ever heard him swear.

Silence hung over the camp for an eternity. Three guns never wavered, and at any moment, I expected them to go off in some bloody shoot-out straight out of a cheap novel. I clenched my fists and ground my teeth, too scared to move or talk.

Suddenly Uncle Cliff laughed. Bibberman glanced at him, and, when their eyes met and locked, my uncle said: "If anyone pulls a trigger, he's fired. Especially you, Amos." The cook smiled and lowered his Dragoon. Begrudgingly Hamilton and Cochrane also holstered their revolvers, and Bibberman helped Uncle Cliff to his feet.

The tension over camp lifted like fog, and Bibberman put his huge pistol back in the drawer, then roared with laughter. He pulled the broken neck of a bottle from the chuck wagon and pitched it to the ground. "Damnation!" he said. "That bottle of whisky was smashed, too!"

Uncle Cliff shook his head and sighed.

It took us three days to round up all of the strays after two consecutive stampedes. We were on short rations and sleep—and quite on edge. Tempers flared at anything, and even Brazos Billy and Murphy came close to brawling before Uncle Cliff popped both in the ears and reminded them of his edict against fighting.

Nor did the attitude change once we got the herd moving north again. We groused at Bibberman about the food, and, believe me, we had reason to complain when we ran out of coffee. Bibberman replaced Arbuckle's by burning grain and acorns, which went down as easy as tobacco juice. Cowhands snapped at their horses, at the longhorns—even Gen'ral Houston—and Pedro O'Donnell when he'd rope a mount.

"I want the claybank, you stupid greaser!" Hamilton barked at the wrangler one night.

"But *señor,*" O'Donnell said, "you always ride this one at night."

"Well, tonight I want the claybank, damn you!"

"Señor."

"Lay off the kid, Hamilton," Santee said.

Hamilton swore back at Red, and the two glared at each other, about ready to pull their revolvers, when Uncle Cliff barked at both of them to shut up. They were still seething after they had mounted, preparing to begin night herding, when Uncle Cliff walked to them.

"You both cool down," he said, " 'cause, if the herd stampedes tonight, I'm gonna figure it was because of you two hot heads. And if that happens, you're both fired."

They rode out in silence, and Uncle Cliff walked toward

Bibberman to refill his coffee cup. For the past few days, it seemed that Uncle Cliff had been living off coffee, or now what tried to pass as coffee, cigarettes, and Star Navy chewing tobacco. He downed the liquid in an instant, sighed heavily, and swore.

I was on my bedroll near the chuck wagon and noticed he was shaking. "Christ, Amos, I could use some bug juice."

"You know better than that, Clifford."

"Yeah, well, I got a trail crew fallin' apart on me, and we ain't even crossed the Red River!"

"Clifford, you been pushing these men pretty hard, especially since the stampedes. You wind the stem too much, you break the watch."

He nodded. "Yeah, but Doug's got a deadline, and we're behind schedule. And travelin' through the Nations ain't no picnic."

"We won't get to the Nations, Clifford, with you pushing on like this. And you won't get there, neither. You're driving yourself to death, man. You and the boys need a break. . . ."

"Break, hell!"

"They need a break, Clifford. So do you. We should've let them go in to town at Saint Jo. Let them spend a day in Spanish Fort before we cross the Red. We have to get supplies anyway, and Spanish Fort's the last place."

"Hell, Amos, we can't afford any supplies."

"Clifford, we're out of flour, bacon, coffee. Face it. The whole crew will be down with scurvy or starving before we make it Wichita unless we stock up."

"How? We don't have enough money to buy nothin', and I know most of the merchants in Spanish Fort. They ain't about to let Doug Simpson go on tick any more. His credit is shot to hell."

This time Amos Bibberman sighed. The two men were silent, when suddenly I cleared my throat. They looked at me, two pairs of intense, but tired, eyes, boring a hole through me.

"What if we sold a horse or two at that town, Spanish Fort, or traded them for supplies?" Neither spoke, and I swallowed and continued: "Pedro says that Cochrane's bay, the one that went lame during the stampede, will get better with rest, but it'll be useless for the rest of the drive. I hardly ever ride the buckskin." More silent stares.

"It's just a thought. It's better than selling Mister Simpson's beeves, isn't it?"

"Son-of-a-bitch," Uncle Cliff said softly.

"Clifford," Bibberman said, "that boy might make top hand yet."

"Top hand, hell," Uncle Cliff said. "Ty's shootin' to be trail boss."

Spanish Fort was a dusty little town spitting distance from the Red River. It didn't have a post office in 1874, not even a church, but it had a number of saloons. And being on the Chisholm Trail, just a quick swim from the Indian Nations, it managed to attract outlaws, strumpets, gamblers, and cowhands.

"It's a regular Solomon and Gomorrah," Brazos Billy said, and John Dalton shook his head.

We rode into town in mid-afternoon—Brazos Billy, John, Fain, Trace, and me—with just a few dollars to spend and each with an agenda. Dalton and I needed new hats and real baths, while Brazos Billy, Fain, and Trace had other pleasures in mind.

Much to my surprise, my proposal worked. Uncle Cliff had sent Fain to town to sell the tired horses. Emmitt returned with less money than we had hoped, but enough for

Bibberman to buy supplies and a small advance for the cowhands. Earlier in the day, Uncle Cliff and Bibberman rode to Spanish Fort with the rest of the crew—*sans* Pedro and Cochrane. The Mexican wrangler promised his mother he would stay clear of cattle towns, except Wichita, our destination; Cochrane had obvious reasons for remaining in camp.

Now we were getting our turn at town, and I was thinking about my hat and bath. But my thoughts stopped when we reined up at the Cowboy Saloon.

"Boys," Fain said, "I think first on the list is to cut the dust."

The saloon was clapboard, like most of the town, its walls ventilated with bullet holes. Most of the tables were empty, but there were a couple of card games going on. An ornate mahogany bar stretched across the back of the room, with layers of bottles and kegs behind it and a huge mirror cracked in several places and shattered at one end. Above the mirror was a crude painting of a naked lady lying on a cloud with a cowboy looking up at her longingly. John Dalton saw the painting and turned beet red.

Fain, Trace, and Brazos Billy treated themselves to beers, while Dalton and I settled for sarsaparillas. Brazos Billy soon turned his attention to a woman at the end of the bar. She was fat, I could smell the lilac from where I was, and she must have applied the rouge and powder to her face with a shovel. Trace had another beer and bought Dalton a second sarsaparilla, and I found myself following Fain, who drifted toward the gaming tables.

I never really understood faro. And I'm proud to admit that I still follow Amos Bibberman's advice. "Tyrell," he had told me before we rode out of camp, "the only way a cowboy can come out ahead at a card game is not to play."

Emmitt sipped his beer and watched the game between the dealer and a reeking, bearded man in buckskins. I tried to pick up what I could as the house gambler, in a brocade vest, white shirt, and sleeve garters, pulled cards from a nickel-plated case. "Soda card," he said, then pulled a card. "The loser." Another card. "And the winner."

"Damnation!" cried the burly man, and the gambler took his money.

"Care to join us, gentlemen?" the gambler asked.

Fain smiled and sipped his beer. "Lemme finish my drink." He watched the gambler lose a small bet. The big, bearded player in buckskins, who smelled of whisky, sweat, and animal guts, yelled in excitement.

We walked to another table, where more people were playing faro, but gradually moved back toward the one-on-one game.

"I'm on a roll!" the burly man shouted, and dumped a handful of silver on the table. Fain quickly pulled a greenback from his vest pocket and placed it on the table.

"No offense, pard," he said, "but I think I'll copper that bet."

The gambler shot Fain an angry look. Quickly, however, he turned his attention to the card case. "Your loser." Another card. "And the winner."

"Damnation! You jinxed me, you lousy waddie."

"Sorry, sport," Fain said, collecting his winnings. He tossed the burly man a coin. "Have a drink on me." We moved to the other table at a fair trot.

"What made you bet?" I asked.

Fain set his empty beer mug on a table. "Gambler's cheatin'. He has a choice, either pay the buffalo skinner a lot of money or let me win some less. We'll wait a few minutes, then go back and win another hand. Then get out of here before the gambler . . . or that louse of a buffalo skinner . . . gets ornery."

It dawned on me while Fain counted his winnings. "Where the hell did you get that greenback?"

Fain just smiled.

"Damn you, Emmitt! You lied to Uncle Cliff. You got more for those horses you sold! Didn't you?"

"Oh, Ty, it's just a few extra bucks. Call it my seller's fee."

"Call you a thief, more like it."

Fain turned quickly, his face flushing, and there was a fire in his eyes that I had seen before and would see a few more times. I braced for the punch that never came. Emmitt took a deep breath and finally smiled.

"Pard, your mouth is apt to get you into trouble one of these days." Laughing aloud, he slapped me on the back. "Let's try our luck once more."

After the buffalo skinner made another big bet, Fain coppered it and walked away with more money. We were at the bar when a giant man with arms like beer kegs approached us. "You gents aimin' to have another drink?" he asked.

"Yep," Emmitt said.

"Have it some place else."

Fain turned and stared into the bouncer's torso, looked up at his face, and smiled. "Sounds like good advice, *amigo*." We tapped Trace and Dalton on the shoulders and left the Cowboy Saloon.

"Now what are we going to do?" Dalton asked.

I heard Fain's winnings jingle in his pocket and couldn't help myself. "Emmitt cleaned house at the faro table, and he's buying everything. Baths, hats, and maybe some more supplies for Amos."

Dalton cheered, and Trace slapped Emmitt's back, and Fain? He just looked at me, defeated, and smiled.

"You're damned right I am!" he shouted. "Only, we got to get Tyrell and Johnny Dalton outfitted proper 'fore we cross into the Nations."

"I said you were buying us hats."

"Hats! Hell, boys, I'm talkin' about iron. You boys are gonna feel a mite undressed in the Nations if you ain't got a six-gun and we're surrounded by Injuns."

Trace joined in, and, although Dalton and I knew—or hoped—they were pulling our legs, we let them escort us to the town mercantile for new hats, gun belts, and revolvers. Dalton picked out another bowler, but Fain made him put it back. He settled for a high-crowned, gray hat, and I donned a black Boss of the Plains, just like Fain's.

Next it was handguns, but Fain didn't splurge there. Dalton excitedly picked up a fifteen-dollar Colt .45, but Emmitt made him put it back. Emmitt bartered with the shopkeeper for an old Spiller and Burr .36 and box of paper cartridges and percussion caps for Dalton. I got an Army Colt .44, converted to take metallic cartridges, and slid the pistol into my new belted holster. It felt heavy and awkward on my hip—I must have looked like a buffoon—but I was ready for adventure, or anything.

Fain tossed in a sack of potatoes and two cans of peaches for Bibberman and began haggling over the bill. Emmitt nickeled and dimed the shopkeeper down to a reasonable price, paid up, and we headed for the door. "How 'bout some target practice?" Dalton suggested, but once we stepped onto the boardwalk, our plans of target practice and baths were shot. Rain began pelting the grimy streets of Spanish Fort.

"Looks like it's settin' in," Fain said.

"Yeah," Trace said. "We'd best find Brazos Billy and get back to the herd."

Chapter Eighteen

"We got some big swimmin' to do," Trace said as the Red River spilled out of its banks. Uncle Cliff had decided pushing the herd across now was the best option because, if we any waited longer, the crossing would be flooded, and there was no telling when the water would subside. So Bibberman and Pedro fashioned pontoons out of cottonwoods, floating the Studebaker across, while Santee and Slaughter marked the crossing.

With a treacherous current and hidden bogs, the Red was unlike any of the South Texas streams we had forded. This was a real river, not a ditch, with steep banks, slippery mud, lined with trees, driftwood, and brambles. Quicksand traps could pull a steer, horse, or man down in minutes. The river stretched across an eternity, and it seemed to be getting wider by the minute.

Even in dry times, the Red's unforgiving. In wet weather, it can transform into the River Styx in seconds, rising like the ocean tide in a hurricane and sweeping cowboys, horses—even entire herds—to the gates of Hades.

"Go!" Uncle Cliff shouted, and we pushed the cattle into the foaming, icy waters.

In the steady rain and fading light, Gen'ral Houston led the beeves into the river. Their bodies disappeared under the clay-colored water, leaving only horns and heads above the surface. Many balled, drifting downstream, fighting the current, but after a while Gen'ral Houston and the leaders reached the far bank.

I spotted something in the corner of my eye and turned to see an uprooted tree barreling toward the herd like a ramming warship. A few steers saw it, too, and they began milling, trying to get out of the missile's way, when the tree slammed into a terrified brindle longhorn and sank it like a cannonball, unleashing hell in midstream.

The cattle began churning, fighting the current, and several more went under. "Break 'em up!" someone shouted, and I forced my mount to the middle of the steers, sloshing through the choppy waves.

Richard Hamilton and Emmitt Fain were there, while on the far side of the herd, Dalton and Murphy slapped cattle with hats and lariats. Hamilton worked his way near me, cutting loose with his hat and a piercing Rebel yell.

A horn suddenly ripped into his claybank's neck, and the horse reared, catapulting Hamilton into the frothy waters as his mount spewed blood and screamed as it sank beneath the surface. I quickly maneuvered toward him, and, when he resurfaced between two crazed longhorns, I held out my left hand. He grasped it, and I pulled, but my own horse unexpectedly tumbled, and I lost my grip and crashed into wet hide and raging currents.

A hoof popped me below my right eye, and I swallowed a lungful of the muddy Red, struggling to find the surface—and air. Despite water-filled boots, heavy gun belt and Colt, I broke clear and tried to tread water. To my right I spotted the herd, still milling, and—out of reach—my horse swimming to the bank. But Hamilton was nowhere to be seen.

I was thankful my rain poncho was in the chuck wagon because I couldn't have survived with it on, but I stupidly held onto my new Stetson. Holding my breath, I sank again, but kicked, broke free, and gasped.

"Tyrell!" Fain shouted. "Grab a tail!"

Cattle darted past me, and I was about to go under once more when I heard Fain. "Damn it, boy, leggo of that stupid hat and grab a tail!"

A spotted steer swam by, and I grasped its tail, letting my Boss of the Plains float toward the terrified herd. Struggling against my weight and the flooding current, the longhorn somehow pulled me across the rest of the river until Amos and Pedro waded into the shallows and drug me to land.

I sucked in air, then threw up.

Fain and the others quickly forced milling cattle to swim in the right direction, while Santee rode downstream yelling for Hamilton. After a few minutes, I staggered to my horse, but Bibberman made me take a sip of whisky before I climbed into the saddle.

"Should I help Santee look for Hamilton?" I asked Bibberman.

Amos shook his head. "Herd comes first, Tyrell. That's the sad truth about this business. Keep the beeves moving."

Tiredly I joined the others, pushing the longhorns a few rods from the Red. The rain had stopped, at least temporarily, by the time we bedded down the herd, but the sun was setting. We left Dalton, Murphy, and Brazos Billy with the cattle, grabbed lanterns from the chuck wagon, and rode back to the river.

Les Slaughter was on the Texas bank and Red Santee rode on our side, but there was no sign of Richard Hamilton.

Cries of "Richard!" and "Hamilton!" pierced the dusk, but the only response was the gurgling waters that had taken him under. Taking two lanterns, Trace and Fain swam their horses across to join Slaughter, while Uncle Cliff, Cochrane, Santee, and I rode along the banks on our side.

Soon it was too dark, even with the lanterns. Rain clouds obscured the moon and stars, so, reluctantly, Uncle Cliff halted.

"Fain! Jesse! Slaughter!" he called out, and from across the river came Slaughter's hoarse reply. "It's no use, Les!" Uncle Cliff hollered. "We'll try again at daybreak."

We met Fain, Trace, and Slaughter at the crossing. Trace held out my hat, water soaked, beaten, and muddy. "Found this, Ty," he said, and I put in on without comment.

Uncle Cliff said: "I need a volunteer to wait here with a lantern, just in case Hamilton shows up alive."

"Aye," Cochrane said. "I'll wait for the lad."

I was shocked. Cochrane and Hamilton loathed each other, but Uncle Cliff only nodded, and the rest of us rode silently back to camp.

Supper was beans, bacon, and biscuits with real coffee, but no one felt like eating. Night birds, frogs, and coyotes punctuated the surrounding darkness, but inside the camp hovered an eerie silence.

"I keep half-expectin' that ornery sum-bitch to walk in here any minute," Brazos Billy said softly.

"Maybe he will," John Dalton whispered.

But no one really believed it. And Hamilton never showed up.

At dawn we skipped breakfast, even coffee, and rode back to the river. This time we spotted Hamilton's horse washed up on the Texas bank. Slaughter removed the Confederate's war bag, and we continued searching.

An hour later, I heard the quick report of three revolver

shots and realized someone had found Richard Hamilton.

John Dalton discovered the body, hung up on an uprooted blackjack, more than a mile downstream on the north bank. He used his new revolver to signal us and waited. Dalton was softly sobbing, head in his hands, when we arrived and pointed to the dead man.

Fain and Santee dismounted and pulled the heavy body clear. Hamilton's eyes were closed, his face colorless, mouth open and full of water. His hair was matted with river débris and mud. One of his boots was missing, along with his old, gray slouch hat. They wrapped his body in a tarp while we watched silently. Santee's horse shied from the burden when they tried to hoist the body onto the saddle, but Trace grabbed the mount and held it tightly, softly singing to the animal while Fain and Santee secured Hamilton's remains.

Santee swung up behind Fain and rode double, pulling Santee's horse and Richard Hamilton's body, leading an odd, quiet funeral possession.

In camp, Cochrane and Santee took spades from the chuck wagon and began digging a grave. Some of us sipped coffee, and John Dalton asked if he could read from the Bible over Hamilton's grave. "That would be fine, and the right thing to do," Bibberman said, firmly gripping the young cowboy's shoulder.

Uncle Cliff brought Hamilton's war bag to me. "There's some letters and stuff in there," he said. "See if you can find some sort of kin, a name and town, so we can notify 'em when we get to Wichita."

I found a small Bible in the bag, which surprised me. I never took Richard Hamilton for a man who would own the Good Book. It was pocket-size, the kind soldiers take to war, and I opened it and found an inscription. The ink had been smeared by the water, but I managed to read it:

To my brave brother Richard:

As you head off with our Lone Star Defenders to fight those Yankee tyrants, may GOD be with you and may You come back safe to us.

Your loving sister,
Elizabeth
20 June 18 and 61

Most of the letters were ruined by the water, but I managed to decipher: **Elizabeth Baxter, General Delivery, Rusk County, Texas**, from a soggy envelope. I assumed that was his sister.

"Write it down," Uncle Cliff said, "and give it to Amos."

It was misting rain as we lowered Richard Hamilton into a shallow grave. When John Dalton had finished reading from the Book of Matthew, Uncle Cliff stepped forward, hat in hand.

"Boys," he said, "this probably is my fault. I made the biggest mistake a trail boss can make . . . never keep a river in front of you. Had we crossed the Red first, then gone to Spanish Fort, Hamilton might still be with us."

"You don't know that, Clifford," Amos Bibberman said.

"Yeah, Boss," Brazos Billy added. "Besides, then we woulda had to swim the Red back and forth. We might all have drowned."

"Maybe," Uncle Cliff said. He was silent a few minutes, staring at the wrapped body. "I guess none of us liked Hamilton much," he said at last. "I guess none of us had reason to like him." He lifted his eyes toward us and continued. "But we didn't really know him."

Thunder softly rolled in the distance.

"But I know one thing about him," Uncle Cliff continued. "Richard Hamilton pulled his weight. He was a good cowman. And this drive is gonna be a hell of a lot harder without him." He nodded toward Cochrane and Santee, who began shoveling muddy earth over the body. Trace started softly singing "Rock of Ages" and a few others joined in, while Uncle Cliff slammed his hat on his head and walked with Bibberman back to camp.

When it was over, I stared at the unmarked gravesite. Here lay Richard Hamilton, a canvas tarp for a shroud, with no tombstone, no epitaph, not even rocks to keep the wolves away. It was humbling to realize his sister would never put flowers on his grave, never know his final resting place. In a few days, even I wouldn't be able to remember its exact location. And I recalled my own struggles in the Red River, how I had almost drowned, and Bibberman's chilling statement that the herd came first. It could have easily been me.

"Ye all right, Ty?" Cochrane asked.

"Yeah," I said after a few moments. "Seems like a lonely place."

"I dunna, laddie. He's got plenty o' comp'ny. I read once where someone said the Oregon Trail is just one long cemetery. And I imagine the Chisholm Trail's just the same."

We walked away.

"Ty." Uncle Cliff motioned me over to the chuck wagon where he stood in a circle with Bibberman, Fain, and Santee.

"You think you can handle flank?" Uncle Cliff asked when I joined them.

"Sir?"

"I'm hopin' with the herd pretty much trail broke, Billy, Murphy, and Dalton can ride drag by themselves. But I need someone to replace Hamilton at a flank."

I stammered some, and Uncle Cliff said: "Son, the Red's flooded by now, too dangerous to cross. And even if it wasn't, there's no guarantee I could hire a decent man in Spanish

Fort. And you're a better cowhand than Murphy or Dalton. Or even Brazos Billy."

"I'll try," I said reluctantly.

"Good. Les Slaughter will tell you what to do. Now let's get these beeves movin'."

The flank position, I found, was much more pleasant than drag. I no longer swallowed pounds of dust and now could see more of the cattle. Ahead of me, where the longhorns swelled, rode Trace and Cochrane at the swing positions. Across from me, on the left flank, was Slaughter, who kept me in good humor with terrible ditties and tales about his friend Amos Bibberman. Making matters even more pleasant was the smooth traveling.

As we moved north, the trail eased up. It was open, rolling prairie that skirted blackjack groves and small streams. Even the weather held, although it was quite cool.

And we seemed to have put Richard Hamilton's death behind us.

"Ya know, fellers," Brazos Billy said during supper the next night. "If I die on a drive and y'all bury me on some forgotten prairie, I got one request. I want a damned tombstone."

"Then you'd better die in Fort Worth or San Antone," Fain said. "Or else buy one now and put it in Bibberman's chuck wagon."

"Nah," Brazos Billy said. "You ain't gotta put the tombstone on my actual grave. Put it in Wichita or Ellsworth. Just so I am remembered."

"What name you want us to put on that headstone?" Fain asked.

Brazos Billy didn't reply. But Red Santee cackled. "Hell, Brazos Billy," he said between breaths. "You don't need no tombstone to be remembered. All the whores you've known . . . they'll keep your memory alive longer than any piece of marble."

We saw the rock piles long before we were near them. Distances deceived you on the plains, because it was another day before we reached Monument Hill. Atop the flat mesa stretched two columns of red sandstone boulders and rocks, some two or three hundred feet apart, reaching maybe ten or twelve feet toward the sky.

"Thing keeps growin' like a weed," Uncle Cliff said, pointing at the rocks. "Doug, Seth, and me started that as a joke. Said it would serve as a beacon for all them other trail drivers. Son-of-a-bitch, we never dreamed others would use it for a marker.

"These days, you waddies think it's some sort of Independence Rock to carve your John Henry in. What it was, was me, Seth, and Doug got us a bottle of illegal Nations rotgut and started throwin' rocks."

After easily fording a small stream and bedding down the herd, Fain and I rode up the mesa and got a closer look at the rocks.

"Take off a spur," Fain said when we reached the top and dismounted.

I dropped to a knee, unbuttoned a strap, and pulled off the spur. Fain pointed to the rocks, saying: "Here's your chance, pard, to become a cowboy for the ages."

Carved into several of the rocks were crude initials, names, and dates. I traced several with my fingers. **B.H.T., '69. M. Withers, May 1871. Jory Kelton, the best. And e. fain, '72.** I laughed and excitedly went to work above Emmitt's marking, using the rowel of my spur as a chisel and knife. It was hard-going, and I skinned my knuckles a time or two, but when I was done, I stepped back and smiled at my sloppy masterpiece.

TYRELL BREEN
cowboy
1874

Emmitt slapped me on the back and howled. "You're damned right, pard. Tyrell Breen! Cowboy!"

And so I stood, spur in my bleeding hand, wearing a battered Stetson, chaps, gun belt, and Colt. I was Tyrell Breen, king of the border men, feeling ten feet high and straight out of a half-dime novel. Ready for adventure. What I didn't know was that more hardships than any of us had imagined awaited us. A grim, savage ugliness. . . . And death.

Chapter Nineteen

It was a damned, miserable way to spend my birthday. At least, I thought it was April 8, but days, let alone dates, had long been discarded along the trail. Bacon was my cake and coffee my punch that morning. By afternoon, I was bone-tired, soaking wet, and shivering in the cold as we sloshed our way toward Hell Roaring Creek.

I was seventeen years old.

Gray clouds hung low across the rolling prairie, and a bitter north wind whipped misting rain mixed with snow. Water poured off my poncho and chaps, and, despite the protective gear, sopping clothes now stuck to my skin. I used the bandanna as a muffler, over hat and ears and tied under my chin and wrapped frozen reins around fingers numb despite heavy gloves. Luckily for me, the chestnut gelding I was riding was a good cow horse, nudging the stubborn longhorns along, headfirst into the wind, rain, and snow. All I did was sit in the saddle with my head bent down, probably rusted and locked in that position.

April in South Carolina meant spring. Flowers blooming. Farmers planting. Verdant pastures and white dogwoods. Maybe the wind would blow hard from the Atlantic and the nights would cool off, but I had grown used to celebrating my birthday in the warmth and comfort of the South.

Now I found myself in the Indian Nations in a frigid wasteland.

Through chapped, blistered lips and frozen nose, I sucked in icy air that set my lungs on fire. I could see my frosty breath as well as icicles forming on the horse's metal bit and bridle chain. Only the thought of Bibberman's coffee and a hot meal kept me going, but God was not kind on this day. In the distance, I made out the high hills that meant our camp and could feel the burned bacon going down my throat, could dream about wrapping myself in my sugan and sleeping for a year.

Ice suddenly pelted my poncho and hat, gently at first, then driving furiously as the wind howled and temperatures plummeted. The gray horizon turned white in an instant, and the cattle did an about face as smoothly as a squad of well-drilled Zouaves. They put the blizzard to their backs and began drifting south.

I fought them for a minute, trying to turn the herd back north, but Slaughter yelled: "Let 'em drift with the storm, Ty! Just hold 'em back as much as ya can!"

Those longhorns were smarter than me. To move north, into the awful sleet, would have meant certain death. With the wind at our backs, the storm's violence seemed to lessen, but that quickly changed as darkness crept around us and the sleet and snow refused to relent.

Time stopped in the darkness. I heard hoofs crushing ice, the droning wind, and moaning cattle, but my body felt nothing. Blood no longer coursed through my body. My fingers couldn't move. Eventually I heard nothing and saw only whiteness in the night. Soon I saw only black.

"Tyrell!"

My eyelids seemed frozen shut.

"Jesus, pard!"

I recognized Emmitt Fain's voice, heard his boots on the ice, felt him lifting me from the saddle. I forced my eyes open as he pried off my gloves and flexed my fingers roughly, then rubbed my hands and face violently until some feeling returned. He lifted me to my feet.

"Stomp your feet, Ty! Else you'll be frostbit. We gotta get them clothes off you and get you to camp. Stomp your feet!"

"I am," I said, but I wasn't.

Fain cursed and carried me to his horse, shoving me up behind the cantle like a bedroll.

"W-w-what 'bout m-m-my h-h-horse?" I stuttered.

"She's frozed dead in her tracks. And you will be, too, if I don't get you to a fire."

Five hours of sleet and snow left ice a foot and a half deep across the prairie. My bones still pang me when the temperatures drop well below freezing, an old reminder of that April in the Nations. Somehow I avoided severe frostbite and kept all my fingers and toes, but it took days before I felt warm again.

Bibberman had made camp in an old blackjack grove. Using chips, dry wood stored in the chuck wagon, and coal oil—and then the blackjacks—he kept a fire roaring constantly.

They stripped me of icy clothes that night, pumped me full of steaming coffee, put me next to the fire with a blanket, and rubbed my body—with horse liniment even—until I thawed out. It was now morning, and I was balled up under my blanket by the fire, holding a cup of coffee and rocking on my heels. I let the steam from the tin cup warm my nose and mouth, but my lips were too cracked to drink.

As the hands rode in from the herd, they gathered around the fire, eating breakfast and drinking coffee while standing, soaking in the warmth. Uncle Cliff walked to me and took the cup from my hands. "You need anything, son?"

I tried to think of some quip, a good joke, but I just shivered and shook my head.

"I count twenty-eight horses and twenty beeves dead," Uncle Cliff told our trail crew.

"I tried with the remuda, *señor*," Pedro said, choking back tears. "But . . ."—he made the sign of the cross.

"Ain't your fault. We're lucky we lost only twenty-eight. But that's gonna play hell on us. Go easy on your mounts 'cause we ain't got none to spare."

"What about the herd?" Santee asked.

Uncle Cliff shook his head. "We gotta round up what strays we can find and get 'em movin' north. Creeks are all frozen solid, and ice is coverin' the grass. We sure as hell can't keep 'em here. We'll need every man in the saddle, and that means you, Ty, if you can ride."

Anything, I wanted to say, to get out of this place quicker. But I could only nod. Slowly I stood up, then put my back to the fire.

"Daylight's burnin'," Uncle Cliff said. "Let's get . . . hey, where the hell is Les Slaughter?"

Silence enveloped the camp for long seconds.

"I thought I saw him before I rode in," John Dalton finally said. "He was ridin' that big dun."

"Lord, not Les," Jesse Trace prayed.

"Red, Fain, mount up and let's go find him," Uncle Cliff said, but I heard the crunching of ice and looked up. Slowly, a horse and rider were heading to camp, and I recognized the big sugarloaf sombrero that swallowed Slaughter's tiny head.

"Here he comes," I said, and you could feel the nervous tension blow away with the wind.

"Slaughter, you better hurry up!" Bibberman yelled.

"Ya done gived us a start!" Brazos Billy added.

Smiles quickly faded as the dun brought Les closer. A blanket draped Slaughter's shoulders, his hands were stuck inside his chaps, and the reins were wrapped around the saddle horn. Ice hung from the brim of his Mexican hat. Frost caked beard stubble. The big horse, with bloody icicles across its bit, stopped in front of us, and we stared up at the young, black cowboy. Les Slaughter, mouth open and head bent forward, stared back with a sightless gaze.

"Damn you all to hell, Lester Slaughter," Amos Bibberman said. He slowly walked to the horse and gently lifted Slaughter's frozen body out of the saddle and laid it on the icy ground. Crying, the cook dropped his massive frame beside his dead comrade.

"Cochrane," Uncle Cliff said, "see to that horse." Then he walked forward and knelt beside Les and the sobbing Bibberman.

"You all right, Amos?"

"Yessir, Clifford." Bibberman sucked in cold air.

"He was a good cowboy. Woulda made a good cowman."

Bibberman bit his lip and nodded. "Ground's frozen solid. We'll wrap him up, put him in the wagon, and bury him up the trail."

"Sounds good. You want Ty to stay with you?"

"I'll ride it out, Clifford. You'll need Ty to help with the herd."

Nodding, Uncle Cliff rose. A muffled pistol shot told us that Ian Cochrane had put the frozen dun out of her misery. "Let's move," Uncle Cliff said.

I got dressed while Amos Bibberman and Jesse Trace wrapped Les Slaughter, only a year older than me, in a bedroll and eased his body into the back of the chuck wagon. After saddling a buckskin gelding, I rode toward the herd with Amos Bibberman's high-key "Swing Low Sweet Chariot" following me out of camp.

" 'Rejoice, and be exceeding glad: for great is your reward in heaven.' "

John Dalton closed his Bible, and Cochrane and Trace began piling stones over Les Slaughter's body in a shallow grave, muddy from the melted ice, near the Little Washita River.

"Seems like we done this before," Fain said softly as he put his hat on his head.

"I'm thinkin' we might be jinxed, after all," Murphy added.

"Knock it off," Uncle Cliff said, and we watched Cochrane and Trace finish their grim chore in silence. The sun finally broke through some clouds—the first time we had seen it in days. I looked up and squinted, letting my face warm.

Bibberman stuck a long stick in the mud at the head of the grave and placed Slaughter's pale sombrero on top, then silently walked back to camp.

"Mount up," Uncle Cliff said after a minute. "We'll try to make five more miles today."

And so we left our second trail hand behind, near a lonely river. I tiredly swung into my saddle and glanced back at the grave. A gust of wind swept up from the south and overturned the stick, blowing Slaughter's sombrero into the brush.

I turned my mount toward the grave, but Uncle Cliff called to me. "It don't matter, Ty. It'll just blow over later anyhow."

We moped along the trail for a couple of days. Brazos Billy, the veteran of many drives to the rails, finally moved off the drag position and took over at flank opposite me, but he was surprisingly silent. A thawing southerly wind, cooperative cattle, and good grass helped improve our spirits, though, and put our troubles behind us.

At our camp, north of Walnut Creek, Jesse Trace pulled his guitar from the chuck wagon. He tuned the strings for a minute, looked at me, and smiled. "Pilgrim," he said, "I fin'ly roped them words. Remember when I first saw you south of San Antone?" That seemed like years ago, but I nodded, recalling how he had tried to explain the phrase "seen the elephant."

Trace strummed his guitar and began singing.

Sittin' in the saddle
On my five dollar steed,
Nothin' else but jerky
On which I can feed.
Out in the horizon
Is them mountains all so blue,
I'm just wishin' that I had a jug
To pull a cork or two.

Now I ain't had a bath
Since I left ol' Alabam'
But my hoss he smells just as bad
So he don't give a damn.
Just like roamin' the countryside
Where the nights and days are still,
I gotta see the elephant
Over the next hill.

Now back in Arkansas
I wedded me a fat Creek squaw.

Didn't have a thing to do
But smoke and drink and chaw.
But that married life just didn't
Take a fancy much to me.
So I loaded up my hoss one night
And rode away scot-free.

Now I ain't had a bath
Since I left ol' Alabam'
But my hoss he smells just as bad
So he don't give a damn.
Just like roamin' the countryside
Where the nights and days are still,
I gotta see the elephant
Over the next hill.

I don't dislike people.
They just don't care for me.
They tarred me in Saint Louie,
And I was shot in Santa Fé.
I just don't care for cities
'Cause there's nothin' else more fine
Than the burnin' heat of the desert
Or the taste of alkali.

Now I ain't had a bath
Since I left ol' Alabam'
But my hoss he smells just as bad
So he don't give a damn.
Just like roamin' the countryside
Where the nights and days are still,
I gotta see the elephant
Over the next hill.

Yeah, I gotta see the elephant
Over the next hill.

The camp exploded in laughter, and Brazos Billy cut loose with a Rebel yell. "That was a good one, Jesse!" he yelled, clapping his hands. We went to bed laughing, but the mood was long gone by breakfast.

Fain shook me awake and told me to hurry.

"What's going on?" I sleepily asked.

"Injuns," he said. "Get your gun."

Chapter Twenty

Fumbling with cartridges, I spilled more on the ground than I loaded in the Colt. Thoughts of the revolver accidentally discharging and blowing off my toes had kept the gun empty since Spanish Fort, but now I was scared, recalling the tales of Indian massacres in those half-dime novels. Would I be able to kill an Indian? Would I be able to hit anything?

"Just remember, Ty," Fain whispered, "save the last bullet for yourself."

My mouth was too dry to spit. I holstered my loaded weapon and picked up the dropped bullets, shoving them back into the cartridge belt while I scurried after Fain toward the hands gathering at the edge of camp. A sweaty palm gripped my gun butt. Uncle Cliff was riding from the herd toward us, followed slowly by two mounted Indians. Several more waited on a bluff overlooking the herd.

"God save us all," I said softly, and Emmitt Fain erupted in laughter.

My face reddened as the other cowboys turned toward us with confused expressions.

"I had you goin', Ty!" Fain roared, his blue eyes gleaming. He jerked a thumb toward the Indians. "Ain't you ever heard of the Civilized Tribes? Them Injuns ain't lifted a scalp in a coon's age. All they want is a toll for crossing their land. This is the Chickasaw Nation, boy. They're as peaceful as your grandma."

"Them ain't Chickasaws, Fain," Uncle Cliff said, reining in his mount. The color drained from Emmitt's face as he turned around and his own hand awkwardly found his Colt. "Cheyennes, I'm guessin'."

"But we're south of the Canadian," Fain said. "I mean, this is Chickasaw country."

"Well, you tell 'em they're trespassin'!" my uncle snapped. "Or ride to Tishomingo and tell the Chickasaws!" He dropped to the ground and handed his reins to Pedro.

"Get your hands off your damned guns! All they want is some beeves." He took a deep breath and forced a smile. "Amos, company's comin'. Get some coffee boilin'."

"Aye," Ian Cochrane said dryly as the two Indians rode their pinto ponies into camp, "they're Cheyennes. Wish me had me howitzer."

He didn't need a cannon. The two men were far from the feared Dog Soldiers I had heard about. Their horses were as skinny as jack rabbits, the riders more skeleton than flesh. One looked as ancient as Egypt. Beneath a battered derby with a feathered headband hung silver hair, braided and wrapped in skins, falling well past slumped shoulders. A hawk nose dominated his hollow, savagely pockmarked face. When he spoke to his companion, I saw that most of his teeth were missing.

The other Indian wore buckskin britches and a red calico shirt. Scars criss-crossed his face, and he was blind in his left eye. Greasy, salt-and-pepper hair blew in the wind, revealing that his right ear was missing. He grunted something and held up his right hand.

Both men carried sheathed knives, and the older one held

a beautiful lance, but those were the only weapons I saw.

"Pave-voona-o," the younger one said in a strange, glottal voice that somehow sounded musical. *"Mohoh-kave na-hesevehe."*

"Light down," Uncle Cliff said cheerfully, motioning our visitors with his hands. He pointed to Bibberman. "Cook," he said, then turned back to the Indians. "Make." He held both hands, open-palmed, in front of him and dropped them a few inches. "Coffee." He pretended to be holding a box and grinding beans.

In a couple of minutes, the two Cheyennes were squatting in front of Uncle Cliff and Cochrane, speaking in vastly different languages but somehow translating with their hands. I was fascinated by the exchange. Suddenly I smiled, remembering my mother admonishing me for talking with my hands. Here, it was the only way to communicate. After a while, Bibberman handed our guests steaming cups of coffee. The older man—I guessed he was the chief—took a sip and grinned.

"Hahoo! E-peva-e!" he said excitedly, rubbing his gaunt belly.

"Hell," Bibberman said as he filed past the rest of us. "I might take to cooking for the Cheyennes. At least, they appreciate good coffee."

Finally Uncle Cliff rolled the two Indians cigarettes, and he and Cochrane joined them in an after coffee smoke. Then all four men rose. The old man grunted something to his companion, who nodded and spoke rapidly to Uncle Cliff. He held out both hands, fingers extended upward, and said: *"Mahtohto."*

Uncle Cliff ground out his cigarette with a boot heel and shook his head. He made horns over his head with his index fingers, then gently glided fingers across his left arm four times. "Five," he said, firmly holding up five fingers.

The chief stubbornly shook his head. *"Mahtohto!"*

"Five," Uncle Cliff repeated, reached into his vest pocket, and pulled out his tobacco pouch and cigarette papers. "And this."

There was a short, guttural exchange between the Cheyennes. Then, nodding, the chief took Uncle Cliff's gift and walked to his horse, followed by the other Indian.

"Trace," Uncle Cliff said, "cut out five head and head 'em toward their camp."

"Yes, sir," Jesse said, "they look like they could use 'em."

I watched the grizzled warriors return to their people. They were the first wild Indians I had ever seen, but they didn't seem too wild or savage. They were starving.

"It's been a tough couple years on a lot of folks, red and white," Uncle Cliff said after forcing down Bibberman's coffee. "Amos, how much sugar did you put in that?"

Bibberman smiled. "Old Iron Belly liked it."

"Yeah. Well, we've burned enough daylight. I don't think this group will bother us any, but let's keep our eyes peeled." He tossed his empty cup at Fain and said sarcastically: "Chickasaws."

"How'd you learn sign language?" I asked while riding with Uncle Cliff and Cochrane to the herd.

"Army," Cochrane said.

"Picked it up on the trail," Uncle Cliff said.

"What was the . . . er?" I tried to copy the last signs my uncle had made to the Cheyenne.

"Sign for cattle," Uncle Cliff said. "Buffalo . . . that's the horn part. Spotted . . . that's with the arm. Spotted buffalo. Learnt that from Doug Simpson. That's my lesson for the day."

"Aye," Cochrane said. "And I've a lesson for you, laddie." He stopped his horse, and I did the same.

He reached over and withdrew my revolver, rotated the cylinder, and ejected a cartridge. "Keep the hammer on an empty chamber," he said, returning the gun to me, along with the bullet. "It's safer. Only fools and desperate men keep six loads in a revolver. Even I dunna do that."

We saw no more Indians that day, or the next. We easily forded the herd across the Canadian River and moved on through the red mud. The sun turned blazing hot—just days after we had been caught in a blizzard—and we swam the North Fork of the Canadian with no trouble from the cattle.

The chuck wagon, however, was another story.

I had never known Amos Obadiah Jonah Micah Bibberman to make a mistake, so I was shocked to see him sitting in the chuck wagon in the middle of the river. He had stopped the wagon in midstream to fill the water barrel, but the added weight sank the Studebaker axle deep in the mud. Water spilled over the wheels, washing over the pots and pans, drenching our sugans and Bibberman's boots.

Drag riders John Dalton and Charley Murphy informed us at camp, but we had already figured something was wrong. Cold camps we weren't used to.

"He's just sittin' there like a hog in a pen," Murphy said.

Uncle Cliff shook his head. "Ty, Fain, Jesse, Ian, let's mount up and go fetch him."

"Mind if I ride with ya?" Brazos Billy pleaded. "I'll help, an' I just gotta see that belly-cheater and give'm hell."

Uncle Cliff laughed and agreed, and we all hooted when we saw Amos. The four oxen were drinking their fill while Bibberman sat unmoving, unsmiling, unfriendly.

It wasn't all that funny after a while. The oxen couldn't budge the wagon, even with Brazos Billy and Jesse Trace whipping their backs with lariats and Bibberman hurling high-pitched oaths and a well-placed whip. Even with me and Fain slopping in the muddy water to our waists, pushing from behind. I slipped in the mud and came up spitting.

Enough was enough.

"Hell's fire, Uncle Cliff! This ain't gonna budge with that tub of lard sitting up there!"

"Damn right!" an equally irritated Fain added. "It's all his fault anyways!"

Uncle Cliff and Cochrane had roped the lead oxen and were trying to pull them forward with their mounts, but the Studebaker refused to give. They slacked the ropes and turned back toward the river.

"They've a point, Capt'n," Cochrane said.

"I ain't moving," Amos Bibberman said. "And Tyrell Breen, you'll pay hell for calling me a tub of lard."

"We got an audience," Jesse Trace softly said, nodding downstream where several Indian women stood on the banks, watching us, giggling and pointing.

"Amos," Uncle Cliff said. "Get off."

"I can't."

"Amos." The voice was no longer friendly.

"Damn it, Clifford, I can't swim."

"For God's sake, Amos, the water's only waist deep!"

"No, sir! I ain't budging."

Uncle Cliff slapped his hat against his leg. "Cochrane," he said dryly. "Shoot that fat bastard."

I wish I could have seen Amos Bibberman's face as Ian Cochrane palmed his revolver, but I was leaning against the side of the wagon. The pistol's report caused me to jump back, and the chuck wagon suddenly leaped halfway out of the water and sprung forward as Bibberman hurled his whale-like body into the river with a mighty cannonball splash.

The oxen panicked and bolted. My feet slipped again as the driverless wagon lunged forward, and I took another dip in the North Canadian. Blinded by the muddy water, I stood up, spitting out water and profanities. Downstream, I heard the Indians howling with laughter. Beside me, a sudden splash told me that Fain had gone under. In front of me, there were shouts of—"Stop that wagon!" and "Get outta the way, Boss!"—along with the jostling of pots and pans. A horse screamed. Uncle Cliff swore. Amos Bibberman cried for help. Water splashed. And Brazos Billy hollered: "Whoa, oxen! Whoa, oxen!"

I didn't want to open my eyes.

Bibberman, Fain, Brazos Billy—how he had fallen into the river, I didn't want to know—and I sat naked by a fire with our clothes drying nearby. John Dalton tried to set Jesse Trace's broken left thumb, and Ian Cochrane fixed coffee and beans while Pedro O'Donnell backtracked his way with a lantern to find the cookware and supplies that had fallen off the chuck wagon during its harrowing, two-mile run.

Night herding the cattle were Murphy and Santee, while Uncle Cliff sat near us, peeling sticky, red clay off his boots with a stick and fingering the cut below his left eye.

A log cracked in the fire. No one had spoken for maybe an hour.

"Ow!" Jesse's scream pierced the night. "You jackass!"

"Well, I'm not a pill roller!" Dalton fired back. "But that should hold you till Wichita."

"Yeah, well I can't play my guitar with a broken thumb!"

"Praise the Lord for that!"

Amos Bibberman began snickering. Brazos Billy quickly chimed in, and it spread to Fain and me, then Uncle Cliff, Jesse and John, even Ian Cochrane.

"You shoulda seen your face when Cochrane fired that shot," Uncle Cliff said, gasping for breath as the snickers turned to giggles, then deep laughter.

"And that splash you made!" Brazos Billy added.

"Hell, the North Canadian's now dry!" someone joked.

I rolled naked across the sand, laughing so hard that I cried. Soon I was on my knees, pressing my head against Bibberman's giant shoulder as he pounded my back and roared and wheezed. We carried on for so long that the coffee boiled over and Cochrane burned the beans.

Chapter Twenty-One

Even though we were short-handed, we made good time over the high, rolling prairie of the Indian Nations, gathering wood, water—and dust. The creeks that we crossed, Deer, Kingfisher, and others without names, became blurry memories as weather turned hellfire hot.

We were four days past the Canadian when we reached Turkey Creek, a small stream with a grove of timbers on the east. The water was cool, so, after bedding down the herd, most of us decided to bathe. I half-expected the creek to turn to mud from all the dirt and grime we removed from our bodies.

Uncle Cliff and Red Santee had ridden out of camp to scout the area, Bibberman was cooking supper, and Pedro O'Donnell gathering wood. Cochrane and John Dalton were with the herd. But the rest of us were relaxing, feeling clean and cool. Fain sprinted naked to the camp and returned with a tin cup, razor, and leather strap.

"Pard, you could use a shave," he said, and began lathering the shaving soap in his cup with his bandanna, in lieu of a brush. I rubbed the meager whiskers on my chin as Brazos Billy shouted: "I wouldn't let Fain near my throat with a razor, Ty."

"I'm not that green," I assured him. Fain smiled and handed me the cup of suds, which I cautiously smothered across my face, nervously watching as he stropped the blade. His eyes were beaming as he handed me the ivory-handled razor.

"Go against the grain, pard," he said, "and watch the jugular."

My beard was far from coarse, so my first shave was not an ordeal. I managed to nick myself only three times, then washed my face in the water, as Fain shaved. Brazos Billy joined us. He had no whiskers—not even fuzz—but he had a small bottle of Gilbert Muir Fine Old Whisky from Liverpool. I splashed some across my face, yelling as the alcohol burned, to Fain's and Billy's laughs. Emmitt applied some to his freshly scrubbed face and followed it with a belt.

"That's good whisky," he said.

"Yep," Brazos Billy replied. "Don't go tellin' Boss Rynders, Ty. There's barely enough in this bottle to wet my gizzard."

I shook my head and headed for the sandy banks, where I slept hard.

We pushed on without incident, until Charley Murphy lost his horse when it stepped in a prairie dog hole the next day and had to be shot. There were more prairie dogs than you could count, but only Murphy had the bad luck to lose a horse, but the village ended and left us facing more creeks and campgrounds. Each evening, Uncle Cliff and Santee would scout the area, something they had only recently started, but I had been too tired to notice.

The heat was sucking the energy from me. Sweat burned my eyes and soaked my clothes, and steam seemed to rise across the northern prairie. I was riding flank, dreaming of

Mattie, caked with so much dust that you would have thought that I hadn't bathed in years. I heard something and looked to my right away from the herd, and my mouth fell open.

Right there, less than fifty yards parallel to us, was another herd of longhorns being driven by cowhands. The wind was kicking up the dust around them, and I could hear the cattle bellowing, cowhands cursing, and the rattling of the chains and pots and pans of the chuck wagon. I wondered how long they had been near us, where they had come from. I glanced at my friends, yet they just ignored the new herd.

But I couldn't help myself. I tugged on the chestnut's reins and trotted toward the nearest cowboy. After months on the Chisholm Trail, I was in the mood for some new conversations. I rode into a dust cloud and pulled my bandanna up over my nose and closed my eyes. When I opened them, the herd had disappeared.

I reined to a stop, lowering my bandanna as a hot wind blasted my face. My throat was dry, and I blinked. The herd had simply disappeared, along with the men and horses and even the wagon. Dizziness overcame me, and I swayed in the saddle, closing my eyes and trying to keep my balance. When the spell passed, I opened my eyes again, hoping to see the herd. But all I saw was the white, glistening bones of cattle and horses—at least two dozen animals.

"Tyrell, what the hell are you doin'?" Uncle Cliff was at my side on his horse. "Boy, you can't just bolt from the herd like that! Fast move like that might spook the herd! Boy, you sick or somethin'?" His voice softened. "You're white as a ghost."

"Ghost," I said. I took a sip of water from my canteen, pointed to the skeletons, and told him what I had seen.

"Mirage," he finally said. "Sun'll do that to a man sometimes. I've been feelin' a mite spooked myself lately, too, like we're bein' followed." He pointed to the bones. "This outfit probably got hold of poison water. I've herd tales of ghost herds before but never seen one. Whole outfit, you said?" He shook his head. "That's one for the books." He jerked his thumb toward our herd. "Now let's get back to work."

I was awake all night, staring at the cloudless sky, thinking about that ghost herd. That was a big mistake for I fell asleep in the saddle the next afternoon—dreaming of the ghost herd, only to be awaked by a real nightmare.

"Stampede!"

My horse was spinning as the herd raced past, and I was pitched to the ground with a thud. The screams of men and animals pierced my ears as I scrambled to my feet, spitting dirt and blood from my mouth and lunging for the reins of my mount. I missed my mark but managed to grab the near stirrup, which I held on to as the horse raced across the rocks and cacti before slowing as my weight pulled the saddle to one side.

I crawled up alongside her, patting her and reassuring her, then moved the saddle in place and tightened the cinch. After clamping my hat down on my head, I mounted and kicked the horse into a gallop toward our fleeing herd. My lip was busted from my spill, my shirt shredded from my drag, and my chest bleeding and raw. A hoof had bruised my right arm, and my left thumbnail was gone, but my instinct was to get to the herd.

Does this make me a cowboy, I wondered, *or a fool?*

It wasn't much of a stampede, after all, and I got the worst of it. We managed to turn the herd and calm them down just south of Cox's Crossing of Bluff Creek. I replaced my ripped shirt with my last shirt after Bibberman treated my cuts and scrapes with salve, then joined the others as we rounded up strays.

A sod house greeted me two miles from Bibberman's makeshift camp. Uncle Cliff and Santee, still mounted, were being furiously yelled out by a massive, bearded man in denim overalls and a muslin shirt. Brazos Billy and Dalton were on top of the sod house working hard at removing a buckskin-colored mossy horn from the farmer's roof.

"I get shotgun and shoot beef! You ruint house!" the man barked in some thick, European accent as I rode into the yard.

"You pull a shotgun and you'll be pulling pellets out of your arse," Santee snapped back, unintimidated by the farmer's massive bulk.

The steer's forehoofs had fallen through the sod roof, and it was balling like a kid while Brazos Billy tried to hold the massive longhorns steady and John Dalton worked to dig the steer free.

"What caused the herd to run?" I asked.

"Damn' coyote bolted in front of the leaders," Santee said. "Even Gen'ral Houston ran like hell. What the hell happened to you? You look like you got trampled."

Uncle Cliff glanced my way, snickered, then looked back at the roof. The farmer began pointing a massive finger at us and bellowing some more, partly in English, partly in some other language.

"Keep your hand on the butt of your six-gun, Ty," Santee whispered. "Make this sodbuster think twice about kicking our arses."

I nodded. "He sure looks like he can do it."

"How's it comin'?" Uncle Cliff asked, ignoring the farmer's complaints.

"We just about got it!" Brazos Billy said.

Those were the last audible words spoken.

The longhorn bellowed, and it, Brazos Billy, and Dalton

disappeared in a cloud of dust as the entire roof collapsed. The farmer almost choked on his curses as he turned to see dust pouring out of his front door like smoke. Santee's horse reared and threw him, and Uncle Cliff and I danced around on our mounts. Chickens scurried across the farmyard, and a pig squealed at the commotion.

Out of the dust came John Dalton, wheezing, blinded and bloodied by the fall. Santee had grabbed his reins and was trying to calm his mount, which was rearing and snorting. From inside the sod house came a loud scream and snort, then Brazos Billy dashed out of the door, yelling like a Comanche and running across the yard behind the chickens. He was holding his arse with his right hand and had a noticeable limp.

The buckskin steer crashed into the door frame, but its massive horns blocked its exit. It bellowed, backed up, and rammed the doorway again, sending more dirt and thatch from the house's frame. Turning its head sideways, the longhorn made another effort, but still couldn't leave its new home. The farmer moaned something in his native tongue, and Santee finally calmed his horse.

Having calmed our own horses, Uncle Cliff and I dismounted and walked past the dazed farmer toward the sod house. The scared longhorn backed up and began ransacking the inside looking for another way out. Uncle Cliff and I quickly entered the hut and grabbed the horns, struggling to bring the steer to the door.

Red Santee suddenly appeared and threw a rope over the steer's head, then disappeared outside. The slack on the rope tightened, and the longhorn, Uncle Cliff, and I were pulled toward the doorway. We managed to twist the animal's head so that the horns cleared the passage, then let go as the animal snorted and was pulled outside.

Uncle Cliff and I glanced at the inside of the destroyed house. Furniture, glassware, pots and pans, and papers, wood, and pounds of dirt were all over what once was this immigrant's home. The sun shown brightly overhead where the roof once was.

"Sodbusters," Uncle Cliff said, smiling, and walked outside.

"That damned steer poked me in the butt," Brazos Billy said, then showed us his bloody hand.

Santee was leading the still-angry longhorn back toward our herd, and John Dalton was mounted and holding the reins to our horses, obviously in a hurry to leave before the farmer realized what had happened to his home.

"If I were you, I'd sit my poked butt in the saddle and light a shuck out of here," Uncle Cliff said. He mounted his horse, and we left the farmer staring blankly at the sign still hanging over his doorway: **Fusse abputzen**.

It was German, Ian Cochrane later told us, for "Wipe Your Feet."

Chapter Twenty-Two

Caldwell, Kansas, was a handful of stores, saloons, and huts in 1874, our first look at civilization, if one could call it that, since Spanish Fort, and calling Spanish Fort civilization took some imagination. In later years, Caldwell would become one of the meanest cowtowns on the Chisholm Trail, so, I guess, it's somewhat fitting that it was here that we met Henry Allison.

We had collected our strays and crossed Bluff Creek, leaving the Indian Nations behind us. In a week or so, we hoped to be in Wichita. After setting up camp, Uncle Cliff, Trace, and I rode into the roughshod settlement. Charles H. Stone owned a store, and, although we couldn't afford supplies, Uncle Cliff wanted to see if there was any mail from Doug Simpson.

The store was a solid log cabin, unlike the filth that surrounded it. Mister Stone wasn't around, but his clerk was a friendly enough fellow, offering us a drink on the house while he checked the mail. Uncle Cliff licked his lips, glanced my way, but settled on coffee, and Trace and I followed his example.

"No mail, sir, sorry," the clerk said. "Y'all need any supplies?"

"Not unless you'll allow us to go on tick," my uncle told

him. "And I expect C.H. would have to put his stamp on that."

"Yes, sir. He's in Wichita, expected back next week, if you'd care to wait."

Uncle Cliff shook his head. "I suppose we can go on short rations for a week."

A strange voice sounded behind us. "Been a hard drive?"

He was a tall man with thick black hair and cold blue eyes, sitting on an oak keg next to the stove despite the afternoon heat. Black striped britches were tucked into long, brown riding boots, scuffed with age, and a cap-and-ball Dance revolver, just like my uncle's, was holstered in a navy blue sash. He wore a bright calico shirt, navy military vest without buttons, light blue scarf, and buckskin hat. He spat a stream of tobacco juice that sizzled against the cast-iron stove.

"They are all hard," Uncle Cliff said. "This one's been harder than others. Lost a couple of men."

The man shook his head. "Sorry to hear that. I lost my whole outfit last year to thieves. Said they was range detectives once, but they weren't. Damned Kansans. Bloody Bill and Quantrill had the right idea. Range detectives!" He spat again.

"Who were you with?" Trace asked.

"Horton Rodgers of Lampasas County."

Trace nodded. "I heard about that. Killed like eight men."

"Yep. Put a ball in my leg, wounded two others, and dragged Mister Rodgers to death."

Uncle Cliff shook his head. "I've had my fill of thieves. If they're gonna rob me, be a man about it and act like thieves. Don't hide behind some kind of range detective title."

"I agree," the man said. "You say you're short-handed. Can you use a man?"

"We're only a week or so out of Wichita. Best you'd get is

ten or fifteen dollars . . . and only if we get our bonus. You're probably lookin' at only seven dollars."

The man slowly stood, smiling. "And free grub and safe passage to Wichita. I been waitin' on the first herd to come through. Henry Allison's the name." He held out his hand.

"Don't know how safe it'll be," Uncle Cliff said as they shook hands. "This is the so-called jinxed outfit. Grab your possibles. We're camped just north of here. Afraid you'll have to start out ridin' drag."

Allison's smile vanished, and he took a step back. He pointed to me and said: "Drag? I'd put the kid on drag. I'm a swing or flank man."

"And you ain't bossin' this outfit. Maybe the next herd through'll fill your bill."

The smile returned. "All right, Boss. Drag it'll be. Damn, I hope you got a good cook."

We rested a day—although Uncle Cliff refused to let anyone sample the whisky in the settlement—and moved northeast at first light. The new hand kept to himself and seemed to know what he was doing on drag, not that it took too much brains to keep your mouth shut and head down.

"I don't like him," Fain told me over supper. "He's got the look of a man-killer, like Cochrane."

"I like Ian," I said.

"Yeah, Ian's one to ride the river with. But you ain't learned your lessons, Ty. His saddle." He looked at me, as serious as I had ever noticed him. "Allison's saddle is in need of a good scrubbin' and mendin'." He collected our empty plates and stood up, looked down at me, and said before walking away: "A good cowhand keeps his saddle clean. Allison ain't no cowboy."

There were other clues that went unnoticed, like how he

studied each of us, his aloofness, and tendency to clean his revolver. I once watched as he loaded all six chambers and remembered Cochrane's telling me that only a desperate man or idiot would keep a six-gun loaded in such a fashion. But I quickly forgot about it. We were nearing Wichita, and my thoughts were of Mattie.

Uncle Cliff decided to let the cattle graze late into the morning, taking advantage of the rich grass near the Ninescah River. We were leisurely enjoying our coffee when Henry Allison rode into camp.

"Damn you, Allison!" Uncle Cliff snapped. "You're supposed to be with the herd."

"I left the Bible-thumper with 'em," Allison said, referring to Dalton, as he swung down near me and filled a coffee cup. "Figured you'd like to know what I seen."

Pedro led his horse away, but all other eyes were on the newcomer. He jutted his jaw toward the southwest. "We're bein' followed. Dozen men, I reckon. Cattle thieves."

Every eye turned away from Allison and toward the horizon.

"Capt'n Rynders and I thought we was being followed," Santee said.

But Uncle Cliff was now looking at the herd. "I don't see Dalton," he said.

The next thing I knew, Henry Allison had dashed toward me and split my head with his revolver. My hat softened the blow and went sailing toward the fire as the black-bearded man shoved his left arm around my waist to keep me on foot and cocked his revolver with his right hand and put it under my chin.

I was groggy, but I understood his words: "Don't try nothin' or I'll splatter this kid's brains across the chuck wagon."

"You thievin' bastard," someone said.

"What the hell have you done with John Dalton?"

"We're gonna string you up, you son-of-a-bitch."

Allison pressed the pistol barrel deeper into my chin. "This is for you, Rynders," he said. "You wanted open robbery, well, this is it. Now you and your waddies toss your hardware at my feet. Do it now, or I send this child and many of you to hell."

"Dalton?" Bibberman asked.

"He's trussed up like a turkey and takin' a nap. Nobody's got to die like Horton Rodgers and his crew."

I'm not sure anyone believed him, because Trace had told me that Rodgers's men had been tied up, then shot, although one or two escaped. Allison wouldn't want witnesses, not this close to Wichita. But slowly, after Uncle Cliff nodded, the cowhands unbuckled their gun belts and tossed them toward Allison.

"You harm my nephew, Allison, and I'll make hell look like a whorehouse to you," Uncle Cliff said as he threw his gun belt and revolver onto the pile.

"You scare me, old coot." He lowered the revolver from under my head and pointed it at Brazos Billy. "Simpleton," he said. "Why don't you ring that dinner bell on the chuck wagon so my friends can join this here fandango? Do it!"

The clanging of the bell made my aching head want to explode. Brazos Billy was ringing that bell as if he were Gabriel blowing his horn. It clanged and clanged until Henry Allison shouted three times for him to stop. Brazos Billy backed up, looking at me all the while. Then we waited.

Riders appeared to the southwest and began loping in toward us. Allison hadn't lied. He had a dozen men. I saw my crushed hat near the fire. At least it hadn't been burned, I thought, then my head cleared, and I looked back up. Brazos

Billy's eyes were locked on me. I couldn't meet his glare. *What the hell is he doing?* I thought.

Hoof beats sounded to my right. Allison and I turned to face it. *Was it another of his riders?* I wondered. *John Dalton?* And then it hit me. *The bell!*

"Jesus Christ!" Henry Allison screamed as the giant Gen'ral Houston rounded the side of the chuck wagon, his massive set of twisted horns glistening in the morning light. The spotted dun longhorn with its scarred face was the last thing the outlaw expected to see, and I took advantage of the situation. Allison was about to fire at the steer, when I slapped his gun hand and threw myself against the chuck wagon.

The revolver discharged. Gen'ral Houston, expecting his treat of sugar or oats, bellowed and bolted toward us. Allison kneed me in the groin, but I caught my breath and shoved him away. He was raising his gun, about to fire, when the Gen'ral's right horn tore into his belly.

I dropped to the ground. A gun fired. *"Move!"* Uncle Cliff was shouting. "Get movin' or we're all dead!"

Allison's screams became strangled by blood as the giant longhorn tossed him up and down. The ground shook around us as the herd stampeded. Another shot sounded. There were more shouts and screams, then gunfire. I saw the Gen'ral's legs dancing as I crawled underneath the chuck wagon. The outlaw's body fell beside me, as Gen'ral Houston raced away, confused and scared by the battle that had erupted around him.

Henry Allison stared at me with sightless eyes. Blood spilled from his mouth, and I tried not to look at his stomach, or what was left of it. I choked on bile, then forced myself to take the revolver from his dead right hand as his band of thieves were charging into camp. I raised the revolver and fired, but it was hard to tell what I was shooting at. I crawled from underneath the wagon and stood up. A bullet whizzed past my ear and banged against the pots in the wagon. I fired again, then tripped on Allison's body, and fell into a lake of blood.

This was nothing like one of the half-dime novels I had read. I rolled over as a man on horseback jerked his roan to a stop. He was bald and toothless with a patch over his left eye. And he pointed a huge shotgun at my face and smiled. I tried to raise my pistol, knowing I was too late, as he pulled the trigger.

A cap popped and fizzled.

"Hell's bells!" the man said. "A misfire!"

His ugly face disappeared in a sea of crimson as the horse reared and threw him. I looked at my revolver, but knew I hadn't fired. Uncle Cliff was suddenly at my side, holding a smoking rifle. He lifted me up and shoved me behind the nearest wagon wheel.

"Stay down!" he shouted, levering the Winchester and running away at the same time.

It was over in a matter of minutes. Uncle Cliff walked toward me, his face blackened by gunsmoke. I slowly rose, glanced at the bald man and Allison, and dropped to my knees and threw up on the fire.

I must have passed out. The next thing I knew Trace was with me by the river, where he had lowered me in the water until the blood was washed from my clothes. He wrapped my head with a torn shirtsleeve. I took a sip from his canteen and asked in a weak voice. "Did we win?"

He tried to smile. "Herd's stampeded. We got most of them murderers, but the rest scattered and took the remuda. We only managed to grab two or three horses."

There wasn't anything else he needed to say. We were almost spitting distance from Wichita, but with three horses we'd never be able to round up the herd and deliver it by deadline. Poor Douglas Simpson. His ranch was lost. And how could I tell Mattie that I had let her down?

"Let's get you back to camp, pilgrim."

I managed to walk in on my own feet. John Dalton, his head also wrapped in a calico shirtsleeve, limped toward us. One eye was swollen shut, and the other was filled with tears. The bodies of Allison and four other outlaws were piled next to the chuck wagon, and our hands were gathered at the far end of camp in the shade. They were standing over Amos Bibberman, who was silently wiping the brow of a cowboy.

"What is it?" I asked.

"It's Brazos Billy," Dalton said softly.

Chapter Twenty-Three

Brazos Billy had been shot twice in the abdomen, and I knew enough about stomach wounds to know he lay dying. He smiled, even though racked with pain, as Bibberman mopped his forehead with a wet bandanna.

"Ya waddies promised," he said, then gasped, shutting his eyes and groaning. After the pain subsided, he forced another smile. "Marble tombstone . . . in Wi . . . Wichita."

"We got most of them sum-bitches, Brazos Billy," Red Santee said, "and I guaran-damn-tee you that I'll track down those other bastards."

"Don't matter," Brazos Billy said. Blood trickled from the corner of his mouth. He coughed some. "Tomb . . . stone matters."

"What's the name, Billy?" Uncle Cliff said.

There was another coughing fit, then Brazos Billy took a deep breath and said: "William T. Sherman."

Uncle Cliff smiled. "Not a good handle for a Southerner, I reckon."

Billy shook his head. "No, sir. It sure ain't."

"It'll do ye right in Wichita, lad," Cochrane said. "You're in Yankee country."

He was silent for a few minutes. "Feels like another

norther, Boss," Billy said after a while. But we were all sweating. "I sure . . . could use some . . . whisky."

Uncle Cliff nodded, and Bibberman rose and walked to the chuck wagon. He uncorked a full bottle of Gilbert Muir Fine Old Whisky from Liverpool and handed it to the dying cowhand. "From your war bag, Brazos Billy."

His eyes widened in surprise. "Belly-cheater." He gasped suddenly, coughed, and grinned. "How long . . . ya . . . knowed?"

"How long you been riding with us?"

Brazos Billy's smile vanished. "Cain't move my arm," he said.

Jesse Trace lifted Billy's head, and Uncle Cliff moved over and took the bottle. He poured a bit into Billy's mouth, but the liquor mixed with the blood and spilled out on his blood-soaked shirt.

"Can't swaller," he said, then coughed violently, and screamed. "Oh, Lordy, Boss, I don't want to die!"

Uncle Cliff lowered Brazos Billy's head and corked the bottle. "We'll save this for you, Mister Sherman," he said, "till you're feelin' better."

Brazos Billy spit up blood, shivered, and let out a deep, ragged breath. Trace silently closed the dead man's eyes and rose. Uncle Cliff sat the bottle on the ground and struggled to his feet. "Fain, Red. Dig a grave for Brazos Billy. Cochrane, Trace. Take them vermin to that buffalo wallow east of here and throw 'em in it."

"Bury 'em?" Trace asked.

"Let 'em rot," Uncle Cliff said. He looked down at Brazos Billy's lifeless body. "William T. Sherman," he said, "you were a hell of a cowboy."

John Dalton sobbed uncontrollably as Fain and Santee

lowered William T. Sherman, known to all this cattle season as Brazos Billy, into a shallow grave. The two gravediggers climbed out and stood near us, and Uncle Cliff bowed his head. He was quiet for a minute. He opened his mouth, but words never sounded. After a while, he bowed his head again. Finally he said, "Dalton, you want to read somethin'?"

"Mister Rynders," Dalton said between sobs, "I can't." And he balled like a child on Amos Bibberman's massive shoulder. Charley Murphy also wiped his eyes.

Ian Cochrane stepped forward and opened his book. I had never been close enough or curious enough to find out what he was reading. I guess, after learning of his military background, I had assumed it was HARDEE'S RIFLE AND LIGHT INFANTRY TACTICS or something along those lines.

He thumbed through some pages and read:

"So saying, he arose; whom Adam thus
Follow'd with benediction. "Since to part,
Go heav'nly Guest, Ethereal Messenger,
Sent from whose sovran goodness I adore.
Gentle to me and affable hath been
Thy condescension, and shall be honour'd ever
With grateful Memory: thou to mankind
Be good and friendly still, and oft return."
So parted they, the Angel up to Heav'n
From the thick shade, and Adam to his Bow'r.

"Farewell, Brazos Billy," Cochrane said as he closed his worn copy of John Milton's PARADISE LOST.

We stood around as Brazos Billy's grave was covered and marked with a stick and bandanna. Then we ambled back to camp. It was fast approaching dusk, but no one was hungry. Walking ahead of us, Emmitt Fain quickly stopped and picked up the bottle of Billy's whisky that Uncle Cliff had left on the ground. He stuck it inside his vest, hoping no one noticed.

"Fain!" Emmitt stopped dead in his tracks as Uncle Cliff bulled his way through us. He stood in front of Fain and held out his left hand. "You are a disgraceful son-of-a-bitch, Fain! Give me that damned bottle."

Fain slowly withdrew the Gilbert Muir, which Uncle Cliff snatched with his left hand, then sent a crushing right into Fain's jaw. Emmitt fell sprawling on the ground. He shot up in a second, though, but he wasn't about to fight.

"Hell's fire, Boss Rynders!" he shouted. "We ain't got but three horses, no chance at gettin' that herd to Wichita. I'd say if anyone deserves a shot of whisky now, it's us! We likely ain't gonna see no pay after buryin' three good men on this damned drive!"

"You ain't gettin' drunk, Fain! You're crazy like a drunk Injun when you get drunk. And you ain't gonna do that when we just buried a fine young man back there. You want to, grab one of those horses and ride out of here." Uncle Cliff stormed away, out of camp, leaving the rest of us dumbfounded.

"Pedro," Bibberman finally said, "let's get some supper going."

"What the hell are we supposed to do now?" Charley Murphy asked. He only got a few shrugs in reply.

But I knew what I had to do, so I followed Uncle Cliff out of camp. I found him by the river, taking a long pull on the bottle. He glared at me, wiping his lips on his sleeve.

"Don't start preachin'," he said, and took another drink.

My face reddened. "Fain can't get drunk, but you can, I guess. Hell, I've seen you drunk, and you ain't no better than Emmitt."

"We're finished, Tyrell!" he shouted. "Doug's lost his

ranch. We've lost the herd. Brazos Billy is dead. I told Doug this was no good, that I can't boss a herd." He shook his head, had another shot. "Jinxed outfit," he said with a sigh. "Next thing you'll know, Mattie will take to whorin' to make ends meet."

I tackled him, and we both splashed into the river. I grabbed the whisky bottle with my right hand, slapped him with my left, and was tempted to fling the bottle across the water. But I stopped myself and stumbled onto the bank. Uncle Cliff was charging out of the river, but he lost his footing and crashed at my feet. As he scrambled to get up, I kicked him in the chest and knocked him on his backside.

He was looking up at me, dazed, the liquor hitting him, and the words of Doug Simpson back in Texas returned to me as clear as the sky.

"All right, damn your yellow hide!" I screamed. "You want to wallow around in a pigpen, you wanna swamp out saloons and spittoons for your bug juice, go ahead! We've got a job to do, a chance for you to do what you're good at! I'm not crazy about the idea myself, but damned if I see another choice!"

I tossed him the bottle, which he caught, spilling only a couple of shots. "I'll be damned, if I'm gonna beg to a drunkard," I said, and left him on the riverbank.

It was full dark by the time he returned. We were around the campfire, eating beans and rancid bacon. He tossed the bottle—with plenty of whisky left—to Fain. "Take a sip," he said, "and pass it around. We've got a lot of work to do come first light."

I smiled.

"Get me some coffee, Amos," Clifford Rynders barked, and this time the cook didn't argue.

"What the hell can we do, Boss?" Trace asked.

"Three horses. That's a start. One of us can ride to Wichita, tell Doug what's happened. We'll send another rider south, find another herd, see what they can do to help us. We'll keep the third horse here."

Red Santee took a sip and handed me the bottle. I decided to sweeten my coffee rather than drink the raw liquor, and handed John Dalton the bottle who politely passed it to an eager Charley Murphy.

"Yeah," Santee said, "but we'll never get that herd to Wichita in time."

"So, we don't get the bonus. We can gather what beeves we can, still get a fair price maybe."

Fain shook his head. "By the time we get another remuda, those longhorns will be scattered across Kansas and the Nations. I ain't sure it'll be worth the effort."

Uncle Cliff shrugged. "Then you can walk back to Texas, Emmitt. With no pay. We do it my way, we'll get something out of it."

"But not enough to save the Simpsons' ranch," I said.

Uncle Cliff shook his head. "Probably not. Unless we get lucky."

"Lucky!" Fain snorted. "It'll take more than luck to help this jinxed outfit."

Chapter Twenty-Four

Our luck came from the south the next morning, so we held off on sending a rider to Wichita. Red Santee loped toward the rising dust far behind us, which could only mean another herd, and we sat around camp waiting for his return, as Jesse Trace sang while awkwardly mending a spur strap with his busted thumb.

And now the farmers and townsmen,
They try to drive us away,
When we feed the nation
Beef and steaks every day.
I only hope I'm in my grave
So I can never tell,
When fences have closed
That lonesome Chisholm Trail.

Three dusty riders rode into camp with Santee a few hours later. One wore a big Texas hat and brown handlebar mustache. Another was the blackest man I had ever seen, with white hair, a neatly trimmed mustache, underlip beard, and a cigar jammed in his mouth. And leading the way was a rail-thin man as tall as a telegraph pole, bearded, in his late thirties or early forties. He was dressed in typical cowboy fashion, but when he spoke, I knew he was in charge.

"Damnation! Joseph, have you ever seen such a raggedy-ass-looking group of waddies?"

It was a booming yet shrill voice, irritating but commanding. Without waiting for a reply, he barked an order to see our trail boss, said it was common courtesy to ask visitors to dismount and offer them coffee, if not food, that it was an interesting concept to drive a herd from Texas to Kansas *without a herd.* He sprinkled his opinions with well-placed profanity; he seemed unable to speak a sentence without an oath.

Pedro led their horses away while Bibberman gave each man a cup of coffee. Uncle Cliff, who had been shaving by the river, walked into camp.

"Hello, Shanghai," he said.

The tall man turned suddenly, swore, and bounded over to my uncle in only a couple of steps. They shook hands violently, and then the man stepped back, finished his coffee, and boomed: "Clifford Rynders. Damn me to hell." He jerked a thumb toward Santee. "This waddie tells me you ran into a hell of a lot of trouble. I'm here to help."

His name was Abel "Shanghai" Pierce, probably the most famous cattleman on the trails. Some said he resembled a shanghai rooster, hence his nickname, but I couldn't see it. There was a touch of Yankee in his voice, but his dress and manners were all Texan, all cowboy. He had ridden from Ellsworth almost two weeks ago to join his herd of "sea lions," so called because the cattle had to swim across so many swollen rivers, and guide it to Ellsworth. He also said that if we gathered our herd, we should bypass Wichita for Ellsworth.

He said this because Ellsworth was paying him good

money to send Texas herds there. Wichita had paid him two hundred dollars a month in 1872 to send herds there. Ellsworth apparently had made him a better offer.

Uncle Cliff told him our predicament. Pierce listened without speaking, tugging on his full beard. "I was kind of worried," Uncle Cliff concluded, "that the herd behind me would be owned by some carpetbagger son-of-a-bitch. Now, I'm really worried."

Shanghai Pierce boomed with laughter. He had bought herds in Kansas during the Panic last fall, paying prices that were basically highway robbery because he had the cash and the other cattlemen were desperate. That was why he was rich.

"Douglas Simpson's damned herd is jinxed," Pierce said. "Everyone in Texas knows that, by God. I'm a hard ass. And by God, everyone in the world knows that. If it was anyone but you, Rynders, I'd buy their herd at fifteen dollars a head and sell them in Ellsworth for thirty dollars. But we go back far, Rynders. What do you need?"

"Horses and help."

Pierce nodded. "Joseph! Get your damned horse and ride back to the herd. Tell Jackson to bed it down and get as many men as can ride here. Bring the remuda!"

"Sir?" the white Texan asked.

"What the hell is that your hat's sitting on, you dumb bastard?"

"Yes, sir," the man named Joseph said. "I'll have every man we can spare here in a flash."

"Hold it!"

Joseph stopped. "D.C. Pearson's damned herd should be right behind ours. Get a fresh horse and ride, tell that son-of-a-bitch what's happened here, tell him that Shanghai Pierce wants him to stop where he is and ride here with every man jack he has that's worth a shit. And tell that damned fool not to tarry, by God, or I'll ruin the son-of-a-bitch. Tell him!"

Joseph was gone in an instant and probably glad to escape his boss. Pierce had turned back to Uncle Cliff, but now he was smiling. "Abilene in 'Seventy. Your men and mine tore up that damned town. Then me and you got into a little old drinking game."

"And you wound up barkin' like a German shepherd."

"Bullshit! I was howling like a coon hound."

Everyone laughed. He turned toward us suddenly and flung his coffee cup at Fain. We were silent as Pierce fumed, his face scarlet. He swore underneath his breath, then shouted: "By God, I'll give you bastards something to laugh at!" And he dropped to all fours, lifted his head, and howled —like a hound.

We laughed until we cried. And after all we had been through the past day, we needed a good laugh. By now, Pierce and Uncle Cliff were resting near the chuck wagon, while his black cowhand chewed on his cigar and we sipped coffee, smoked or chewed tobacco . . . and listened.

"Your herd will be back on the trail soon, by God," Pierce said. "We'll cut out enough damn' horses for you, on a loan. We'll pick them up when we swing through Wichita on the way to Ellsworth. And if you need some damn' help on the drive, you've got it. Hell, I'll ride drag for you."

"No need. We're two days from Wichita. I think we can get there without trouble, jinxed or not. But I appreciate the offer, Shanghai, and the horses."

Pierce nodded. "Sure you've missed your damned bonus?"

"Tomorrow's Friday, May Second," he replied. "That's the deadline."

"Tomorrow," a quiet voice said, "is April Thirtieth."

It was the first time the black cowboy had spoken, mainly because Shanghai Pierce had a way of dominating a conversation. Every eye was now on the old cowboy.

Days of the week were hard to keep up with on the cattle trails. Somehow we had lost two days, but Wilbur Boone said he kept a journal and knew that today was April 29th, 1874. Shanghai Pierce thought back. He had left Ellsworth on a Monday. Nine days ago—not two weeks, April 20th.

Uncle Cliff was on his feet, dumbfounded. "How could I have been so wrong?" he said softly, and suddenly his eyes blazed with excitement. "Maybe," he said, "just maybe."

"Hell," Pierce said, "it probably doesn't matter. I don't see how we can round up two thousand stubborn ass beeves and get you to Wichita in time. But, hell, there's a chance. Where the hell are those damned horses?"

Pierce's men arrived soon enough with fresh mounts and a chuck wagon. "Smart thinking, Jackson!" Pierce told his ramrod, and Shanghai Pierce wasn't one to praise often. "Their cook will need extra help, especially when Pearson gets here."

He explained the situation to his men while we saddled. With ten extra men, we rode north, following the trail left by our stampeding herd. Four miles north, the cattle had split, and so did we. In the rolling flint hills, Douglas Simpson's jinxed outfit finally got lucky. Below us stood, at best guess, more than two-thirds of our cattle, lowing and grazing on tall grass.

Charley Murphy yipped in excitement, and we eased our way to the longhorns. By early afternoon, we had the cattle bedded down north of our camp. Others brought back pockets of cattle that had been found grazing. Only five dead steers had been sighted. Late that night, D.C. Pearson arrived with eight men. Our luck was changing. Maybe, just maybe, we had a chance. We ate well, then got an early start the next morning to find the rest of the cattle.

I rode north with Uncle Cliff, Cochrane, and Pierce's black cowhand Wilbur Boone. We were driving ten steers back to camp late in the morning when we spotted a covered wagon in the distance. Boone pulled a spyglass from his saddlebags. "By God," he said, "I believe they've killed one of your beeves!"

Boone and Cochrane loped forward while Uncle Cliff and I drifted the cattle toward the camp. Boone was furious that some homesteader would kill a branded steer—I guess that was the Shanghai Pierce in him—but Uncle Cliff seemed to take it all in stride. But not for long.

A dun steer with dark face and forelegs was on the ground about thirty yards from the wagon. It kept trying to rise, but couldn't, and thick blood soaked the ground around it. A middle-age woman stood at the side of the wagon, both arms firmly on the shoulders of a crying toddler. A black kettle of soup sat on the campfire, and nearby lay an ancient flintlock rifle.

Still on horseback, Boone and Cochrane towered over a bearded man in black pants and hat and white muslin shirt. Boone's pistol was drawn, but Cochrane and the immigrant talked in a harsh, foreign language. The immigrant was excited. He kept pointing at the downed cow, then at his family, at his rifle, at the heavens, at us.

"Oh, no," Uncle Cliff said, and rode toward the longhorn.

It was only then that I realized the immigrant had shot Gen'ral Houston.

I left the stray cattle grazing nearby and trotted toward Boone and Cochrane. The immigrant's eyes were wild with fear, and I recognized some of the words from our run-in with the German farmer a few days before. Wilbur Boone holstered his pistol and rode back to the cattle. This, I guess he figured, was our fight.

"What happened?" I asked Cochrane.

"Mennonites," Cochrane said. "They'll be taking over the trail, lad." And he added with contempt: "Turning it into farmland."

That didn't tell me anything. Uncle Cliff rode up. "Well?" he said. I glanced back at Gen'ral Houston. His lows were pathetic, as he kept trying to rise.

"Capt'n," Cochrane said, " 'twas an accident. This Mennonite says his wife was preparing their sup, rang the dinner bell, and this beast appears out of nowhere, charging into camp. He shot it. Been afraid to go near it."

"Supper!" Uncle Cliff shouted, his ears red with anger. "The Gen'ral's been like this since last night?"

"Aye. Farmer did a poor job of shooting, Capt'n."

Uncle Cliff jerked his Winchester from his scabbard, and the immigrant backed up so fast that he tripped and fell to the ground. His wife screamed. The baby's cries intensified. And I thought I was about to witness the murder of an entire family. But Uncle Cliff whipped his horse back to Gen'ral Houston and swung from the saddle. Slowly, sadly, I followed him.

I dismounted, picked up the reins to my uncle's mount, and stared at the dying steer. He balled again weakly, trying to raise his head. Flies were gathering at the wound in his side. The ground had been ripped by his massive horns. With his one good eye, Gen'ral Houston looked up and seemed to plead for mercy. This was the steer that had guided so many of Uncle Cliff's herds to Kansas, so valuable that they had always brought him back to Texas. And now it had charged into a camp of farmers upon hearing a bell ring, expecting a treat only to be shot down. It was all so unfair.

Uncle Cliff wiped his nose and levered the Winchester. He brought the stock to his shoulder and aimed. The ancient beast moaned, and the rifle lowered, unfired. "Damn," my uncle said softly.

"Uncle Cliff," I said. "You want me to . . . ?"

"No, Tyrell." He took a deep breath and jacked a fresh shell into the chamber, forgetting or not caring that he had already cocked the rifle. My eyes followed as the unspent cartridge was ejected and flipped into the air, landing awkwardly on the brim of my uncle's hat. It stayed there as Uncle Cliff aimed the Winchester again.

"Good bye, Gen'ral Houston." The gunshot tore through the morning. Uncle Cliff didn't look at the dead longhorn. He turned sharply, sending the unused bullet on his hat to the ground, slammed the rifle in the scabbard, took the reins from my hand, mounted his horse, and galloped back to Cochrane and the German immigrant.

"Ask him if he knows how to butcher a cow," Uncle Cliff was shouting when I arrived.

Cochrane spoke, and the panic-stricken German could only nod.

"Tell him to do it! Tell him that I don't want one part of that steer to go unused. Tell him to skin it and keep the hide for something. Tell him to hang the longhorns over his fireplace when he finally builds his miserable farm. Tell him that the meat will probably be tough but that it's prime Texas beef. Tell him!"

He whipped his horse away from us.

Ian Cochrane translated my uncle's orders to the German, who was still on the ground. The man's head bobbed after each sentence.

"Tell him," I said, "that it wasn't his fault."

"Aye, laddie," Cochrane said.

Chapter Twenty-Five

"We're twenty-five head short," Uncle Cliff said, and let out a deep sigh. Douglas Simpson's contract with the cattle buyer from Kansas City called for two thousand beeves in Wichita by May 2nd in order to earn a bonus of five dollars a head, or forty dollars per steer. That was an exceptional price considering that it was the year after a financial panic. But, according to the contract, if the herd arrived after May 2nd or with fewer than two thousand beeves or with cattle of poor quality, the seller had the option of lowering the price to the average in Wichita for the previous month.

"Prices aren't good," Shanghai Pierce informed us. "Wichita hasn't recovered from last year. Neither has Ellsworth, anywhere." It was the first time I had heard him speak without swearing.

"Well, we've pretty much done what we can do. The rest of the cattle could be anywhere by now."

"Probably feeding some Injuns in the Nations," D.C. Pearson said.

"We're moving on, D.C. I appreciate your help, the horses, everything. It was a long shot that we could make it to Wichita by May Second to begin with. We'll still have to push 'em hard. Hell, maybe we can exaggerate our tally and get away with it. Or maybe we can buy a few head in Wichita. It's only twenty-five steers."

Shanghai Pierce boomed with laughter. "Hell's bells, Rynders. You can be a stupid son-of-a-bitch!" He turned to his men. "Jackson, Boone, Joseph. Ride back to our camp, cut out thirty of those extra sea lions and mix them with the Bar DS Bar herd." His men smiled.

"Now, damn your sorry-ass hides! Don't laugh! *Move!*"

"Shanghai," Uncle Cliff said. "Don't. . . ."

But Pierce cut him off. "Rynders, tell Simpson he'll get my damn' bill next year. And don't worry about my damn' herd. The thirty my men are cutting out didn't start out with us. Damned fools just seemed to wander in with my sea lions." His eyes beamed.

D.C. Pearson and his men returned to their camp after a noon meal of bacon, biscuits, and coffee. Pierce's men left soon afterward, but Pierce stayed behind for a few more farewells.

"Last chance, Rynders," he said as he swung into the saddle. "Ellsworth, you damn' fool. Drive them to Ellsworth."

Smiling, Uncle Cliff shook his head. "Got to go to Wichita. But maybe next year, we'll try Ellsworth."

Shanghai Pierce laughed. "Hell, Rynders. Next year, I might be singing the praises of Great Bend!" He turned his horse on a dime, yelled—"Good luck, you sorry ass waddies!"—howled like a hound to our cackles, and galloped back to his herd.

Uncle Cliff mounted his new horse. "Let's drive *our* sea lions to Wichita!"

We had the herd up and moving north quickly. We knew we didn't have much time.

The contract specified the date of delivery as May 2nd.

There were no other terms, which meant if we got the herd to Wichita before midnight, we were in the clear. So we didn't rest except for a cup of coffee while we got fresh mounts and moved on, taking advantage of the moon.

I chewed tobacco. When sleep threatened to take over my body, I spit the smelly, brown liquid in my hands and rubbed my eyes. It burned like coal oil, blurred my vision, and made me yell. But it kept me awake.

Bone-tired, eyes puffy and red, stomach empty, I forced myself to stay in the saddle. I lost track of time, of reality. I remember little of those last hours on the trail. Did we sleep, or did we drive through the night? I honestly have no idea. Did we eat breakfast the next morning? Who can tell? How many plugs of tobacco did I use?

We crossed the Arkansas River below the toll bridge, pushed on past grazing herds that were waiting to be sold. These were vague memories, almost dream-like. And we bedded down our herd and rode to Bibberman's chuck wagon. I was in camp, sipping coffee, when I asked: "How much farther?"

Amos Bibberman laughed. This I do remember clearly, and his answer: "Young Breen. We're here. This is Wichita."

The sun was setting when Uncle Cliff and I rode down muddy Main Street. I had envisioned a celebrated ride into Wichita, pistols drawn and firing, as we whooped it up and "treed the town." But this was nothing like one of those half-dime novels. There would be no shooting up Main Street, I knew, because the first sign I saw said:

EVERYTHING GOES IN WICHITA.
Leave your revolvers at police headquarters
and get a check.

CARRYING CONCEALED WEAPONS STRICTLY FORBIDDEN.

Besides, I was too worn out for any horseplay. And we were in town on business. We had to find Mister Simpson in a matter of hours, and Wichita was a big, busy town of more than two thousand, especially on a Friday evening.

"Doug's supposed to be at the Munger House. If we can't find him, we've got to find that buyer, Ferguson," Uncle Cliff told me. "We'll try him at the hotels. If no luck, you'll hit the stockyards and I'll try the saloons. If he's not at the stockyards, hit every other place you can think of. But don't cross the river into Delano. I don't want you gettin' killed on your first night in the trail town."

Delano was the red-light district, full of saloons, card houses, and brothels. Not that Wichita proper was without sin. Saloons were commonplace. A brass band belted out tunes from a corner establishment at Main and Douglas. There were shouts and screams echoing through the night, and Uncle Cliff and I were almost rammed by two Texas cowboys galloping down the street.

"The horse track's north of town!" someone shouted. A whistle shrieked, and a fat police officer, panting like an old dog, ran after the horse racers.

Uncle Cliff shook his head and led me to the Munger House, but it was a goose chase. The kindly clerk informed us that Mr. Simpson and his daughter had gone to supper, and he didn't know where. Nor did he know the buyer from Kansas City, and no Ferguson was registered there. He suggested the Empire House, a three-story frame building on Main Street.

The smell of roasted meat and fresh bread knotted my stomach as we secured our horses in front of the hotel. My mouth watered. A chalkboard outside informed us of the night's menu: **ROAST ANTELOPE, BUFFALO TONGUES, SWEET POTATOES, CRANBERRY SAUCE, OYSTER SOUP, OYSTER PIE, CHARLOTTE RUSSE, PEACH TARTS, RAISINS, STRAWBERRY ICE CREAM.**

Now Amos Bibberman was a fine cook, but. . . .

A strange sound stopped me as we walked inside. Uncle Cliff turned, waiting, and I turned red and laughed when it dawned on me. I pointed at my boots. "It's been so long since I've heard boot heels on a wooden boardwalk. . . ."

Uncle Cliff laughed. The Empire House was another failure, though. A one-legged man and young lady had not been seen. A cattle buyer named Ferguson was not known.

We were back on the boardwalk, unfed, dodging pedestrians. Uncle Cliff looked up and down the streets, then pointed to the horses. "Let's try the Texas House."

That was the same story, and so was the Douglas Avenue House, catty corner from the Texas on Douglas and Water. The clerk at the Douglas Avenue House had suggested The Occidental Hotel, which had just opened on Second Street near the *Beacon* offices. We were riding toward the hotel when I heard the voice.

"Tyrell!"

I reined my dun to a stop and turned, my heart pounding. She stood behind a hitching rail on Douglas Avenue, wearing a bright yellow dress and a smile. Her father, in black broadcloth suit and wooden leg, stood by her side.

I slid from my saddle and dashed across the street toward her, dodging a whisky wagon whose driver pelted me with oaths and a clod of mud. I was so excited that I forgot to be intimidated by her overbearing father. "Mattie!" I yelled, threw my hat off, and wrapped my arms around here. She squealed playfully as I twirled her around on the boardwalk, almost knocking down a minister and his wife, who both smiled and walked on as Mr. Simpson offered an apology.

I spun her until we were both dizzy. Then I stopped and leaned against a wooden column. Uncle Cliff had gathered my horse's reins and eased his way across the street to the hitching post in front of us.

"Young'uns," Douglas Simpson said, shaking his head.

Mattie Simpson leaned against me, smiling, and laid her hands on my shoulders. "Tyrell," she said softly, "you smell."

I wasn't as devastated as I could have been. Fact was, I smelled. I smelled bad, but that was to be expected after weeks with cattle and cowboys who smelled just as bad. As soon as I was paid, I planned to burn my remaining clothes, spend a day in a hot bath, and then buy a new outfit.

But first I had to be paid. And first we had to find the buyer. Our reunion was short. "Where's the herd?" Mr. Simpson asked.

"Bedded down west of town. Where's Ferguson?"

"Don't know where he's staying, but I'm sure he'll be at the Keno House. He's there every night."

Uncle Cliff looked at me. "Douglas and Main, Tyrell. Find him and get him to the herd."

I patted Mattie's hand and hurdled the hitching post. I swung into the saddle and loped down the street toward the two-story saloon, guided there by that brass band playing on the second-floor porch.

The hitching rail was full, so I had to tie up a block away. My spurs jingled as I raced down the boardwalk and bolted into the exquisite saloon and gambling parlor. It was crowded, and after a quick glance I realized that I didn't fit in. I was a dirty cowboy, and most of the men here were buyers and other businessmen. Cowboys did their drinking in Delano or in lesser saloons.

A somber-looking man with dark hair and well-waxed handlebar mustache approached me. "Gent," he said, "what can I do for you?"

"I'm with a Texas herd," I told him, "looking for a buyer from Kansas City named Ferguson. I have to find him quickly."

The man tugged on his mustache, looking me up and down. The brass band bellowed "Little Brown Jug" and someone yelled: "Keno!"

At last the man turned and shouted: "Wyatt, you know a buyer named Ferguson?"

Another somber-dressed man with an equally impressive mustache left a faro layout and approached us. The two men were obviously related. The man named Wyatt took a sip of brandy and asked his relative to repeat the name.

"Ferguson. Cattle buyer from . . ." He looked at me for help.

"Kansas City. He's supposed to be here every night."

"Man calls himself Ferguson's over in the corner playing poker. Playing badly. We'd like him to stay." But he smiled, and pointed out a tall man in a gray coat and brown derby. I thanked the two men and hurried to the cattle buyer.

I expected him to argue, to try to get out of the contract, to refuse to leave the poker table. He would argue that the deadline was 5:00 p.m. or something like that. But he didn't. He seemed relieved that we were there, maybe because he was losing at cards.

"I thought y'all would never make it," he said, tossing in his cards. "Deal me out, gents. My herd has arrived."

His suit was ill-fitting, and he was taller, tanner than I had imagined. Rather than rent a horse from one of the livery stables, he simply swung up behind me, and we trotted out of town to the herd. Douglas Simpson and Uncle Cliff were already there, but Mattie had gone back to the Munger House.

Ferguson enjoyed some coffee, and offered Uncle Cliff and Mr. Simpson a cigar. They both accepted, and after a few minutes of chitchat, they got to business.

"Two thousand head of beeves delivered by May Second," Ferguson said. "Forty dollars a head. I'd say that means Plankinton and Armour's Packing Establishment owes you eighty thousand dollars."

"You'll want to inspect the herd," Uncle Cliff said, but Ferguson shook his head.

"You're trustworthy Texicans," he said with a chuckle. "Drive your herd at first light into the stockyards. I'll issue you a draft when the bank opens Monday morning. I sent you two hundred dollars in earnest money in January." Douglas Simpson nodded. "Plus, I advanced you a hundred dollars when you arrived in Wichita last week." Again Mr. Simpson nodded. "I assume your men would like a little spending money." He turned back to Uncle Cliff. "How many men have you?"

"Just ten."

"Ten. That's all?"

"We lost a few on the way."

Ferguson withdrew his cigar. He was silent for a minute. "I'm sorry," he finally said. "I have fifty bucks on me," he said as he reached into his coat pocket. "It's not much, but it might please some of your men. And I'll give you another fifty at the stockyards tomorrow morning." Then he turned back to Mr. Simpson.

"That'll be four hundred dollars total. So your bank draft should amount to seventy-nine thousand, six hundred dollars. I'll draw up the paperwork and meet you and your lovely daughter at the Munger Hotel after breakfast Monday. We'll head over to the First National Bank and get everything settled." He held out his hand.

"Congratulations, Mister Simpson. It's been a pleasure doing business with you."

I smiled. Emmitt Fain yipped, and Charley Murphy and Jesse Trace did a jig around the campfire. It was finally over, I thought.

Chapter Twenty-Six

The herd was up at first light, and we pushed the tired longhorns through town along Douglas Avenue, past a crowd of gawking spectators outside the Douglas Avenue House. We were the first herd to reach Wichita that year, although many herds had been grazing out of town since last season, their owners waiting for the prices to recover from the Panic.

In southeast Wichita we found the stockyards. A train whistle screamed, but our cattle were too tired to be frightened. The smell of smoke and cinders overwhelmed the odor of cattle, dirt, and sweat, and a sudden gust of wind blew that thick, black smoke from a locomotive in our faces.

The pens were full, as another herd was being loaded, but we drove our cattle into an enclosure fixed to the stockyards. Ferguson sat on a top rail with a stockyard official who took a count of the cattle as we pushed them inside. When we were finished, Ferguson handed each of us a five-dollar gold piece.

"My count's exactly two thousand and seven head," the stockyard man said, and Ferguson nodded. I wondered if we had picked up a few extra steers in two days, or if our tally had been wrong. "I'll add seven steers at forty a head to the price," Ferguson said, then noticed that he had three extra gold pieces.

"Three of our men are back in camp," Uncle Cliff said, referring to Bibberman, Pedro, and Cochrane, who thought it in his best interest to avoid a thriving metropolis full of Texans and law men.

"I'll take 'em to 'em," Fain offered, but I quickly stepped in front of him and took the money.

"It might take you a while to give it to them," I said, and slipped the coins into my pocket.

Ferguson shook hands with Uncle Cliff and Mr. Simpson and hurried away. The cowhands had gathered around the holding pens, waiting. Ten dollars wouldn't go that far in Wichita, but the money was burning a hole in their—or rather, our—pockets.

"We're done," Uncle Cliff said, and everyone whooped. "We'll stay camped where we are if y'all would care to sleep outside some more, or once y'all have spent your money. Meet us at camp at noon Monday to get the rest of your pay. Enjoy."

The men scattered like excited ants, and I was about to follow when Mr. Simpson yelled my name. "Tyrell, I have a young girl who is in need of an escort tonight, if you'd care to."

I grinned. "Yes, sir. I'll be at the Munger House at dusk. And I'll be clean!"

I joined Charley Murphy and Emmitt Fain for a beer on Douglas Avenue, then we split up. Fain went searching for a faro game, Charley for what he called "horizontal refreshments," and I found the New York Store on Douglas near Main and bought a pair of gray striped pants, new underwear and socks, and a pillow-ticking shirt. That set me back some financially, so I decided new boots, bandanna, and vest would have to wait.

With my package of clothes, I wandered aimlessly around

town until I found a bathhouse. And for twenty-five cents, I enjoyed soaking and scrubbing myself clean in a hot tub. It had been a long time since I knew what it really felt like to be clean. Next came a haircut and shave, and I realized that if I wanted to be able to buy Mattie supper and maybe a flower or ice cream, I had better end my spree now and head back to camp.

Camp was deserted, except for Uncle Cliff and Cochrane. Bibberman had gone to town after I gave him his gold piece, and Pedro O'Donnell left in search of a priest for confession. Cochrane was asleep, so I sat around the campfire, sipping cowboy coffee, when suddenly Uncle Cliff asked a question I had never contemplated.

"What do you do next?"

I sat silent for several minutes. "I don't know," I finally replied.

My uncle smiled. "Well, I've been doin' some heavy thinkin', son. When Brazos Billy died, and then Gen'ral Houston, I started to realize this way of life will be over before we know it. Nothing lasts forever," he said, and I recalled the message of my dead father. "I ain't put away nothin', but I got a decent spread," Uncle Cliff continued. "Could raise some horses, I was thinkin'. There will always be a need for horses, and maybe some cattle. But I sure could use a partner."

I stared at him for a minute. "Are you asking me?"

He smiled, his eyes filling with tears. "Hell, nephew, I couldn't have made it without you. I think we make a good team. I don't even want a drink no more." He stood up, I guess to hide his tears, and said as he walked to the remuda: "Think it over, Tyrell."

"Uncle Cliff," I said, and he stopped but didn't turn around.

"I couldn't have made it without you. I'd like that a lot."

Mattie wore a blue bonnet and dark blouse and skirt when I picked her up at the Munger House. She smelled of lilac, and we walked briskly down the busy streets of Wichita until we found a pleasant-looking café. We ordered chicken and dumplings and coffee, but the coffee, after spending so much time on the range, was awfully weak for my taste. Next, we found an ice cream shop and splurged. That was quite tasty, but by then I was down to only a couple of dollars, so we just walked and window-shopped and talked and held hands.

It was a beautiful evening, and I was enjoying myself immensely, when suddenly I had to sit down on the boardwalk. I pushed my hat off my head. "What's the matter?" Mattie asked.

Everything had hit me at that moment. Tears streamed down my face. I felt stupid, but I couldn't stop crying. For Richard Hamilton and Les Slaughter. For Brazos Billy and Gen'ral Houston. I had joined the cattle drive expecting some romantic adventure, but it had been nothing but hardship and pain, boredom and violent death. I remembered the bald outlaw firing a shotgun in my face. If his gun had not misfired, I would be dead.

I explained this to Mattie between sobs, and she simply stroked my hair and pulled my face onto her shoulder. A couple of cowboys walked by, and I heard one say: "Always hate to see John Barleycorn wasted on some greenhorn."

Mattie's reply was far from lady-like.

When my tears ran their course, I pulled myself up, wiped my eyes, and put on my hat. I apologized, but Mattie patted my cheeks and told me everything would be all right. Her eyes were watery, too. "I cried my heart out when Papa told me about Les and the Gen'ral, but all the while I was just thankful that nothing had happened to you."

I pulled her close, then kissed her gently.

"Better?" she asked.

"Much," I said, smiling.

"Good, let's go see the stockyards!"

The massive holding corral where we had left our herd was empty, though. Confused, we walked by the pens and saw men leading Bar DS Bar beeves through runways and chutes into cattle cars. An engine was puffing smoke.

"I didn't think they'd ship the cattle out until later," I said to Mattie, but she just shrugged. I saw Ferguson talking to a stockyard official in the distance, then he took off toward the dépôt, carrying two valises. I scratched my head, bewildered, then was thunderstruck.

"Stay here!" I shouted and hurdled the rails into the holding pens. I maneuvered my way through the longhorns until I found a black man punching the steers with a rod to keep them moving toward the loading cars.

"Hey!" I shouted. "Where are these beeves going?"

"Mac, I dunno," he said. "I just load 'em!"

I ran out of the pens on the far side and chased down the stockyard man I had seen talking to Ferguson. He was on the tracks in front of the engine when I caught up with him. I had to shout to be herd over the engine's mechanical belches and gasps of steam.

"This herd!" I shouted. "What's going on?"

"Shipping it to Chicago, son! That's what we do here!"

"Chicago? Not Kansas City?"

The man checked a note pad. "Chicago. Herd owned by Daniel Stevens of Seguin, Texas."

I took off like a stampeding steer. I found Mattie and caught my breath, my eyes wide. "Go find your dad or Uncle Cliff. Tell him that Ferguson is trying to steal our herd! Tell them to get the police and hurry!" She picked up her skirt tails and raced away, and I ran in the direction of Ferguson, or Daniel Stevens.

At the dépôt, I learned that he had just bought a ticket for the 10:00 P.M. train. Final destination: Chicago. But he wasn't around the dépôt. The cattle train being loaded was set to depart at 9:30. I checked the clock behind the clerk's head. It was 8:45. Ferguson had been seen heading toward Douglas Avenue, so I sprinted in that direction. I rounded the corner in a flash only to slam into a solid figure and went sprawling to the boardwalk. Through blurred vision, I saw a dark-clad figure land in the muddy street.

He was up in a minute and had a firm grasp around my neck. He had lifted me off the boardwalk and was choking me, pressing my head against the door of a mercantile. I gagged, gasped, staring into a pair of angry eyes and flaring nostrils above a thick mustache.

"I remember you," the man said, lowering me so that my boots touched the ground and releasing my windpipe. My hands went to my aching throat, and I sucked fresh air into my lungs. "You're that pup from the Keno House last night. Boy, you owe me a new suit."

It was the gambler who had pointed out Ferguson. Wyatt was his name. "What's the hurry?" he said.

I told him the situation, and he took action. "Follow me!" he ordered, and we walked briskly down Douglas Avenue, peering into the dram shops and card houses. "There!" I said, when I spotted Ferguson inside a rawhide saloon, railroad ticket in front of him and a *Wichita Eagle* stuffed into his outside coat pocket. He was gulping down whisky, sweating, his bags at his feet, and was motioning to the bartender for another round, when the gambler and I barged in.

Ferguson recognized me, or maybe he was scared of the

gambler, because he tried to run through us, leaving his bags. Wyatt shoved him aside, and, when Ferguson reached into his coat pocket, a massive revolver appeared in the gambler's right hand. He swung the barrel, which caught Ferguson with full force against the temple, and Ferguson dropped to the floor without a sound.

"Hey, by whose authority are you pistol-whuppin' my customer?" the drunken bartender said.

Wyatt smiled, returning his handgun to a hidden shoulder holster, an obvious violation of the ordinance against concealed weapons.

"By Smith and Wesson's," he replied, grabbed the collar of the unconscious Ferguson, and dragged him out of the saloon.

Chapter Twenty-Seven

He confessed rather quickly, holding a rag against his bloody head and telling the gambler Wyatt Earp, Assistant Marshal Daniel Parks, Uncle Cliff, Mr. Simpson, Mattie, and me his story in the jail.

His name was Fred Dickinson, and he had pulled his cattle-buying flim-flam before, in 1871 in Abilene and in 1872 in Newton. Last year, he took a vacation in San Francisco and lost most of his stolen fortune in the casinos and in some legitimate investments that collapsed during the Panic. By December he was back in Kansas, where he heard tales of a hard-luck rancher in South Texas named Douglas Simpson. And so he decided to try his cattle scheme again. For five hundred dollars or a little more, he would get a herd, ship it as his own, and sell it in Chicago, Kansas City, somewhere, and turn a tidy profit.

"I knew forty a head was too good to be true," Mr. Simpson said softly.

Assistant Marshal Parks thanked the gambler for his help, and Wyatt Earp returned to the Keno House. "I've got your herd unloaded," Parks said, "but I suggest you get it out of the stockyards and bedded down nearby until you can find a legitimate buyer. I'm sorry."

"Yeah," Mr. Simpson said, pulling himself from a jury chair and walking out the door, followed by his sobbing daughter.

"Tyrell," Uncle Cliff said, "find as many of the boys as you can, have them meet me at the stockyards in the mornin'."

Without much conversation, we herded our two thousand steers out of the pens and back to our camp. Mr. Simpson settled his bills at the Munger House and other places, bought a tent at a mercantile, and joined us with Mattie at camp. He had to save as much money as he could, and the Munger House cost two dollars a day. We were in trouble. I knew that.

Mr. Simpson was broke, and soon Shanghai Pierce would be in town to collect his horses. But a few days went by, and Pierce never showed up. D.C. Pearson's herd arrived that Tuesday, and he rode into our camp with a note. Uncle Cliff handed it to me, and I read it aloud, to him, Simpson, and Mattie, and the rest of our despondent crew.

Rynders:

Those horses I loaned you are damned nags, just like you. Sell them when you're done at Horsethief Corner and have Simpson wire me the cash.

Good luck,
Shanghai

"Well, something's finally goin' our way," Jesse Trace said.

But little else did. A buyer from Illinois looked over our herd on Wednesday and offered seventeen dollars. "I could sell 'em in Texas for that!" Mr. Simpson yelled, and threw the man out of camp.

Fain became increasingly bitter. He was ready to tie one on, to do some fine whoring, drinking, and gambling. But he had spent all of his money on our first night, so he sat around camp, brooding. Once he and Charley Murphy got into a fight before Bibberman cuffed both of them.

I wondered if we really were jinxed.

On Friday, Ian Cochrane mounted a horse and rode up to Uncle Cliff and me.

"Capt'n," he said. "Me thinks it's time to travel. Too many herds are arriving from Texas. Someone might recognize me pretty face."

"Cochrane," Uncle Cliff said, "I owe you wages and haven't got a dime."

"I'll take the horse, if ye dunna mind."

"That horse ain't worth much."

"Aye, but she'll get me to the Seventh." He held out his hand. Uncle Cliff shook it, and then I did likewise.

"Laddie," he said, "ye'll always be welcome in me camp."

"Likewise," I told him, and he rode north, singing some Scottish ballad until he disappeared across the horizon. I never saw him again. Two years later, I was in Ogallala, Nebraska, with a herd when we received word of the massacre of Custer's 7th cavalry in Montana. Later, I learned that Cochrane's friend, Myles Keough, had died there. I scanned the lists of casualties, but found no Cochrane, no MacNab, but I knew he would have enlisted under another name. Maybe he didn't die there. Maybe he never joined the 7th cavalry, never went to the Little Bighorn. But my heart tells me that he did, that he died there, and that it was the way he would have wanted to go.

Fain galloped into camp Sunday evening, smiling and

laughing. He pulled out a handful of greenbacks and coins. "I won thirty bucks at the horse track!" he shouted. "And I'm in the mood to tree the town! Who's game, boys?"

"How?" I asked. "You didn't have a plug nickel to bet on? How. . . . ?"

"They didn't ask to see my capital, and, when that roan won, it didn't matter!" He laughed. "How 'bout it, pard? Delano's callin' our name!"

I turned down the offer. Surprisingly, so did everyone else but Charley Murphy. They disappeared to enjoy the comforts of the red-light district while we supped on bitter coffee, cornmeal, and potatoes.

Shouts woke me that night, and I sleepily rolled from my blankets to see several men in our camp, brandishing torches and weapons. I quickly reached for my revolver, but a boot crunched my hand as I grasped the butt. Groaning, I looked into the malevolent eyes of a tall man in his nightshirt, holding a blazing piece of timber in his left hand and shotgun in his right.

"Where is he?" the man yelled.

It was confusion. I heard Mattie scream and tried to rise, but I was pinned. "Where is he?" the man yelled again. "Tell us or we'll string every one of you sorry Texicans up." Again, Mattie screamed. I heard Mr. Simpson shout and then a gunshot. I struck like some venomous cobra, swinging my body forward and tripping my captor with my left arm. He dropped his shotgun and torch, and I pulled my pistol into my bleeding, but not broken, right hand. I yelled Mattie's name and took off for the tent.

A gunshot exploded, and I felt a bullet *zing* past my left ear, but on I ran, past other strangers holding torches and guns. Then someone blind-sided me and sent me to the ground near our dying campfire. Again, torch-wielding men towered over me, and someone wrestled the gun from my grasp.

"Is this the sum-bitch?" a strange voice asked, and someone jerked my hair, pulling my face into the light.

"Nah, too young."

From the corner of my eye, I saw Mattie running toward me. I struggled to free myself, but someone jammed a shotgun butt into my stomach, and I gasped for breath. "Leave him alone!" she cried, kicking at a bearded man who grabbed her arms and fastened them behind her back.

"She's a fiery devil!"

I struggled again, and this time the butt struck my head, and I dropped to the ground. Mattie screamed. Strange voices sounded. There was another gunshot.

"Let's burn these bastards out!"

"Look at this big darky!"

"Where the hell is he?"

I stared at the orange flames, leaping off the torches, until the flames disappeared, and I saw only pitch blackness.

"Ty?" A cold towel on my knotted forehead brought me out of unconsciousness with a jerk. Mattie was over me, and I slowly saw a lantern, ceiling, and then bars. Jail?

"What happened?" I said, groaning.

Assistant Marshal Parks, Uncle Cliff, Mattie, and Mr. Simpson were in the narrow cell. I was on a cot, and slowly sat up. Charley Murphy was locked in a cell next door, and the swindler Fred Dickinson was across the pathway. But my cell was unlocked. Mattie gave me a cup of hot tea, and I sipped it, holding the hot tin cup carefully in my bandaged right hand.

"What happened?" I asked again.

When Uncle Cliff told me, I fell to my knees and threw up.

* * * * *

Emmitt Fain and Charley Murphy had gone to a brothel in Delano, gotten drunk, then crossed the river into Wichita proper, with two whores, another Texas cowboy, and their firearms. When a special deputy tried to disarm them, Murphy and the other Texan complied, but Fain was drunk and belligerent. He drew his Colt and opened fire.

The policeman had a bullet in his leg but was expected to survive. The Texas cowboy was dead, with a bullet in his brain. Who fired that shot wasn't clear, but witnesses, including the two prostitutes, swore that when Rebecca Alexandria ran screaming from her house across the street, Emmitt Fain turned and shot her in the breast, then fled. She was dead before she hit the ground.

A mob had raided our camp looking for Fain, who apparently had stolen a horse outside a dram shop and lit a shuck for parts unknown. Marshal William Smith and two policemen had interrupted the mob, just after I was knocked out, and prevented further bloodshed. But Wichita was in a near riot.

"You Texans can kill each other in Delano from now until Judgment Day," Parks told us, "and no one in Wichita will bat an eye. But this man of yours killed a decent woman in the city limits. And that we won't tolerate."

"Charley Murphy?"

"He's being held. We might charge him as an accessory. He will be charged with violating the weapons ordinance. And it's probably best that we keep him locked up for his own safety. If we catch Fain, I doubt if your cowboy will be in any trouble. If not. . . ." Parks paused. "This town wants blood."

"The herd?"

Parks shrugged. "You're free to go, everyone but Murphy. I'd suggest that you take this jinxed outfit to Ellsworth.

Wichita doesn't want your business, and no cattle buyer will offer a nickel a head for your herd now."

We staggered outside. A crowd of unfriendlies had gathered opposite the jail, so we went back to camp in the Simpsons' rented wagon. "I'm ruined, Cliff," Mr. Simpson said. "No one will buy my herd in Wichita, and I can't afford to move it." He sighed heavily, brokenly. "Tell the men to take the horses and go. I don't think it'll be safe for 'em." He put his arm around his daughter.

"Mattie," he said softly, "I want you to go back to Texas with Cliff and Ty. I'll be back as soon as I can, but you had better pack what you can."

"No, Papa!" Mattie cried, and buried her head in her father's shoulders.

"There's one chance," I said weakly. Uncle Cliff and Mr. Simpson turned toward me. I reined the wagon to a stop and faced them, as Mattie lifted her tear-stained face.

"If *we* bring Emmitt in to stand trial."

Chapter Twenty-Eight

It was never my intention to become a manhunter, but I didn't see any other options. If we brought Fain in ourselves, Mr. Simpson would have a chance of selling the herd at a reasonable price. Right now, with Fain on the run and Wichita bloodthirsty, the townsmen and cattle buyers were without reason.

But I had no illusions of what tracking down Fain would entail. This wouldn't be like something out of Beadle's library. Fain was desperate. He was facing the gallows, and I knew he would fight for his life. Maybe he would kill me. Yet it was our only chance.

Marshal William Smith had led a posse out of town shortly after the tragedy, and we doubted if he would have wanted any Texas cowboys along with him, especially Fain's friends and co-workers. At camp, Uncle Cliff explained our situation and asked for volunteers.

"You didn't hire on as law men," he said, "or gun men. If you want to stay in camp, I won't hold it against you."

Only Red Santee and Jesse Trace agreed to go. John Dalton and Pedro O'Donnell were too religious, too young. Physical conditions prevented the one-legged Simpson and overweight Bibberman. So the four of us mounted up, armed, reticent, and rode south.

"He'll cut across the trail herds," Uncle Cliff guessed. "Hope the cattle hoofs wipe out his tracks, and they will. Head to the Nations. After that, I don't know. Texas? New Mexico? It's a big country. That's why we need to catch him quickly."

We found his trail south of town, and lost it later that afternoon, sure enough, where the ground had been broken by a recent herd of longhorns from Texas. The Wichita posse seemed to be making a beeline for Caldwell, but we cut southeast, through the flint hills, then split up. Uncle Cliff and I rode together, while Red and Trace headed westward, between us and the posse.

"Fire three quick pistol shots if you find anything," Uncle Cliff told them. "We'll do the same."

Uncle Cliff swung from his horse and studied horse tracks an hour or two later. His right hand touched his pistol butt, but he didn't draw the gun and fire a signal. He touched a brownish-red spot on the ground with his fingers and rubbed it around. "Blood," he said. Then he reached over and grabbed some horse apples and broke them open. "We're close," he said, wiping his hands on his chaps. "He's runnin' that horse to death."

My throat was too dry to spit as we followed the trail. Uncle Cliff pulled his Winchester, cocked it, and cradled the rifle across his lap as we rode away from the sinking sun. A flash glinted in the distance, and we dismounted, muzzling our horses and walking cautiously.

There he was! In a gully, his horse was down, and he was trying to remove the saddle. We picketed our horses and moved forward silently. His back was to us, and he was furiously working on the saddle. The horse was dead, its throat cut, and he jerked the saddle away when Uncle Cliff stood up and shouted: "Don't move, Fain!"

Emmitt turned suddenly, his eyes wide with fear, and reached for his Colt, but stopped when Uncle Cliff tightened the rifle stock against his shoulder. Slowly he held up his hands, and we moved forward.

"I didn't mean to hurt that lady!" he shouted.

Uncle Cliff kept the rifle sighted on Emmitt as we closed in. I tightened the grip on the butt of my holstered pistol with my bandaged right hand, trying to keep my arm from shaking, but it was no use. "Shuck the hardware, Emmitt," Uncle Cliff said, "we're takin' you back."

"Back? Come on, Boss. Y'all owe me somethin'. I can disappear in the Nations. Give me a horse, and, I swear, y'all will never hear from me again."

The rifle never lowered, and Uncle Cliff solemnly shook his head. "No chance, Fain. You killed a woman back there. You're standin' trial."

Fain's eyes went from fear to anger. He unbuckled his gun belt, wrapping the belt around the holster and staring at me. "Judas!" he said, and walked toward my uncle and offered the gun belt.

It happened fast. Uncle Cliff lowered the rifle and went to take the gun belt and holster from Fain. Why he didn't ask me to do it, or why he didn't just order Fain to drop the belt, I don't know. It was stupid. It was green. But Uncle Cliff was a trail boss, not a law man. And Emmitt Fain was a desperate murderer.

In a flash, Fain, grasping the holster with both hands, swung the gun belt over his head like some Biblical slingshot. The belt unwrapped, and, as Uncle Cliff was raising his rifle, Fain stepped forward and cracked the belt like a whip, the buckle catching Uncle Cliff under his right eye, tearing a gash and sending him to the ground with a thud and a groan, the Winchester landing at his side, unfired.

Quickly Emmitt grabbed the butt of his revolver and jerked it from the holster, which sailed across the prairie. The hard, metallic *click* woke me from a daze as Fain cocked the Colt quickly and pointed it at my prostrate uncle.

"No!" I shouted, and drew my weapon.

Fain glanced my way, his face contorted with rage. He didn't even pause, or turn. The only parts of his body that moved were his head and outstretched right arm, which suddenly was pointed at my direction as my revolver cleared the holster and I jerked back the hammer to full cock.

My ears rang at the explosion, and something struck me hard in the left shoulder, dropping me to the Kansas sod. My revolver landed at my side, and I tried to suck in air. I didn't feel anything, but my other senses were keen. I could taste and smell the bitter, sulphuric gunpowder, and, when the ringing left my ears, I swore that I could hear distant lowing of a cattle herd heading up the Chisholm Trail.

I looked up to see that Fain's expression had changed. He took a few quick steps and stopped. "Pard?" he shouted, and, when I lifted my head, he looked like an apologetic kid. My head dropped back to the soft grass, but I heard another sound and forced myself to look up.

Fain was turning back toward Uncle Cliff, the angry look returning, and was thumbing back the hammer of his Colt. But Uncle Cliff was sitting up, swinging the Winchester like a club at Fain's legs. The stock connected with a solid *whack,* and Fain's groans were drowned out by his pistol shot as he fell. Then Uncle Cliff was on top of him, his face bloody, flailing his arms in a rage.

They rolled over out of my sight, and I dropped my head back to the ground, taking short gasps of air. I brought my bandaged right hand to my chest and rested it on my left shoulder, felt a warm stickiness, and lifted my hand. It was covered with blood. I tried to swallow, but couldn't, and next tried to raise my left arm, but it wouldn't respond. I heard the savage groans as Uncle Cliff and Fain fought, the pounding of flesh, both men sucking in air. I looked up again.

They were standing, faces bloodied, but Uncle Cliff was wearing down. He was much older than Fain, and Emmitt was fighting for his life. My head collapsed again and fell sideways as I closed my eyes. When I opened them a few seconds later, I saw my revolver.

With my right hand I reached for it, groaning as I forced my aching body to move closer. My fingers touched the butt, and I pulled it forward until I could grasp it, slipping a finger into the cold trigger guard. The Colt felt as if it weighed forty pounds. The move exhausted me, and I had to catch my breath. My right knee raised, and I struggled to raise my head and arm, resting the barrel on the top of my knee. The gun was already cocked, which was good, because I lacked the strength to pull back the hammer.

Fain had dropped Uncle Cliff to the ground, some yards in front of me, and had picked up the Winchester, raising it over his head like a battle axe. He was about to let loose on my uncle's head, when I said: "Fain." But it was barely a whisper.

He must have heard me, however, because he paused. Emmitt looked at me as I pulled the trigger.

The rifle dropped behind him, and he fell forward to his knees. His mouth moved. "Pard," I think he said, but I couldn't hear him or tell, and he fell forward. My head collapsed again, and I turned, feeling the wind blowing through the grass in the gully. And I focused on Fain's black Stetson that was being carried away by the wind. Toward Texas maybe. I didn't know. I watched the hat until it disappeared, sailing out of the gully and across the prairie.

Three pistol shots fired suddenly, and next Uncle Cliff

knelt at my side. Grass stems and dirt were caked to his bloodied face, but he didn't seem to care about his own condition. He unfolded a pocketknife and ripped open my shirt.

"Christ, Tyrell," he said, "you're in bad shape."

He ripped off his bandanna and jammed it against my shoulder, then pressed my right hand on it. "Hold it there, tight," he said. "I gotta get a fire goin' and cauterize this or you'll bleed to death before I can get you back to Wichita."

I fought back nausea and listened as he rustled around, gathering dried dung. He was back in a few minutes with a canteen, and gently lifted my head and gave me a drink. Most of it ran down my chin, but it tasted good.

"Uncle Cliff," I said weakly. "How's Emmitt?"

He didn't answer, and I knew Fain was dead. But I couldn't cry. Uncle Cliff checked the fire, then lifted the blood-soaked bandanna, and began probing the wound. The bullet had entered above my lung, bounced off the shoulder blade, and exited under my left armpit. Had it turned the opposite direction, I would probably be dead. Uncle Cliff had found a jug of whisky in Fain's saddlebags, and he poured it into the wound.

I groaned, and now tears filled my eyes. "Bury him," I whispered. "Bury Emmitt."

"Tyrell," he said, "don't talk or I'll be buryin' you."

"Bury him," I repeated.

"I will, son," Uncle Cliff said. He reached over to the fire, picked up his knife, and pressed the hot blade against my shoulder. I heard the sizzling of flesh and blood, the odor almost forcing me to vomit, and again I swore that I could hear distant cattle. I shivered.

"Emmitt," I said faintly before drifting into a deep sleep. "I'm so cold."

Chapter Twenty-Nine

E. FAIN
Died 1874

The words had been scratched into a plank from Bibberman's chuck wagon with a knife, and the makeshift tombstone shoved into the grave overlooking the gully where Emmitt Fain had died. I left the buckboard on my own and stood silently as the wind whipped my face. Then I knelt, untied my bandanna, the same piece of cloth that Fain had stolen for me back in San Antonio—a lifetime ago, it seemed like—and fastened it to the wooden marker. It flapped in the late summer breeze.

Brazos Billy, that is William T. Sherman, had received his marble monument in Wichita. The stonemason swore it would last one hundred years. With the wind, rain, and snow, I knew that Fain's probably wouldn't make it through the winter. But I would always be able to find this spot, I thought, and, as long as I came up the Chisholm Trail, I would stop here to pay my respects.

Emmitt Fain. He was the first friend I had made in Texas, yet he had also been my first enemy. He was my partner, but also my rival. He had saved my life, and had tried to murder me. I had loved him, despised him, defended him.

And, finally, I had killed him.

"There was a lot of good in Fain," Mattie had told me as I lay on a doctor's cot in Wichita, "but there was a whole lot of bad in him, Tyrell. You did what you had to do."

So now I stood over his grave, tears running down my face, my left arm still in a sling, as I prepared to leave Kansas for Texas, my new home. I fought my emotions, trying to understand what had happened, to justify my actions. In time, I would be able to accept what I did, but I would never wear a handgun again. Killing a man was far from anything described in those half-dimers I read as a kid. Killing a former friend was something unfathomable.

The cattle I had heard while wounded were not figments of my imagination. A mixed herd of three thousand head was coming up, which probably helped save my life. The trail boss allowed Uncle Cliff, Trace, and Santee to ferry me to town in the outfit's hoodlum wagon, used for carrying bedrolls and assorted tack. Later, Uncle Cliff returned to the gully with Marshal William Smith and Assistant Marshal Daniel Parks and a witness to Rebecca Alexandria's murder. The body of Emmitt Fain was positively identified, and Uncle Cliff buried him that evening.

I was slow to recover. At one point, my doctor swore that I would die and suggested that Uncle Cliff buy a coffin. Uncle Cliff informed the doctor that should I die, the sawbones himself would be in need of the coffin. Someone was constantly at my bedside, usually Mattie or Uncle Cliff, but I vaguely recall hearing Jesse Trace strumming his guitar and softly singing, and once I briefly awoke to Amos Bibberman's snores. Mattie said she always held my hand when she watched over me. Uncle Cliff whittled or chewed tobacco, but he said he never even thought about taking a drink and never doubted that I would get better.

Mr. Simpson sold the herd to, ironically, a legitimate buyer from Plankinton & Armour's Packing House at thirty-one dollars a head. He paid off the crew, bought Brazos Billy's tombstone, and everyone headed back to Texas—after blowing most or all of their wages—but first said good bye to me. All except Charley Murphy, who paid his fine for breaking the firearms ordinance and left town at dark. We never heard from him again.

Amos Bibberman bought me a new pair of boots, told me to get back to Texas soon because he needed some wood chopped. And then he, Pedro, and John Dalton left with a few horses and the chuck wagon. Jesse Trace bought a train ticket, said he was tired of traveling horseback, and Red Santee, broke, joined a group of buffalo hunters as a skinner. Uncle Cliff took the rest of the horses to Horsethief Corner, an empty lot on Douglas Avenue, and sold them, then wired a draft to Shanghai Pierce in Ellsworth.

At last, Mr. Simpson said his good byes, and, with stage-coach ticket in hand, departed Wichita for his ranch. He had some Texas creditors to pay off. But Mattie stayed behind. And so did Uncle Cliff. When I was well enough to travel, we bought train tickets to Dallas, but first I rented a buckboard and rode to Fain's grave with my uncle and sweetheart.

Eventually I wiped the tears from my face and took a deep breath. I caught the aroma of lilac soap, and felt Mattie take my right hand in hers and squeeze. She said nothing, waiting patiently, until I was ready.

"Let's go home," I finally said.

I returned with Uncle Cliff on a drive to Wichita the following year. It became a pattern. We would breed horses at his ranch, run a few head of longhorns ourselves, and join trail drives once, sometimes twice, a year. In 1876, I rode swing on one of Shanghai Pierce's herds, driving through Kansas to Ogallala, Nebraska.

By 1877, the year I married Mattie Simpson, Wichita was dead as a cowtown, so we took the Dodge City cut-off in the Indian Nations and headed west to what became the Queen of the Cowtowns. But whenever I was close to Wichita, I would ride to Fain's grave. No one argued with me; they simply understood that it was something I needed to do.

Uncle Cliff and I herded Douglas Simpson's steers to Dodge City in 1878 and 1879. Amos Bibberman left us after the 1879 drive, moving to the Black Hills of Dakota Territory to try his hand at mining. And in 1880, Uncle Cliff and I drove to Caldwell, where again I rode toward Wichita to pay my respects to Emmitt Fain. Red Santee won part of a saloon in a poker game, but he wouldn't let Jesse Trace sing there. Red stayed behind, and Trace married a dressmaker in Gonzales that winter and gave up his cowboy ways, working in a hardware store and giving guitar lessons on the side. The following year, I served on two trail drives, riding point for D.C. Pearson's twelve hundred mixed head to Caldwell and swing for Shanghai Pierce's eighteen hundred steers to Dodge. One of our drag riders drowned in the Canadian River on the Dodge City job, the first time I had seen a cowboy buried since my first drive. It was also the last.

By now, the cattle trails had moved west, so it was no longer feasible to visit Emmitt Fain's grave. And I had accepted what I did, putting it behind me. In 1882, Uncle Cliff said he was too old to be trail bossing, so I took over and led another herd to Nebraska. My daughter was born the following year, and Uncle Cliff and I merged our ranch with Mr. Simpson's and sent a combined herd of two thousand, with me again serving as trail boss, to Dodge City in 1884.

I bossed one herd the next year, driving eight hundred

head of breeding stock all the way to Wyoming, where John Dalton owned a ranch north of Fort Laramie. In 1886, Mattie gave birth to another daughter, and I had to drive a small herd to Fort Reno in the Nations.

It had been twelve years since Emmitt Fain's death, and, after I collected a draft from the fort's commander and paid off the men, I felt compelled to seek out Fain's grave one more time. The days of the long drives were ending. I realized this, and now with two young daughters and several business interests in South Texas I knew that this would be my final cattle drive, so I mounted a blood bay gelding and rode north. In Caldwell, I stopped at Red Santee's saloon for a beer. The town, once as wild and woolly as Dodge and Wichita combined, was now hushed. So quiet, that Red had sold out his interest and moved to Montana.

So I pushed on toward Fain's gully. But I failed, reining in my horse and staring ahead, the words of Jesse Trace's song dancing in my head and the wind stinging my face.

Now, pard, the trail days will end soon
And we'll have to say good bye,
But first we'll raise glasses
Of whisky, beer, or rye,
Then we'll toast our friends and horses
And maybe wish them well
And recall stories
Of the old Chisholm Trail.

I was stopped, probably only a couple of miles from Emmitt Fain's final resting place. Ahead of me, where once our cattle grazed on and trampled the tall grass prairie, summer wheat rippled in the Kansas breeze. White farmhouses could be made out on the horizon, as well as a few windmills. This was farmland now, much as Ian Cochrane had predicted a dozen years earlier. Strands of barbed wire blocked my path. As far as I could see stretched fences, criss-crossing, and closing the lonesome Chisholm Trail.

Author's Note

Most of the characters in this novel are fictitious, but there are some historical figures. Wyatt Earp and Shanghai Pierce are well-chronicled, while Doc Burts of Fort Worth and Daniel Parks and William Smith of Wichita also lived outside my imagination.

This novel could not have been written without help from the archivists at the Texas State Library and Oklahoma and Kansas state historical societies. I am also deeply indebted to the many cattle drivers of the 19th Century who left behind personal remembrances of their treks along the various cattle trails of the American West, particularly the narratives compiled by J. Marvin Hunter in THE TRAIL DRIVERS OF TEXAS. Other primary sources include HISTORIC SKETCHES OF THE CATTLE TRADE OF THE WEST AND SOUTHWEST by Joseph G. McCoy, THE CHISHOLM TRAIL by Wayne Gard, THE CHISHOLM TRAIL: HIGH ROAD OF THE CATTLE KINGDOM by Don Worcester, THE CATTLE TOWNS by Robert R. Dykstra, and COWBOY CULTURE by David Dary. They are responsible for any strengths in this book. Its weaknesses are entirely my fault.

I must also thank my wife, Lisa, for her proofreading and encouragement.

Johnny D. Boggs has worked cattle, shot rapids in a canoe, hiked across mountains and deserts, traipsed around ghost towns, and spent hours poring over microfilm in library archives—all in the name of finding a good story. He's also one of the few Western writers to have won six Spur Awards from Western Writers of America (for his novels, *Camp Ford,* in 2006, *Doubtful Cañon,* in 2008, and *Hard Winter* in 2010, *Legacy of a Lawman, West Texas Kill,* both in 2012, and his short story, "A Piano at Dead Man's Crossing", in 2002 and the Western Heritage Wrangler Award from the National Cowboy and Western Heritage Museum (for his novel, *Spark on the Prairie: The Trial of the Kiowa Chiefs,* in 2004). A native of South Carolina, Boggs spent almost fifteen years in Texas as a journalist at the *Dallas Times Herald* and *Fort Worth Star-Telegram* before moving to New Mexico in 1998 to concentrate full time on his novels. Author of dozens of published short stories, he has also written for more than fifty newspapers and magazines, and is a frequent contributor to *Boys' Life* and *True West*. His Western novels cover a wide range. *The Lonesome Chisholm Trail* (Five Star Westerns, 2000) is an authentic cattle-drive story, while *Lonely Trumpet* (Five Star Westerns, 2002) is an historical novel about the first black graduate of West Point. *The Despoilers* (Five Star Westerns, 2002) and *Ghost Legion* (Five Star Westerns, 2005) are set in the Carolina backcountry during the Revolutionary War. *The Big Fifty* (Five Star Westerns, 2003) chronicles the slaughter of buffalo on the southern plains in the 1870s, while *East of the Border* (Five Star Westerns, 2004) is a comedy about the theatrical offerings of Buffalo Bill Cody, Wild Bill Hickok, and Texas Jack Omohundro, and *Camp Ford* (Five Star Westerns, 2005) tells about a Civil War baseball game between Union prisoners of war and Confederate guards. "Boggs's narrative voice captures the old-fashioned style of the past," *Publishers Weekly* said, and *Booklist* called him "among the best Western writers at work today." Boggs lives with his wife Lisa and son Jack in Santa Fe. His website is www.johnnydboggs.com